IT'S IN THE
CARDS

IT'S IN THE CARDS

Pamela Fudge

ROBERT HALE · LONDON

ISBN 978-0-7198-1369-6

Robert Hale Limited
Clerkenwell House
Clerkenwell Green
London EC1R 0HT

www.halebooks.com

2 4 6 8 10 9 7 5 3 1

Typeset in Minion Pro
Printed in Great Britain by Berforts Information Press Ltd

Dedication

This book is dedicated to my wonderful children, Shane, Kelly and Scott, whose love and support has always been unstinting, to my lovely son-in-law, Mike, and daughter-in-law, Jess, who couldn't be more perfect if I had chosen them for myself and, finally, to my gorgeous grandchildren, Abbie, Emma, Tyler, Bailey, Mia and newest addition, Lewis, who fill my life with love and laughter. You're the reason I wake up each morning with a smile on my face and I love you all dearly.

Acknowledgements

My thanks, as always, go to all at Robert Hale Ltd for making my dream of becoming a published author a reality and for continuing to enjoy my novels enough to keep publishing them.

My grateful thanks go to Sarah Petty for all the beautiful personalized greeting cards she has sent to me since I've known her. They gave me the idea to give Ellen Carson, the main character in this novel, a similar talent. Sarah generously shared many of the finer details of the card-making process and her cards were pinned above my desk as I wrote.

To my wonderful family, near and far, and friends, old and new, I do know how lucky I am to have every single one of you in my life. When I count my blessings – which is often – I always count you twice.

www.pamfudge.co.uk

Chapter One

STEPPING THROUGH THE door, I scarcely had time to note that the restaurant was obviously a very popular one, before the whole place erupted: the diners rose as one to their feet and roared in my direction, 'Surprise!'

I was so shocked that I felt my heart literally leap in my chest, slamming so hard against my ribs that it actually hurt. In my panic, I took a swift involuntary step backwards. My mother neatly side-stepped my reversing feet to stand grinning at me like the proverbial Cheshire cat.

'Happy birthday, Ellen,' she said.

My siblings appeared as if from nowhere, dragging me further inside and surrounding me, echoing my mother's sentiment, as 'diners' with familiar faces burst into a noisy rendition of 'Happy birthday to you'.

I know when I've been beaten and pinned a smile on my face, but in truth I was absolutely mortified. 'No celebration of any kind,' I'd insisted, 'definitely no party,' but when had my family ever listened to a single word I said?

'Just a quiet meal with your father and me, Ellen,' my mother had pleaded. 'It doesn't seem right to let your fortieth birthday pass unnoticed.'

The 'quiet meal' my parents had promised obviously included all of my four siblings, their partners, my nephews and nieces, aunts, uncles, cousins and, apparently, everybody I'd ever know from primary school onwards. It was so typical of my noisy, sociable family. I couldn't think for the life of me now why I had believed for one minute that they were ever going to respect my wishes in the matter of how my birthday should be spent. This celebration wasn't about me – it was about them.

'You don't really mind, do you, love?' my father was looking down at me anxiously, probably the only one in the whole noisy room who actually understood that this really was the last thing I would have wanted.

I took a deep breath, made a much bigger effort with the smile, swallowed my chagrin, and assured him, 'Of course not, Dad. I just didn't expect everyone to go to all this trouble.'

There was worse to come as all the tables were pushed out of the way and curtains swished back to reveal that a disco had been set up. It was immediately clear that I was expected to begin the proceedings by taking to the floor for the first dance – which predictably was a slow one. I was pushed into the arms of a brother-in-law well known for his two left feet, and so the evening began.

Common courtesy forced me to make a tour of the room to accept the many gifts gratefully and thank everyone for coming. It would actually have been lovely to see relatives and friends I hadn't seen – in some cases for a very long time – but their comments were horribly familiar.

'Not married yet, then, Ellen?' was a favourite, and always said after a sly glance at my third finger, left hand.

'No,' I replied brightly and repeatedly, 'nor even engaged.'

'You'll be thinking of settling down now,' was another remark, always made as if it must now be a foregone conclusion that I was officially over-the-hill.

'Actually, no,' I responded firmly without hesitation, and moved swiftly on.

'Still on your own, Ellen?' my Auntie Vi peered round me, as if I might have Mr Right tucked away behind my back.

'Just the way I like it,' I murmured sweetly and wondered how much more of this I was going to be able to stand and how soon I could make my escape.

'You look as if you could do with a drink.'

I turned to find someone I took to be a stranger, but with a winning and vaguely familiar smile, holding out a glass of champagne.

I took the proffered glass, said 'Thank you,' and took a sip, glancing up at the tall, rather pleasant-looking man over the rim of the glass but, no, I still couldn't place him.

'You don't remember me, do you, Ellen?'

His smile became rueful and something tugged at my memory, but I pursed my lips and shook my head.

'St Bart's,' he prompted, 'I used to sit behind you, and we lived a couple of streets apart.'

'Simon,' I found myself beaming up at him. 'Simon Weller, you used to pull my pigtails and steal crisps from my lunch box.'

'*And* carry your books.'

'So you did.'

By this time my glass was empty and from somewhere he procured another one. The second drink followed the first, slipping down easily, the tension began to drain away from me as he chatted idly, giving me a potted history of almost everyone who had ever been a class-mate. When he followed that up with some wicked impressions of the teachers we'd shared, I actually found myself laughing out loud.

'So,' he said eventually, 'why the Spanish inquisition from the oldies about your marital status?'

'Have you been following me round?' I stopped laughing immediately and glared at him.

'Yes,' he said, with a disarming lack of embarrassment. 'I was waiting for you to recognize me and fall into my arms in transports of delight. I must have been the first boy ever to buy you a present.'

'I don't remember any present.'

'Oh,' he clasped both hands to his chest, and gasped, 'I'm wounded now. How can you have forgotten the Crunchie bar, and the copy of *Jackie* magazine I bought for you out of my paper-round money?'

I burst out laughing again, I just couldn't help myself, and then admitted ruefully, 'It was a shame you couldn't run to an engagement ring, I know we were barely in our teens, but my family would have been in transports of delight at seeing my future secured at such a young age. They've always thought being married was the be all and end all – they still do. Obviously they despaired of me long ago.'

'Oh, good grief.' His face was a comical mixture of horror and dismay. 'Don't tell me you're–' he paused for dramatic effect and then continued in a hushed tone – 'an *old maid.*'

I gave him a stern look. 'You can take the Mickey if you like, but let me tell you, you've placed yourself in a very precarious position just by standing talking to me for so long. Don't look round now, but all eyes are upon us. They've earmarked you as husband-material, have already mentally measured you up for a morning suit, decided on the style of wedding dress I will wear, and are now in the process of visualizing us walking down the aisle to the appropriate organ music.'

'You're kidding me, right?' he gave a show of peering nervously over his left shoulder and when my Auntie Vi gave him a little wave and a huge smile, he shrugged and said, 'Well, then, let's give them all something to get excited about, shall we?'

Before I knew what he was about, he had spun me onto the dance floor. The couples already dancing parted before us like the Red Sea, and then immediately closed ranks behind us effectively trapping us in the centre of the dance floor.

Simon had certainly chosen his moment, it was near the end of the evening – though I wasn't sure where the time had gone – and the DJ was playing music of the slow and romantic variety. Seeing me in a man's arms – especially for the last dance – was bound to cause the maximum amount of excitement in my family. As far as they were concerned such a thing hadn't happened in a very long time – I had made sure of that.

I should have been furious, instead I just felt reckless. That could have been the effects of the alcohol, or it might have been Simon's carefree attitude rubbing off on me. When he pulled me closer and pressed his cheek to mine I made a great show of cosying up to him. Let them think what the hell they liked, I was past caring.

It must have been the drink because, by the third sibling phone call next morning, I discovered that I did care what they thought, and was back to my 'spinster of this parish and proud of it' best.

'Oh, for goodness' sake, Alma,' I knew I sounded completely exasperated, because I was, 'he's a friend from school. We had a laugh and a dance, nothing more. Don't start looking for a hidden agenda.'

'Well, that's not how it looked to me or the rest of the family.' My eldest sister sounded so smug that it took me all my time not to simply press the red button on the receiver and disconnect the call.

'That's because you're all so desperate to marry me off that practically anyone will do,' I fumed. 'When will you all get it into your heads that you're wasting your time and accept that I have absolutely *no* interest in entering the marital state. If Brad Pitt, himself, got down on one knee I would turn him down.'

'Now you're just being ridiculous,' she huffed, 'everyone knows he's happily settled with Angelina Jolie.'

'Why does everyone have to be "happily settled"? There's absolutely nothing wrong with remaining single – I can heartily recommend it.'

'It's just not natural. Everyone wants to marry – or at least live with someone – have kids and live happily ever after.'

'Not me,' I said flatly, 'and may I remind you that not everyone who marries goes on to live "happily ever after". Our own family provide excellent examples of what can go wrong. Even *you* have been married twice, Alma.'

'Everyone is entitled to one mistake.' She sounded huffy and I could tell she was making a determined effort not to rise to the jibe.

'Of course,' I agreed, 'but I don't intend to make *any*.'

'That's just silly.'

'It's not. I have a sister who's been married twice, one who leaves her husband so regularly that the front door of their house should be a revolving one, a brother who spends so much time at Relate that I'm surprised he hasn't been issued with a season ticket, and another who has had so many wives and partners that I'm not even sure what my latest sister-in-law's name is. Hardly recommends itself to me with all my reservations, does it?'

Alma was silent for all of two minutes and she drew her trump card with a metaphoric flourish. 'What about Mum and Dad?'

I wasn't fazed and had my answer all ready. 'Mum and Dad are the exception rather than the rule and you know it – even if you won't admit it. How many couples do *you* know who are completely happy? Oh, and when you answer that, try and be totally honest for once.'

I knew she wasn't about to give up, it wasn't in her tenacious nature. She ignored that question and quoted the facts and figures she always seemed to have at her fingertips. I tuned out and let her earnest words wash over me. You'd have thought after all these years she would have realised she was preaching to someone who would never be converted.

The youngest of the five children in the Carson family, I had already decided before I'd even reached my teens that matrimony wasn't for me. Growing up in the chaos of a crowded family home had given me a longing for my own space, and watching the ups and downs that besieged my older siblings relationships, not to mention listening to arguments involving children and lack of money, convinced me that family life just wasn't for me.

I had never felt the least desire to change my mind over the years and my family had never given up trying to make me do just that.

When Alma finally hung up, having talked herself to a standstill, I reminded myself sternly that she meant well. She would go back to the husband who seemed to do very little when he wasn't working, except sit guarding the TV remote control as jealously as a dog with a bone, and share with him her exasperation that her little sister couldn't be as happy with someone as she was with him. He would nod sagely, tell her she had done her best and wonder aloud if there was any tea left in the pot.

I went to put my own kettle on, just as she was undoubtedly doing on the other side of town, and breathed a heartfelt sigh of relief that her lot in life wasn't mine. Besides the husband whose desirable traits weren't at all apparent to me, her house always seemed to be filled with grown up children and step-children together with their many off-spring and she appeared to spent all her time running around after them. In my, admittedly rare, visits I had never seen anyone so much as drop a teabag into a cup in her house. Yet in her many arguments she often said she pitied me for that very reason.

'Who is there to make you a cup of tea?' she asked with monotonous regularity – as if that were a valid reason for getting married.

I was quite capable of making my own tea, thank you very much. Not exactly rocket science, was it? I questioned as I poured boiling water over the teabag in my two-cup pot.

It was October, but it was one of those gorgeous autumn days that always take us by surprise even in the south of England. I carried the tray out into the garden. Putting it on the little wrought iron table, I sat down to pour the tea with a sigh of relief, determined to ignore the phone if it rang again. Unlikely, I thought, since both of my sisters had already had their say and even one of my brothers – the other brother would probably be too busy sorting out his own marital affairs to concern himself with the lack in my life.

I had only just raised the cup to my lips, not even taken a sip, when the tinny sound of a mobile phone ring tone assailed my ears.

It wasn't a tune familiar to me – I didn't go in for fancy ring tones or even fancy mobile phones – and I realised the sound was coming from the other side of the hedge.

Obviously not Mrs Hitchins because she was in her eighties, didn't own a mobile phone and technically didn't live next door any longer, either, since she had recently moved to a nursing home. Her son, however, had voiced his intention of putting the house on the market, so it could be him.

I stood up and put the cup down. 'Roger,' I called, 'is that you?'

I was ignored as the mobile was answered by someone with a deep, very masculine voice. A fairly lengthy conversation ensued, which became distinct and indistinct as the recipient apparently paced backwards and forwards across the garden. The clipped tone sounded as unlike Roger's plodding speech as it could be and I wondered who it was and what right they had to be wandering round Ivy Hitchins' garden. Full of neighbourly concern – and, yes, I confess perhaps a tiny hint of plain old nosiness – I decided to go round and find out.

I automatically checked my reflection in the hall mirror before leaving the house. I worked from home and, although technically Sunday was my day off, I had been intending to catch up on a couple of orders and was aware I wasn't really dressed for what might prove to be a confrontation. Creating greetings cards required dressing for comfort rather than show.

I found myself hesitating, because I always felt that in such situations it was best to have the upper hand in every way that mattered, and that included appearance as far as I was concerned. However, clean jeans and t-shirt were generally seen as an acceptable mode of casual dress and, flicking my fringe out of my eyes, I decided my dark hair look smooth enough, the touch of make-up gave much needed colour to my otherwise pale complexion, and I would do.

The telephone conversation was still going on as I made my way up the garden path next door. It sounded as if heated words were being exchanged. I squared my shoulders, reached for the latch on the side gate and stepped determinedly through just as the person on the phone came round the corner of the house. We both came to a rapid halt and eyed each other warily. My first impression was of a tall, dark man wearing what appeared to be a very expensive suit and a shirt so white it positively gleamed. I immediately bitterly regretted the jeans.

He said abruptly into the mobile, 'I'll have to go. We'll continue this later. And *you* are?' he demanded of me with barely a pause.

'I think that's my line,' I returned dryly. 'I happen to be a good friend of the lady who lives here and I feel I have a right to look out for her interests.'

'If you were such a "good friend" of the lady who lived here,' he said grimly, 'you would know that she is now resident in a nursing home. I am now the owner of the property.' Cold grey eyes raked over me scathingly, and I could feel a flush creep over my cheeks, which made me angry with myself for feeling even a little bit intimidated.

Just who the hell did he think he was? I fumed, and then realised, to my horror, that I had said the words out loud.

'And just who the hell do *you* think you are talking to?' he demanded furiously, and I had to force myself to stand firm and not back away.

'Well, I don't know that, do I?' I said, looking haughtily down my nose and squaring my shoulders, 'or I wouldn't have asked the question. I have a perfect right to be concerned about my neighbour's property.'

'You're a neighbour?' he said, and seemed to step down from his high horse with a speed that I found disconcerting to say the least and, smiling down at me, he put out his hand. 'Bruce Redman, Redman Construction. We seem to have got off on the wrong foot and I apologize for being short with you.'

Still firmly seated up on my high horse, I ignored the proffered hand, and let the full implication of the word "construction" wash over me.

'You'll be getting "off on the wrong foot" with me, and every other resident in this close, if you're thinking of redeveloping Ivy Hitchins' property into something that won't fit in.' I stood my ground and glared at him until my courage finally deserted me, and then I spun on my heel and went back through the gate, slamming it hard behind me.

Only when I had closed my own front door behind me did I realise that my legs were shaking so much I was in danger of sliding to the floor. Remembering the gleam in those steely eyes I couldn't help thinking I might have made a very serious enemy.

Chapter Two

A QUICK CHECK ON the internet told me all I needed to know about my new neighbour. Then trying hard not to recall the furious look on Bruce's – Redman Construction's – face, I did what I always did in a crisis and turned to work. It was the one thing in my life that never caused me problems.

Card making of the greetings variety had been my passion for a very long time. It had been just an enjoyable hobby until the day, five years before, when I had taken the massive step of giving up a well paid career with a pension at the end, to turn it into a business that would be my only source of income. Formerly an exceedingly stressed tutor at an inner–city college I had reached the point when I truly believed that my health – both mental and physical – was at stake and taken the plunge to become my own boss. My family, predictably, were totally against it. The main reason for the concern was exactly what I might have expected.

Without even varying the words, they had each said, 'It's not as if you have a man to support you if you fail,' and Alma had even added, 'and you'll never meet anyone if you don't get out of the house.'

I'd gritted my teeth and informed them, individually and together, 'I don't intend to fail. I know what I'm doing and I do not need a man to support me.'

My maternal grandmother had left a small legacy to her

grandchildren and my share was just enough to clear the mortgage left on my modest house. Reminding myself that I could actually live on very little, I just went for it. Knowing I wouldn't be the only one running such a business had not deterred me, because I had steadily been building up a local and very loyal client list through the years of making cards in my spare time. I had also built up a good supply of stock and, thanks to my time in teaching and my frugal ways, I wasn't entirely penniless.

I invested in the advice of a recommended PR lady, who introduced me to the intricacies and advantages of Facebook and Twitter, and then I went the whole hog and hired a web page designer. The final inspired decision to add personalised verses when required was my masterstroke, though, and Ellen Carson's Complete Card Service (greetings for all occasions) was born. Not very original or even catchy, I was aware, but it did what it said on the tin as far as I was concerned. I hadn't looked back since. I might not be rich, but neither was I living on the breadline or suffering from stress.

As a bespoke card began to take shape in my hands, and a sleeping cat came to life as the layers were carefully built up, I felt the tension drain away. I was actually humming along to a song on the radio playing softly in the background when the jarring ding-dong of the doorbell made me jump. I was lucky not to ruin the card at such a crucial moment in its creation.

Muttering crossly I was stamping my way to the door when I suddenly realised it was probably my new next door neighbour paying me a return visit. If I'd given the matter any real thought I'd have realised sooner that he hadn't seemed the sort to let me get away with having the last word.

I wasn't sure I was quite ready for another confrontation, or indeed that I ever would be with *that* man. However, I psyched myself up by imagining him as a stroppy teenage boy. I'd had years of experience dealing with them.

I swung the door back and barked, 'Yes, what do you want?'

'Crikey, Ellen.' Simon Weller looked shocked and almost fell backwards off the step, 'I'm glad I'm not the one who upset your apple cart. Erm, I'm not, am I?'

'No,' I managed a short laugh, which was cut even shorter when I caught sight of a movement in the next door garden out of the corner of my eye. 'Come in,' I said, practically yanking him through the door which I then shut with a decisive slam. It was only a step from the small entrance porch into the sitting room.

'Nice,' Simon nodded approvingly as he looked around.

'Well, it's what you might call bijou but it's home to me. What did you want?'

'Has someone really rubbed you up the wrong way or are you always this abrupt with your visitors?' Simon was looking down at me with an amused smile on his face.

'Not when I've actually invited them to call or when I'm not working.' I refused to smile back because I really wasn't in the mood. I was probably being unfair because that wasn't his fault, but then I hadn't asked him to call, had I?

'Working?' he sounded quite horrified, 'on a Sunday?'

'Needs must when you're self-employed,' I lied, since I could choose my own hours and generally did.

'Business booming, is it, or nothing better to do with your time, Ellen? All work and no play, you know.'

'I actually like what I do, so it doesn't feel like work to me. I'm quite happy to do it anytime – and the business is doing very well, thank you.'

Simon nodded and said in a serious tone that seemed at odds with what I assumed to be his permanently jovial nature, 'I'm not surprised. I've seen some of your cards – had a quick look on your website, actually – and they're quite beautiful.'

'Thank you, Simon.' I couldn't help being pleased, and even managed a little smile.

Taking full advantage of the slight lightening of my mood, he said cheekily, 'I'll put the kettle on, shall I?'

I tutted, shook my head, and then told him, 'Oh, go on then.

Don't feel guilty about hindering me.'

He made his way into the kitchen through a narrow archway and was soon opening and closing cupboards a bit too noisily for my liking.

I sighed deeply and going after him, pushed him out through the back door, saying, 'Oh go and sit outside. I'll do it.'

'You could do a lot more with this garden,' he told me the minute I put the larger teapot on the tray beside the smaller pot of tea I had made earlier – stone cold now, of course – and added two mugs.

'Yes,' I agreed, looking round at borders sporting far more weeds than flowers and overgrown bushes that were keeping the sun from my small patio, 'I probably could, but I don't feel inclined and I certainly haven't got the time.'

'I could sort it out for you, if you'd like me to,' Simon said, surprising me.

'You?'

'Yes – me, Ellen, I am a gardener by trade now, you know.'

I sat back in my chair and stared at him. 'But weren't you. . .' I searched through a memory that wasn't always very reliable, 'something high up in banking or similar?'

'Probably, like you, I reached the point when it was clear the rewards didn't in any way make up for the lack of job satisfaction, and the pressure was horrendous. The offer of redundancy came at exactly the right time and the package allowed me to return to college and retrain.'

'Oh.' I didn't know what else to say.

'So, what do you think?'

'I think I'm quite stunned. It's refreshing to meet someone who understands where I'm coming from – having done exactly the same thing himself.'

'Besides that,' Simon said with a hint of impatience. 'What do you think about letting me loose on your garden?'

'How much would it cost?' I was tempted, but doubtful, and not just about the expense.

'I can work it out for you, mate's rates, of course.' He looked around speculatively. 'It's a nice little patch, but could be so much more.'

It wasn't difficult for me to agree about the latter, so I said I was prepared to consider his ideas as long as they weren't too radical or too expensive. He seemed satisfied and we moved on to swapping stories about life in banking and in education respectively. In some ways it seemed amazingly similar.

So,' he eventually asked nosily, when I'd drunk one mug of tea to his three, and he had devoured the best part of a large packet of chocolate digestives. 'What are you going to do with the rest of your Sunday?'

If he hadn't been such amusing company I might just have told him to mind his own business, but he'd had me laughing as I hadn't for ages. He was also the first person in a long while to understand that a lucrative career wasn't the be all and end all. Both had succeeded in making me warm towards him quite considerably.

'Actually,' I said, 'I've been invited to a neighbour's barbeque. They decided to risk it because the weather has been so unseasonably mild. It looks very much as if they might get away with it.'

We both looked at the sky which was a steady deep-blue with just the odd fluffy cloud and a bright sun that was making it a very pleasant day.

'I thought you didn't like parties.'

'I don't like family parties,' I corrected him, 'which have been arranged for the sole purpose of fixing me up with a man.'

'Ah, yes,' Simon said, 'and now you've brought the subject up, what exactly is your objection to becoming joined in holy matrimony?'

'Do you want a list?' I demanded shortly, 'because I have a fairly comprehensive one. Are you married?'

He looked taken aback, which pleased me, but he answered easily enough.

'I was once.'

'So you are one of the statistics I am trying to avoid becoming. Basically – very few marriages really work so the divorce rate is high and, of the couples who stay together, very few are really happy,' I paused, and then added, 'Shall I go on?'

'No,' he laughed, 'you're OK. I take your point.'

'I have no objection at all to anyone in my family choosing to get married, as many times as they wish, so why they think they have the right to object to my desire to remain single is beyond me.' I could hear the tension in my voice so I shut up and changed the subject. 'Come to the barbeque, if you like. You'd be very welcome.'

'Aren't you afraid they'll think I'm your boyfriend and start making assumptions?' he challenged.

'My neighbours aren't like that. They know me very well indeed and would accept that even if I introduced you as my boyfriend it would only be a temporary state of affairs – no pun intended.'

'In that case, I would love to come.'

'Good,' I said and I was pleased, Simon was proving to be very easy company, though one thing bothered me. 'You haven't actually said what brought you here today or,' I added, 'how you even knew where I lived.'

'Easy,' he was laughing again. 'At the party someone put a scrap of paper in my pocket with your address and telephone number on it. I was just checking that it wasn't you who did that. It wasn't you, was it, Ellen?'

Words failed me for a moment, and then I also laughed. It was so absurd that it seemed like the only thing left to do. In truth, though, my family and their determination to get me married off were a joke that had long ago ceased to be funny.

'I actually knew it wouldn't have been you,' Simon admitted, 'but I thought I would call round anyway. I knew you would have no compunction about telling me to push off if you didn't want to talk to me. I'm flattered to find myself still here and even invited to stay and go to a barbeque with you.'

'Well, I find I still like you, even after all these years, and just as long as the M word – marriage,' I added for clarification, 'is never mentioned between us we shall get along just fine.'

'God forbid,' he shuddered theatrically, and then asked cheekily, 'what about the A word – affair?'

I laughed, slapped him on the arm as we went indoors. 'No chance – behave yourself or I won't let you come to the barbeque after all.' Dumping the tea tray on the draining board, I bent down and reached into the fridge. 'You can carry this,' I said thrusting a chilled bottle of Pinot at him and then advised, 'Just give me a minute to spruce myself up a little.'

It didn't take long to change into a smarter top and fresh jeans, touch up my lipstick and mascara and run a brush through my hair and then, grabbing a jacket in case the evening got chilly, I pushed Simon out of the door in front of me.

There was just the one imposing house in the close, at the centre of the bowl of the cul-de-sac, the rest of the dwellings were more modest bungalows and small houses – little more than cottages really – of which one was mine. The owners of the large house were the ones hosting the barbeque.

I hadn't touched either bell or knocker before the front door was thrown open. I was immediately enveloped in a bear hug that squeezed the breath from my body, before finding myself being hustled into the impressive hallway.

'Greg, Greg, stop.'

He stopped and looked down at me quizzically. Everything about Greg was big. He was a tall man, well built, and gregarious and the biggest thing about him was his smile.

'I've brought a friend along,' I laughed, 'and he's in danger of finding the door closing in his face.'

'A friend, eh – and better yet, bearing a bottle? Come on through, young man, any friend of Ellen's, and all that. I'm Greg.'

'Simon.' He put his slimmer hand into the great paw that Greg offered and found it gripped and shaken as Greg urged. 'Come on through both of you.'

We were taken straight through to the large rear garden, where a huge gas barbeque was belching and spitting ominously while various cuts of meat were being poked indiscriminately by Greg's partner, Jasper, who was brandishing tongs as if they were medieval instruments of torture.

Both men were in their fifties, but they couldn't have been more unalike with the one so big, broad and loud, and the other quietly spoken, slight of build and so slim that he looked as if a stiff breeze would blow him away. Where Greg was clean shaven – even his head – Jasper had a good head of hair and a neatly trimmed beard. They may have looked an unlikely couple but if anyone could have convinced me that a relationship *could* work, it would be Greg and Jasper, because they were the happiest couple I knew, bar none. Owners of a bookshop, they lived and worked together with never a cross word as far as I was aware.

'Move over, love,' Greg bid Jasper now, 'or you'll be getting your fingers burned and we'll be eating charcoal for supper. Now, let's turn that gas down a tad, shall we? I expect Ellen could see the flames from all the way down the street.'

Jasper relinquished his tongs with evident relief and hurried over to kiss me on both cheeks. 'As you know, Ellen, cooking isn't my strong point – it's one thing you and I both have in common. I find heating a tin of soup stressful – and cooking al-fresco holds absolutely no interest for me at all. Oh, hello,' he looked at Simon. 'Now, who's this?'

'This,' I said, 'is Simon. I knew him at school and he was at my surprise party last night.'

'A surprise party? Oh, no,' he was all sympathy, 'you were worried it might turn out to be something like that, weren't you? Was it ghastly, darling?'

'It could actually have been far worse,' I admitted with a rueful smile, 'if Simon hadn't been there to wind my family up. They were getting ready to order their hats and buttonholes by the time they saw us on the dance floor together. It was very cruel of us really.'

Jasper clapped his hands. 'Brilliant,' he said, and went on to tell Simon, 'Had you down as husband material for Ellen, did they? They had me down for that dubious honour once. You should have seen the looks on their faces when they realised they were barking up entirely the wrong tree.'

While he'd been talking to Simon, I glanced around the garden, recognizing most of my neighbours among those gathered in small groups around the garden. Several raised a hand and others a glass in my direction. I had a feeling it would be a good night, as Greg's and Jasper's affairs usually were – and then I spotted a familiar face I certainly hadn't been expecting to see, and did a double take.

I couldn't believe it, because chatting easily to Fiona – one of my best friends in the close – was no other than Mr Redman Construction, himself.

'What on earth is *he* doing here?' I asked, cutting across Jasper and Simon's conversation. I knew I sounded rude, but I couldn't help myself.

'Who?' Jasper followed my horrified gaze. 'Oh, you mean Bruce? Well, he is going to be our new neighbour, darling. It would have been churlish not to invite him.'

'But you do know he's some kind of a property developer, don't you?' I asked appalled. 'He's bought Ivy's place and is probably going to pull it down brick by brick and build a block of flats there.'

Jasper threw back his head and roared with laughter. 'Whatever gave you that idea, love? He's just going to tidy the whole place up – and you have to admit it badly needs it because Ivy hadn't spent a penny on it in living memory – and then he's going to live there.'

'He told you that – and you believed him?' I scoffed, scarcely able to believe that anyone could be duped so easily.

'Well, he got us all together last night – of course, you weren't at home or you'd have been invited too – and explained his plans very carefully. Apparently, he spent his very early years here, so the house and the area are special to him. The place does need modernising – well, to be blunt it's a damn eyesore and practically falling down – but that's all he intends to do. He didn't even mention an extension, though we could hardly object if he did since most of us have extended our properties somewhere. Oh, Bruce,' he called across the garden before I could stop him, 'come and meet Ellen,' and I wanted nothing more than for the ground to open up and swallow me.

Chapter Three

'Please don't.' I pleaded with Jasper, but it was already too late because Mr Redman was turning our way, and Fiona was saying brightly, 'Oh, Ellen's arrived, you must come and meet her,' and then they were both making their way towards me.

Desperate for a distraction, I looked around wildly and thankfully a new arrival caught my attention.

'Oh, there's Miles.' I skipped nimbly from between Jasper and Simon with a quick 'Excuse me,' and shot across the garden with all the speed of a greyhound released from its trap, 'How lovely to see you.'

I knew that my display of joy at seeing someone who could loosely be described as an ex-boyfriend was over the top, but my relief at escaping an introduction that would be at best awkward, and at worst highly embarrassing was such that I didn't even care.

'Ellen, how are you and how was your birthday?' Miles smiled down on me from his six foot height. He was suited and booted because Miles didn't do casual – not even for a barbeque. 'A meal with your parents to celebrate, wasn't it? How did that go?'

'I'm fine and it was fine. Thank you for the card.' Miles was inclined to rattle off his questions at a rate of knots, but as I rattled back the answers a sudden suspicion popped into my head. 'Erm, the meal turned out to be a bit of a party. You didn't get an invitation by any chance, did you, Miles?' He turned a bit pink around the ears, which told me all I needed to know, and I assured him, 'It's all right you don't have to answer that.'

We made our way over to speak to Greg, and filled our plates while we were there. Miles kindly went to fetch a glass of wine for me and I started to relax and enjoy myself, especially when I hooked up with Simon again. He had quickly cottoned on to the fact that I was avoiding Mr Redman and took great satisfaction in steering me in another direction whenever there was the remotest chance of our paths crossing.

'Enemy approaching from a south-westerly direction,' he would chortle, and we would rush to another part of the garden and mingle with a group there as if that had been our intention all along.

After the unseasonal warmth of the day, the evening began to cool rapidly once the sun went down. When the goose-bumps appearing on my exposed arms could no longer be ignored I finally gave in, and slipped into the house for the jacket I had left hanging on the coat stand in the hall when I arrived. I had my arm in one sleeve and was groping behind me for the other when someone held the jacket so that I could slip my other arm into it.

'Thank you.' I turned, expecting it to be Miles or Simon, and found myself face to face with Mr Redman who, I was quite sure, had been part of a merry group at the very bottom of the garden when I had come inside.

'You're welcome,' he said, and then added before I could turn away, 'Are you trying to avoid me, Ellen?'

'Of course not,' I denied instantly and rather too emphatically, 'don't be so ridiculous. I scarcely know you. Why on earth would I do that?'

'Exactly what I was thinking myself,' he said coolly, 'but, somehow, we seem to have got off on the wrong foot. Could you, perhaps, have gained the wrong impression of me and particularly about my intentions regarding the property I've just purchased?'

I cursed the fact that I could literally feel my face burning, all too aware that I was probably turning an embarrassing beetroot red under his steady gaze. I knew I had to do something, say something and, going along with the oft heard saying that attack is the best form of defence, I jumped in with both feet.

'You can hardly blame me now can you, Mr Redman, for expecting a block of flats to be erected on the site with all possible speed, when your reputation for ruthlessness precedes you?'

I didn't tell him, of course, that his reputation had only became apparent to me after our first meeting when I went indoors and immediately Googled him. However, he looked so amused that I was quite sure he knew exactly what I had done – and when.

'My reputation is largely unwarranted, I can assure you.'

'So,' I folded my arms and glared at him fiercely, 'it wasn't *your* company that was responsible for tearing down the row of beautiful and quite historic terraced houses in the oldest part of a certain well-known town and erecting a bloody ugly monstrosity in its place.'

'If you have a problem with the design of that particular building I suggest you also speak to the architect and to that particular town's council for passing the plans,' he suggested, quite mildly, but I got the distinct feeling he was becoming rattled.

'So, it was you,' I stated triumphantly. 'I rest my case.'

With that I turned on my heel and marched back out into the garden where Simon took one look at my stormy face and said with a satisfied smile, 'I don't need to ask who came off best from that little confrontation. I did see him go after you but, without an undignified scramble to get through the door before him, there wasn't a lot I could do about it. I didn't give much for his chances anyway. I still remember your dirty tactics on school sports days.'

For a fraction of a second I bristled, and then I laughed and told him, 'So far, if this was a tennis match, it would be thirty love – to me. You know me, Simon, always in it to win it.'

'I almost have it in me to be sorry for the guy,' he said, not sounding remotely as if he meant it.

The rest of the evening passed without incident and this time I made no effort to avoid Mr Redman's company. He knew I had his number and that was good enough for me. I even made a reasonable show of laughing at his jokes, but though I knew I wasn't fooling Simon for a minute I hadn't realised he wasn't the only one to see through me.

'What on earth has the lovely new neighbour ever done to you?' Fiona said in my ear, looking at me quizzically as she waited for my reply.

'You know who he is, don't you?' I hissed as we wandered off together to replenish our glasses.

'Well, yes, I Googled him,' she admitted predictably. I wasn't surprised, because we were quite alike in some ways and that was probably why we were such good friends. 'Owns his own construction company, I discovered. In other words, he's a builder, and I must admit to having a soft spot for builders.'

I gave her a look that told her what I thought about that statement. 'I can think of a soft spot that would do nicely for Mr Bruce Redman,' I said nastily. 'He's the man, Fiona, who has been responsible for the changing face of a town not too far from here – and it wasn't a change for the better.'

'Not single-handedly responsible,' she pointed out, and I gave her another look. 'What?' she said, 'Well, he isn't. Town planners, architects etc.' she started ticking them off on her fingers.

'Yes, yes,' I interrupted, 'but it's the likes of him and his cronies that are taking the great out of British architecture. Every town will look the same soon.'

'Bit harsh,' she said mildly, slopping wine with a generous hand into both of our glasses, adding, 'You shop in the new precinct, don't you? And even you have to admit it's a vast improvement on the tatty old high street with its tumble-down shops. People come from miles around to shop in Brankstone now and that has to be good for the area. We can even give Poole and Bournemouth a run for their money these days and they're far better known.'

'It's killed the high street,' I pointed out, refusing to give in without a fight.

'Brankstone high street was already on its last legs and needed finishing off,' Fiona's tone was emphatic, 'and I think you'll find Redman Construction have won the tender for the intended make-over to said high street.'

I groaned. 'You're kidding me! He'll probably make it look like something constructed from Lego bricks and Plasticine.'

She laughed at me. 'Give the guy a break, Ellen, apparently he grew up here and will obviously be staying around, at least for a while, now he's bought a property. He says he has a fondness for the area and, therefore, is hardly going to put his name to something tacky. He must be about your age and you both grew up here – do you remember him at all?'

'No,' I said, probably a little too quickly, because I suddenly found that I did remember him – only too well – and I couldn't think why I hadn't realised who he was sooner. If he remembered me at any point I was going to be absolutely mortified.

'Do you?' Fiona looked at me, and then she looked harder, 'You do, don't you? Don't tell me you went out with him at some point.'

'Don't be silly,' I said adding abruptly, 'He was at school with my brothers and friendly with them. He was far too old for me.'

It didn't stop you fancying him though, did it? An annoying little voice inside my head reminded me. As if I needed reminding of the embarrassing way I had used to follow him round like an eager-to-please little puppy.

'Was he just as good-looking as a school boy?' Fiona asked and I found myself waiting for her to lick her lips. She didn't, but she might as well have because it was becoming increasingly clear that she fancied the pants off the damn man.

'He was good-looking, yes, if you like that sort of thing,' I said in what I hoped was an off-hand way, and changing the subject, waved my glass under her nose and told her, 'The bottle you're holding so tightly is empty and I need another drink, I don't know about you.'

Thankfully she took the hint and we went to where Jasper was dispensing wine in generous measures. Sipping the chilled wine from a glass so full that it threatened to spill over I watched Bruce Redman over the rim and wondered why I hadn't recognized him before. Of course, it was a very long time ago, but he had been a familiar figure in our crowded house from when I was quite tiny and throughout my growing up years.

It was hardly surprising that I had absolutely adored him, I acknowledged, when he treated me so differently from the way my bothers did. They were impatient, off-hand, and always teasing me – not always in a kind way. Bruce, on the other hand, always took time to greet me with a smile, to admire whatever toy I was playing with when I was young, and to notice a new haircut or a new outfit when I was a little older.

He'd gone away to university at eighteen, continuing to meet up with my brothers during the holidays so I still had those limited opportunities to idolize him. Then he had suddenly seemed to disappear from our lives entirely by the time I was thirteen and I was bereft for a while, but I was young and there were other boys. I hadn't set eyes on him since – until now.

I couldn't think why I wouldn't have immediately placed his name – even after twenty-seven years – and then I remembered how the boys had been great on nicknames and I doubted on reflection whether surnames were ever mentioned at all.

Now, what was it they'd called each other? Oh, yes, the names had to end in 'o' for some reason. So my brother Richard became Richo, Jonathon became Jono and Bruce was. . . ? I couldn't think. Surely not Bruco. I shook my head and then nodded, that was it – they'd called him Bruno. No wonder I hadn't connected the names.

'You OK?' I looked up to find Simon staring at me in a fascinated way. 'Only,' he went on unkindly, 'you look like one of those nodding dogs they sit on parcel shelves in cars.'

I managed a light laugh and said mildly, 'Flatterer.'

'And,' he went on as if I hadn't spoken, 'you were looking at the builder guy as if he was a specimen you'd like to be dissecting.'

'Well, she's not keen on him, that's for sure,' Fiona stated the obvious and they both laughed, 'but then she is known to be fussy about her men. How come you slipped under her radar?'

'Old school friend,' Simon explained.

'So is . . .'

I knew what Fiona was about to say and I gave her a sharp nudge, causing her to spill most of her drink. When she looked at me I frowned a warning. I didn't want everyone to know Bruce Redman and I had an historical link, however tenuous. I certainly didn't want Bruce himself to be reminded and that's what I told her while Simon went to refill Fiona's glass and stayed talking to Jasper for a moment.

'He's nice,' she nodded towards Simon.

'Yes,' I agreed, 'he's a good friend.'

'And does he know that's all there is on offer?'

'I've told him.'

'Loud and clear, I'll bet.' Fiona grinned. 'It won't make a scrap of difference, because when you offer a guy friendship their brain computes it into something else entirely. You must know that better than anyone. Most go for the friends with benefits option and hope the benefits will soon be on offer, but a few – like Miles – go the whole hog, fall madly in love with you and try for the complete marriage package. I don't know how you do it?'

'I don't do it on purpose,' I told her crossly, 'and I just don't understand why relationships have to be so complicated.'

'You should be like me, Ellen. Love 'em and leave 'em, that's my motto. Nothing complicated about that.'

But we both knew – even if we didn't admit it – that it wasn't Fiona who did the leaving. She'd had her heart broken more times than I cared to remember, yet still she kept up high hopes of the man of her dreams turning up bearing the diamond ring and the marriage licence. That was despite the fact her one and only marriage had ended in disaster when her husband had disappeared leaving her with a string of debts she knew nothing about. He'd even managed to remortgage her house. She was still recovering financially – even after down-sizing – and it would probably take a lot longer for her to recover emotionally.

I kept up the pretence for her sake. 'Yes, you're right, I should,' I agreed, and just remained even more determined to keep my life relationship free and uncomplicated. It was easy really when I hadn't felt any over-whelming attraction towards a man in so long I had a job to even remember who that was. I looked up to find Miles standing in front of me and was absolutely certain it hadn't been him.

'Can I get you another drink, Ellen?' he said in his courteous way.

'Too late, mate.' Simon removed the empty glass from my hand and replaced it with a full one. I didn't remember drinking all that wine and thought I had better slow down, though I found myself sipping the fresh drink anyway.

It was getting late and people were beginning to leave and those remaining gathered into one group nearer to the house, so there was no hope of avoiding Bruce who was part of it. Most were making noises about having to get up for work the next day and I joined in. I had a complicated job to do in the morning and I wasn't looking forward to doing it with the hangover I was certain I would have.

'Oh, what is it you do, Ellen?' Bruce Redman made a very obvious attempt to appear interested, or that's how it seemed to me, and it was on the tip of my tongue to tell him bluntly that I con-structed beautiful things – which was quite the opposite to what he did for a living.

It was probably a good thing that Fiona managed to get in first. 'Oh, Ellen makes the most gorgeous greetings cards *and* as part of the service she also provides the verse to go inside when required.'

Simon chipped in with, 'I know it's not really a bloke thing, but I had a look on Ellen's website and can tell you that her cards are really quite something.'

Some of the others joined in to say how thrilled their various family members had been with the ones they'd purchased for them and in the end I pleaded, 'Stop, stop, you're all very kind, but are embarrassing the life out of me. I must go or I won't be up early enough in the morning to complete the urgent commission waiting in my in-tray.

'I'll see you home.'

The offer came simultaneously from Simon, Miles and, to my surprise, from Bruce Redman, too.

I couldn't have been more delighted when Greg stepped in before I could say a word and insisted, '*I* will personally be making sure Ellen gets home and is not kept up half the night chatting on her doorstep. She also has a commission from Jasper and me for some more of those attractive little book marks for the shop and I don't want to give her any excuses for a late delivery.'

'Thank you.' I tucked my arm through Greg's and smiled up at him.

'No need to thank me. I saw the expression on your face, and being unsure of exactly who it was you wanted to walk you home least, I thought it best to step in myself. Had it been Fiona I could have left her to sort it out all by herself with a clear conscience.'

I laughed. 'She'd probably have accepted all three offers, although,' I paused and then went on, 'I think Mr Bruce Redman might have the edge.'

'You don't like him much, do you, Ellen?' Greg held my gate open for me and gave me a straight look as I walked past him.

I shrugged. 'Nothing personal, I just don't like his type, that's all.'

'And his type is?'

'Ruthless, self-serving, arrogant – do I need to go on?'

'I think I get the picture and you're usually a good judge of character.' He took my key from me, unlocked the front door and pushed it open for me. A kiss on the cheek, a quick hug and he was on his way back down the garden path. Pausing at the gate, he said, 'But I do think on this occasion that you're quite wrong. Goodnight, love.'

I didn't sleep easily that night because my conscience was troubling me – but not over Bruce Redman, no, definitely not. In fact, I was feeling guilty over Miles and it was all that I could do to stop myself labelling him in my mind as poor Miles.

I'd been an idiot ever to be tempted to date a neighbour, but he had seemed so nice, so normal, and so absolutely fine about there being only friendship on offer on my part. He could be a bit pedantic and a fuss-pot which, if I'm honest, could get the teensiest bit wearing. I do quite like a man to have a mind of his own but not when he always thinks he's right.

If anything, Miles was also a little bit staid for me and took every flippant remark I ever made seriously – though I didn't realize that at the time. I'd been clear, right from the start, as I always was, about marriage not being on my agenda.

'Not ever?' he asked in his solemn way, and I'd replied lightly and without any real thought, 'Oh, I might change my mind when I'm old and grey or maybe in the very unlikely event that I get totally swept off my feet and become convinced that it's a good idea after all.' I'd almost laughed myself sick at the thought, so I was stunned when he repeated that all back to me word for word several months later and suddenly produced an engagement ring from somewhere.

When I'd recovered somewhat from the shock, I reminded him, 'But, Miles, I told you right from the start that there was only friendship on offer. I can't think for the life of me what might have given you the idea that I had have changed my mind.'

Had he really thought that he'd swept me off of my feet or, alternatively, that he'd convinced me that marriage was a good idea? Apparently he had. Despite the fact the closest we'd ever got was holding hands – and I was never really totally comfortable with that, because to me it implied an intimacy between us that didn't actually exist. My problem had been how to tell a very sweet man that you would never fancy him in a million years?

I'd struggled and could only come up with a feeble, 'Miles, I did tell you from the very start that I didn't see us as a couple.'

'I thought you would change your mind once you knew me better,' he'd said sadly. 'We get on so well, Ellen. Don't you think that. . . ?'

'No.' I said it so sharply that he jumped a little, and so I added in a kinder tone. 'I *like* you, Miles, I don't *love* you and even if I did I still wouldn't consider marriage.'

'What about living together?' he immediately pounced on that as an option.

'That's the same thing to me and the answer is still no.'

After that it was difficult for us to even stay friends because I could see in his eyes that he was still hoping for more. I blamed myself, of course, because on reflection I could see that over time he had been gradually becoming possessive, wanting to know where I was and whom I was with when he clearly had no right to question me. The trouble was that the change in him had happened so gradually that I barely noticed what was happening until it was too late.

No wonder I had become ever warier about relationships of any kind – it had been proved to me over and over again that friendships between men and women didn't work – cross the line into intimacy and it all became too complicated for words, as I knew to my cost. It hadn't been such a problem when I was younger when everyone was just out to have a good time. Then you could enjoy a sexual relationship without commitment but that, it seemed, was no longer the case.

My family were convinced I just hadn't met 'the one', and that when I did everything would change. I, on the other hand, was totally convinced that 'the one' for me only existed in their imagination.

By the time I finally fell asleep in the early hours I'd begun to question the advisability of the friendship with Simon, and I woke to grey skies and a mood to match.

I'd been assured many times that a full English breakfast was just the thing for a hangover. However, I disagreed – the very thought made me feel queasy, and I sat down to a piece of dry toast and a hot sweet cup of tea with a couple of paracetamol. Even that held no appeal, but I still hoped it might do the trick because working with a headache wouldn't be great for my concentration or my creativity. What a pity I had chosen today of all days to try out a complicated new design.

I had just given myself a good talking to and gathered all my card-making bits and pieces around me when the banging started and it didn't take a genius to work out that it was coming from my new neighbour's property.

Just about ready to commit murder, I rolled my sleeves up meta-phorically and went outside.

Chapter Four

THUD, THUD, THUD.
The minute I stepped outside the sound became even louder, and I was sure the headache was going to become a stubborn migraine if the pounding didn't let up fairly soon. I felt my temper rise a few more notches and I turned out of my gate ready to let Bruce – bloody – Redman have it with both barrels.

It rather took the wind out of my sails to find that he wasn't actually the culprit and, in fact, he was nowhere to be seen. Instead, it was a much older and stockier man laying into the front wall of the next door property with some kind of huge hammer, and there wasn't actually very much left of the wall. When he caught sight of me mid-swing he quickly lowered the long-handled implement to the ground.

'Nothing scientific about knocking a wall down,' he explained. 'Brute force and ignorance always gets the job done in half the time. Not that it needed much knocking down,' he went on. 'A slight push would probably have done the trick.'

'And been a lot quieter,' I suggested. 'I'm actually trying to work in there.' I pointed to my house.

'Work from home, do you?' he leaned on the long handle of the great hammer, and taking a large white handkerchief from his overall pocket wiped the perspiration from not only his face, but also from a head that sported very little in the way of hair.

'When I can,' I replied shortly with a meaningful glance at the hammer.

'Well, I'm sorry about the noise, but I've almost finished now, as you can see. Bruce said it had to be done sooner rather than later because it was a danger to anyone passing and shouldn't be left.'

Remembering the long cracks and the crumbling joints that had never been attended to, I could see the truth in that statement but still couldn't leave it without getting a dig at the new owner into the conversation.

'Mr Redman didn't think about doing the job himself, then? You know, as he's going to be the one living here. But then I suppose dismantling a garden wall is a bit beneath his touch.'

'Oh, Bruce doesn't mind getting his hands dirty,' the man said immediately, 'but he's in town sorting out some problem to do with the high street plans this morning and, anyway, he knows I'm glad of anything to keep me busy.' He screwed his nose up. 'Retirement doesn't suit me one little bit.'

I laughed then, finally unbent, and told him, 'You sound just like my dad. Can I get you a cup of tea? That looks like thirsty work.'

'That'd be grand,' he beamed. 'While you're gone I'll just get this last bit of wall down and then you'll hear no more from me.'

True to his word, by the time I returned with the tea and chocolate digestives, the wall had been completely demolished and a number of the bricks had already been thrown into the skip which I hadn't even noticed was now standing on the drive.

'Told you it wouldn't take long,' he said with a smile and, after wiping one large hand down his overalls, he held it out, saying, 'Jack.'

I put the tray on top of the brick pillar that was part of my own wall and my fingers were swallowed up into the large calloused hand of a man who had obviously worked hard all his life.

'Ellen,' I said, 'and I won't hinder you any longer, Jack. Just leave the tray where it is when you've finished and I'll collect it later. Nice meeting you.'

'Probably see a bit more of me yet,' he smiled, 'because I'm hoping to be the one re-building this wall and if I get the job I promise to do it quietly.'

I grinned back. 'I can see we're going to get on famously.'

Once I started work, as always happened, I completely lost myself in what I was doing. The headache receded and finally disappeared. The card I was working on was for a wedding and, if I said it myself, it had been quite an ambitious work of art. I wasn't surprised to find that hours had passed unnoticed or that I was actually very hungry since nothing had passed my lips since the cup of tea I had made for myself at the same time as Jack's.

I'd have liked to set to work right away on the verse that would be included as part of this commission, but I could feel the headache returning and knew it could be down to dehydration and the fact my blood sugar had probably dropped to a non-existent level.

I was poking around in the freezer looking for something quick and easy to prepare when the doorbell rang. I assumed it was Jack bringing the tray back, though it was a bit late for him to be still working. I was partly right, because it was the tray – but it was Simon carrying it.

'Yours, I presume,' he said, bringing it with him as he walked inside without waiting for an invitation.

'Come in,' I invited belatedly and, injecting a heavy dose of sarcasm into my voice, I added, 'I was actually working,' and followed him through to the kitchen.

'You always say that. Don't you ever stop? I don't have to remind you again what they say about all work and no play, do I?' he questioned, 'and I bet you haven't eaten.'

'I was just about to,' I said, contradicting my earlier statement in favour of the truth.

'So I see.' He indicated the meal for one sitting, still frozen solid, on the worktop. 'Tagliatelle, eh? Good choice if you were sitting in an Italian restaurant. Do you fancy joining me at Marco's or would you prefer to share a Chinese take-away?'

'I told you I was working,' I said stubbornly, despite the food quite clearly sitting there waiting for its trip into the microwave, and the fact I was practically drooling at the thought of either of his much more tempting options.

'You have to eat, Ellen. You can't be creative if you're starving. Am I allowed to see what you've been working on?'

I shrugged, though I could be quite precious about my work, and followed his tall figure into the sitting room and then through the archway into my dining room-come-workroom.

'Wow,' he stopped and stared at the card sitting on my work table. Seeing it through his eyes even I could see that it was absolutely beautiful with the happy couple built up to give the impression that they were walking through the arched doorway and right off the card.

'You like it.' I said, not quite managing to hide the pleasure I felt.

'It's so much more than a card,' he said almost reverently, and then, 'It's a wedding card.' He sounded surprised.

'Well spotted,' I said. 'I'd have thought that was pretty obvious.'

'How could you come up with something so special when you don't even believe in marriage? Don't you feel even a little hypocritical?'

'It's a job, Simon,' I reminded him. 'Do you only plant the things you like when you're gardening?'

'Point taken,' he nodded and then went on surprisingly, 'that would be a bit like our friend, Bruce Redman, only constructing the kind of buildings he prefers.'

'That's entirely different,' I said sharply. 'My work and yours is usually only temporary, his buildings can change a whole landscape for many years.'

He followed me back into the kitchen, saying, 'Well, strictly speaking so can mine if it's trees I'm planting,' and then, before I could climb even higher up on to the high horse that was making yet another appearance, he said, 'Are we going out to eat, or not?'

I gave in then. I was too tired and too hungry to argue. Throwing the frozen meal back into the freezer for another day, I said, 'Come on then, what are we waiting for?' Barely pausing to run a brush through my shoulder length hair, I snatched up a jacket and ushered Simon out through the front door.

As we climbed into Simon's Land Rover, a four-by-four pulled up at the kerb of the house next door, and I didn't need two guesses to realize just who the driver was. Simon paused half in and half out of the vehicle to call a greeting. For a horrifying moment I thought he might invite the builder to join us, I certainly wouldn't have put it past him, but the next minute he had climbed into the driving seat and started the engine. Before we drove away I had time to notice the immaculate suit and shiny shoes that said, loud and clear, that Bruce Redman hadn't dirtied his hands with any manual labour that day.

Now I know that ready meals have their place, but twirling the steaming mushroom tagliatelle round my fork, I knew there was going to be no comparison to the one I had left at home and as I took the first mouthful I was proved right.

'We can do this more often now that I'm going to be working next door for a while,' Simon suddenly said, out of the blue.

I had just taken a mouthful of the water I had chosen over wine, given my dehydrated state, and I choked as it went down the wrong way.

'Next door?' I queried using a deceptively calm tone. 'Would that be the next door I think you mean?'

'Yeah,' Simon said easily, 'we ended up chatting after you left last night and when Bruce found out what I did for a living he offered me some work. It'll be mostly tidying and clearing at this stage, until the alterations on the house have been completed, but I'll be glad of it because gardening work slows down quite a lot at this time of the year. I can also make a start on yours if you're willing – we can have it looking great by the spring.'

I bit my tongue, realising I could hardly object to his accepting employment that he obviously needed, however much I might object to his choice of employer.

'Right,' I said, 'you come up with a plan and some idea of the cost and we'll talk about it some more. Just make sure you keep those nice tall shrubs along the boundary, especially at the back, so that I can enjoy my privacy.'

There was no doubt in either of our minds exactly which boundary I was alluding to, but Simon wisely didn't comment and we thoroughly enjoyed the rest of our meal.

He came in for coffee when we got back and, while I was making it he had a wander around the back garden and made a few notes. Then he had another admiring look at the wedding card and I thought how unusual it was for a man to take so much interest.

'I suppose something like that is quite pricey?'

'Well, yes, because of the time it takes to put it all together, but I find people – especially women – are quite happy to pay more when it's for a really special occasion. This one has been commissioned by the mother of the bride and will include a verse.' I thought the look he gave me rather telling so I said defensively, 'I can write a romantic verse as well as the next person, Simon, and probably better than most in fact.'

'I didn't actually say a word.'

'No,' I agreed, 'you didn't need to.'

'So,' he began when we were sitting in the living room with cups of coffee on the table in front of us, 'what, exactly, do you have against your new neighbour?'

'Apart from the fact he's set on ruining the town I grew up in,' I shrugged, 'not a lot.'

'Not single-handedly,' he pointed out just as Fiona had and, to be fair, I knew they were both right, but it didn't make me dislike Bruce Redman any less.

'You actually prefer the milk-sop that is Miles?' he queried in a curious tone.

I didn't deign to give him a reply, but was aware that he was very probably right. I knew where I stood with Miles since he'd already been put in his place. Putting Bruce Redman in his place wasn't going to be anywhere near as easy as I already knew to my cost.

After an excellent night's sleep, followed by an early start and a good morning's work – which included getting the verses for several cards completed – I set off for Brankstone high street where Greg and Jasper's shop was situated, armed with the book marks they had ordered. I had to admit it was sad to see the once bustling street now almost devoid of shoppers, and every other store either boarded up or a charity shop now that most of the original businesses had moved to the smart new precinct.

I noticed several men with hard hats and high visibility jackets poking around and was relieved not to recognize my neighbour among them. Finding him inside the shop I was visiting was the last thing I had expected and I immediately turned round to go back out again.

'Ellen' – I cursed as Greg spotted me and came to usher me right inside, encouraging, 'come and look at the plans for the future of the new look high street. Bruce has just brought them in.'

'I really have to . . .' I began, and then started again, 'I was just dropping these in on my way to . . .'

Bruce Redman looked at me in that knowing way he had, and I immediately changed my mind about rushing off. I wasn't going to give him the satisfaction of imagining for one minute that I was avoiding him.

'OK, I have a few minutes. Let's have a look at what our historic high street is destined to become.'

I allowed Greg to guide me over to the table and watched Bruce deftly unroll the plans and spread them out. Jasper fussily placed a small paperweight on each corner to keep them flat. It all looked double-Dutch to me, though I wouldn't have admitted that in a million years. However, when Bruce began to outline his ideas and bring them to life for us on the plans I stopped poo-pooing it all in my mind and began to listen – and started to like what I was hearing.

'So,' said Greg, rubbing his hands, 'it means, basically, that the high street will be restored to its former glory.'

'Pretty much,' Bruce nodded his dark head. 'It won't even be that costly, being mostly cosmetic, because the buildings are pretty solid Victorian dwellings. I've already applied for permission to install new shop fronts in keeping with that era and discussed my plans with the council who have become very involved and are keen to support me in this venture. We want the high street to be a feature for the town, a real alternative to the modern precinct, with traditional businesses – such as this one – that will fit right in with the image we want to project.'

Greg and Jasper were beaming. They had been losing business for months to the well-known book shop in the precinct, not to mention the on-line competition, even I could see that this was going to make all the difference to them. Not everyone wanted modern and convenient, and old-fashioned personal service would surely keep the customers returning once they were encouraged to come back and take a look.

'It *sounds* great,' I admitted, hating myself for sounding doubtful in the face of Greg and Jasper's enthusiasm, 'but there aren't many traders left here since the majority moved to the shiny new precinct, how are you going to tempt them back?'

'Most of them wouldn't come back if you paid them,' Bruce admitted with refreshing honesty, and I found myself warming to him slightly even against my better judgement, 'but that's not necessarily a bad thing. I see the new – or old-look street being populated with little tea-shops, old-fashioned sweet shops, boutiques and more specialist businesses. We want it to be an alternative in every way.'

'You could open that card shop you've always talked about,' Jasper said, and warming to his theme he went on, 'that would be exactly what Bruce has in mind.'

'A specialist card shop,' he nodded. 'I like the sound of that. You'll have to show me exactly what you do some time.'

'Show Bruce the bookmarks,' Greg encouraged, explaining, 'They're only a sideline of Ellen's but our customers absolutely love them.'

I had no alternative but to pass them over, and they were quickly arranged in a fan shape on top of the plans. Bruce spent so long looking them over, picking them up and putting them down again, that I could have screamed.

'These,' he said finally, 'are really beautiful.'

I could feel myself blushing with pleasure, was then immediately cross with myself and dismissed off-handedly, 'They're nothing, really. I only came up with them because Jasper thought something like that might help book sales.'

'And I was right.' Jasper was quite happy to take the credit he was due. 'A book is a book and always a great present to a reader, but the bookmarks make the gift that bit more special. We can't get enough of them.'

'I'm not surprised,' Bruce said, smiling down at me.

'Yes, well,' I said briskly, 'I have to be off.'

'Somewhere nice?' Greg asked nosily.

'Just to my parents' house.'

'Can I give you a lift?' Bruce offered, rolling up his plans once he had collected up the book marks and handed them to Jasper.

'That's very nice of you, but no thank you,' I said carefully polite. I might like his plans for the high street but that didn't mean I liked the man. 'I prefer to walk, it's not far.'

'And the fresh air will do you good, Ellen. She spends hours over those cards,' Greg explained to Bruce.

'No longer than you spend poring over books,' I reminded him and, after hugging my two friends and picking up my bag, I made for the door, only to find Bruce right beside me.

'You should think about that card shop,' he said when we were out on the street.

'I doubt very much that I would be able to afford the rent, council tax and utility bills on what I make,' I dismissed. 'I am only a one-woman business.'

'Perhaps you should look at expanding then,' he suggested, 'you could give talks, maybe run workshops. Think of the extra revenue.'

'Not everything,' I said tartly, 'is about money,' and with that I marched off along the high street. It was only when I had gone quite some distance that I realised I was heading the wrong way and, rather than retrace my steps and risk bumping into him again, I kept going and went a long way round.

Dad was weeding a front garden that was already completely weed-free. The grass was also clipped to within an inch of its life with not a blade out of place.

'Our Ellen's here, Lydia,' he called in the direction of the open front door as soon as he spotted me and in less than two seconds my mother popped out.

''Well, thank goodness for that,' she beamed, 'I had begun to think no one was bothering with us today. Come away in, and I'll put the kettle on. Leave that, Michael, and come and see what our Ellen has to say.'

'Will do,' he said obediently, 'I'll just finish this border and I'll be with you.' He straightened up and put a hand to the small of his back with a grimace.

'Backache, Dad?' I asked, knowing it was unusual for him to suffer aches and pains because, despite his advanced years, he kept himself fit and active with the gardening and long walks with their old dog.

'Just a twinge I get now and again,' he answered, dismissing my concern easily, 'that and a touch of indigestion.'

'It'll be all those years as a bobby on the beat,' my mother said as she ushered me through to the kitchen, 'he walked miles and lived on doughnuts from the old bakery.'

I laughed and reminded her, 'Dad hasn't seen a beat in donkey's years. He was a desk sergeant until he retired.'

'Well, it'll be his age then,' she said comfortably. 'He's bound to get the odd spasm now he's nearly eighty.'

'Get him to make an appointment with the doctor if it doesn't improve,' I advised, making a fuss of Oscar the Labrador who had wandered over to rest his black head on my knee the minute I sat down.

'Mmm,' she agreed absently, and I made my mind up to keep my own eye on him. Every twinge couldn't be blamed on his age.

'If the gardening is getting a bit much I could always ask Simon to call round,' I added, trying to be helpful.

'Oh, is that your friend from the party? The one you went to school with?' Mum pounced. 'You're still seeing him, then? Alma said she thought. . .'

'Yes,' I cut in, 'I can guess what Alma thought, and I can tell you quite plainly that she's wrong. Simon is just a friend. That's all he was and all he ever will be.'

She looked disappointed and I wondered why it bothered her so much that just one of her five children remained unmarried and childless. It was as if she thought she had failed with me in some way, yet I'd had a successful career and now ran a flourishing business and was probably the one of all her family most contented with my life.

'Well, you know,' I could tell that Mum couldn't help persisting even though she knew from bitter experience that it would do her no good where I was concerned, 'friendship is as good a basis for marriage as any other'.

'Lydia.' We hadn't heard my dad come in and his voice was stern for once, though he usually let my mother get away with murder. 'Leave the girl alone.'

'I was only saying.'

''Yes, well don't,' he advised, 'unless you want to drive Ellen away. She's grown up now with a mind of her own and she doesn't need telling what's what. Now,' he said, turning to me, 'what have you been up to since the party?'

'Besides sleeping off the hangover?' I joked.

'You enjoyed it then?' Mum asked eagerly. 'Only I know you said you didn't want a party, but forty is when life begins, Ellen, and we couldn't just ignore your big day.'

I gave her a look, but made an effort not to show how infuriated their high-handed disregard of my wishes had made me. 'It was fine, Mum, but I shall make quite sure that I'm out of town for my fiftieth.'

'Good girl,' Dad laughed, and sat down to enjoy the tea Mum was busy pouring.

Funny how everyone was always entertained in the kitchen in my parents' home, but it had always been the hub of the house and few visitors ever made it through to the comfortable sitting room. Little had changed and the big old table and mismatched chairs still held pride of place.

I told them about the barbeque, but purposely neglected to add that Simon had been there at my invitation, or that I had gone out for a meal with him the previous night. I could just imagine the furore that would have caused, especially when it reached the ears of my siblings.

'I dropped some bookmarks into Greg and Jasper at the shop on the way here,' I mentioned in passing.

Dad shook his head, 'So sad to see the decline of that bit of the area.'

'Yes,' Mum looked upset, 'it used to be a hive of activity. I did all my shopping there when you children were growing up. All the businesses were family run, the butcher, the baker. . .'

'The candlestick maker,' Dad grinned at his own joke, 'or iron-monger – to give it a proper title. You don't even see an ironmonger nowadays.'

'Well, that might be about to change,' I told them, pleased to have a bit of good news for once. 'There are plans afoot to give the high street a facelift, but in a more traditional way and keeping the shops smaller and more personal.'

'Oh,' Mum clasped her hands together and beamed, 'I like the sound of that. I know the precinct is more convenient for some, though I find it all too big and impersonal, but then I know I'm old-fashioned.'

'Nothing wrong with that,' I said, 'and according to the construction guy the modern precinct and the traditional high street will complement each other and give people a wider choice.'

'I've noticed the boards up around town. Redman Construction will be doing the work, won't they?'

As Dad said the name I could almost hear the penny drop with a deafening clang and I cringed as I waited. It didn't take long. I might not have recalled Bruce's surname but nothing much escaped my parents.

'Redman?' Dad turned to my mother. 'Wasn't that the name of the boy that used to be round here all the time years ago? You know, the one that was as thick as thieves with our boys when they were at school. What was his name?'

'Oh, yes, same name as that lovely boxer that always said, "Know what I mean, 'Arry?" all the time.'

'Bruno,' my dad said triumphantly, and I realised with a sinking heart that when my family understood that this highly successful builder was unattached and actually living right next door to me there would be absolutely no limit to their match-making attempts.

Chapter Five

THE WALK HOME after visiting my parents was fraught with danger because I was ducking behind bushes and parked cars every time I saw a four-by-four that remotely resembled Bruce Redman's. It was amazing how many black ones there suddenly appeared to be in Brankstone.

It was with a feeling of profound relief that I turned into the cul-de-sac I called home and then I almost jumped out of my skin when someone fell in step beside me.

'Miles,' I said, more sharply than I'd intended, 'what are you doing creeping up on me like that?'

'Was I? Sorry, I thought you would have heard me coming.'

I laughed. 'No, I'm sorry for biting your head off. Car broken down, has it? We don't very often see you walking around here.'

'No, the car is fine,' he said in his precise way. 'I've decided I need more exercise in the interests of keeping fit and healthy, and the walk to and from the station is a step towards that.'

'A bit more than a step,' I joked, but I could see he didn't get it. Miles wasn't known for his sharp wit.

'I've also started a healthier eating regime.' He waved a carrier bag with green leafy bits sticking out of the top and offered, 'I'm trying a new recipe tonight. Why don't you join me?'

I couldn't actually think of anything worse, and had already opened my mouth intending to decline his offer politely but firmly, when Bruce Redman's gleaming black vehicle swished up to the kerb just in front of us and he jumped out.

'Miles,' he greeted him abruptly and then, 'Ellen,' he turned to me with a smile that would have made anyone think we were the best of friends, 'I was hoping I'd see you. OK to pop round tonight with the plans I've had drawn up for the house? Nothing too radical, I promise, but it will give you the chance to have your say before the architect applies for planning permission.'

His smile, all white teeth and twinkling eyes, widened and he looked so pleased with himself that I'd have done anything to keep him from stepping over the threshold of my house on that or any other night. Luckily, I had just that minute been given the perfect excuse and decided Miles' offer was the lesser of two evils.

'I *am* sorry,' I said in a voice that I hoped conveyed the fact I had never been less sorry in my life, 'but I've just accepted Miles' kind offer to share a meal with him tonight.'

'Oh,' Bruce looked nonplussed for all of about two seconds, while he took in the loaded carrier bag in Miles' hand. 'Bit of a dab hand in the kitchen, are you, Miles? I wish I could say the same about myself.'

It was typical of Miles that he started going into tedious detail about what he was going to cook and how he would go about it, while Bruce feigned a very creditable interest in every herb and spice that would be added at the correct and very crucial moment.

I don't know how he managed it, but to my complete horror, the next minute Bruce had inveigled an invitation out of Miles to join us for the meal. I don't think even Miles knew how it had happened, either, but he could hardly retract the offer once it had been made. I couldn't believe I was now going to have to spend an evening with the very two people I wanted to avoid most.

'Great, I'll bring the wine,' he was saying and opening the car door he reached for a bottle enclosed in a smart-looking box.

I mean, who else would buy a boxed bottle? It was, of course, champagne, and probably a very expensive one. I wasn't enough of a connoisseur even to recognize the name, being far more used to Asti Spumante. A drink which was probably more to my taste.

'Something to celebrate, have you?' I said sourly.

'Oh, I certainly hope so,' he smiled down at me, just laughing lightly when I refused to smile back. 'Can I give you a hand with that bag?' he asked Miles and took it without waiting for an answer.

I noticed that Miles looked every bit as disgruntled as I felt but, to give him his due, he recovered his good humour far more quickly than I did. Miles always had loved to show off his culinary skills to anyone who exhibited the slightest interest, and the thought of swelling his audience obviously helped him to put a brave face on the gatecrasher at his table.

Miles' home was one of the nicer bungalows in the close and was much roomier than my house – it was also much neater. He was a big fan of a place for everything and everything in its place. It was just one of the things that had started to drive me mad about him when we were seeing each other. You could never find *anything* because it would have been put away the minute it was done with. I swear he actually put his book back in alphabetical order on the bookshelf if he wasn't actually reading it at that precise moment. The easy-going attitude that had first attracted me to him had, of course, turned out to be a complete sham.

'Come on through,' he encouraged, immediately adding, 'after you've put your coats in the closet, and you'll probably want to wash your hands, the cloakroom is over there.'

I was used to Miles, but Bruce threw a startled glance my way, before doing as he was bid and I then followed suit.

It was like watching one of those interminable cookery programmes the TV channels are so full of these days, as Miles took us through all his meticulous preparation and then offered step by step instructions regarding the actual cooking. I wondered if he actually believed we would go home and try out anything as complicated as this obviously was for ourselves.

I looked at Bruce only once, when I accepted a glass of barely chilled champagne from him, and the quizzical expression on his face was almost the undoing of me. From then on I studiously ignored him until we were actually sitting at the table.

There was no denying that the meal, when it was finally ready, was absolutely delicious and Bruce and I were extremely loud and extremely lavish in our praise – which was probably due in part to the amount of champagne we had been steadily imbibing during the interminable cooking process.

This obviously wasn't exactly the evening Miles had envisaged when he'd invited me to eat with him and, as soon as the meal was over, it was made clear that he'd be glad to see the back of us both. Plates and cutlery were whipped out from under our noses the minute the last mouthful was taken, and Miles scoured and polished around us so thoroughly that I was sure we were the only things left in the dining room that weren't gleaming. The night was still very young when we found ourselves out on the street with the door closed firmly behind us.

'Do you think it was something we said?' Bruce whispered as we watched the hall light go out through the glass door behind us.

'More like something we drank,' I confessed guiltily. 'Miles likes his gourmet feasts to be consumed in a sober state – so that full enjoyment is not impaired in anyway.'

Bruce stared at me with such a look of amazement on his face that I had to rush down the path and out on to the street so that I could laugh out loud without Miles hearing and being so mortally offended that he would never forgive me.

'What will he do now?' he asked. 'Go to bed in a huff?'

I shook my head. 'Probably play opera at full volume – with head phones on so that he doesn't disturb the neighbours.'

'Good God,' he said, shaking his head. 'I need a drink, I don't know about you.'

I hesitated, realising even in my inebriated state that neither more drink, nor more time in Bruce's company was a good idea.

'I have a supplementary bottle of champagne in the fridge,' he said and then added using a coaxing tone, 'chilled to perfection, unlike the slightly tepid vintage we have just *enjoyed*, if that's the right word.'

Suddenly and for no good reason that I could think of, I just gave in. 'Oh, go on then,' I said, 'lead the way.'

In the darkness we tripped and stumbled our way past the skip, which appeared to be filling up nicely with all manner of things.

'I didn't know Mrs Hitchins owned a bike,' I marvelled, peering in at the old bone-shaker lying in there on its side on a set of rusty bed springs.

'Neither did she,' Bruce said very seriously, 'it was buried under what might once have been a flower bed. Of course, she may just have parked it there once and forgotten all about it.'

Well, once we started laughing we found we couldn't stop and ended up clutching at each other to stay on our feet and then more or less held each other up until we reached the front door. I'd somehow forgotten all about keeping my distance.

'Mind you wipe your feet, and don't forget to hang your coat up and wash your hands,' Bruce advised, as we stepped inside, and when I saw the state of the place I laughed even harder.

'Surely you're not staying here,' I managed when I stopped to mop my eyes on a crumpled tissue I found in my coat pocket, 'it's an absolute tip.'

'That's a bit harsh,' he said. 'It's home to me, you know,' and that set us off all over again.

In fact, the kitchen, though very old-fashioned, was fairly reasonable and a creditable attempt had obviously been made to make it liveable. He found two glasses, dusted off a couple of chairs, and fetching the champagne from the fridge he popped the cork expertly and began to pour.

'Not too much for me,' I protested, 'I've already had enough – obviously.'

'Spoilsport.'

'You know I'm a working girl and I need a clear head and a

steady hand for what I do.'

'Of course you do. Just half a glass each then and I'll get the plans shall I?'

'Perhaps not tonight – my concentration might wander.'

'Mmm, a bit like mine when Miles was doing his Gordon Ramsey tribute – minus the profanities or anything else remotely interesting. Is he always like that?'

'Pretty much,' I sipped the champagne, and even I could taste the not very subtle difference between the room temperature stuff we'd imbibed earlier and this cold and crisp nectar slipping down my throat.

'And did you really go out with him?'

I didn't need to ask how he knew that because I was sure Fiona would have told him. 'For a while,' I agreed, adding, 'he's a nice enough guy, just a bit. . .'

'Boring,' he put in helpfully.

'I was going to say pedantic.'

'I thought that was the same thing.' Bruce looked perfectly serious apart from a barely noticeable twitch to his lips.

'We *were* only friends,' I said, 'and he was a very kind one.'

'And that's the nicest thing you can find to say about him, is it?'

'Wouldn't you want to be known as kind?' I asked.

'I would prefer something a little more. . .' he paused, and then added, 'exciting.'

'Mmm,' I nodded, 'but then I don't suppose "kind" is a word very often used about someone in your line of work.'

'Ellen,' he came right up to stand in front of me and so that I didn't have to strain to look up at him, I stood up as well. I was a little startled when he took both of my hands in his and continued, 'contrary to popular belief and whatever you might have read, I don't spend *all* my time knocking down pensioners' houses and replacing them with monstrosities.'

His hands were warm, his grip on my fingers firm, and the grey of his eyes was far from the flinty hint of cold steel I had previously encountered and more like the soft gleam of molten lead. For an extraordinarily long moment I found that I couldn't look away.

I had to do something to break the spell and forced myself to joke, 'I'll believe you, thousands wouldn't, I'm sure.'

'I hope you do,' he said, releasing my hands and taking a step back.

'Yes, well,' I became brisk and businesslike, 'I must make a move.'

I turned quickly, too quickly, tripped on the uneven floor and would have fallen forward if a pair of strong arms hadn't snaked out and caught me around the waist, hauling me back against the long lean frame of my host.

'Whoops,' he murmured, very close to my ear.

'Thank you,' I said, in what I hoped was a cool tone, 'I'll be fine now, so you can let me go.'

It sounded like he said, 'Pity,' but he released me immediately and I was probably wrong anyway.

'I'd better walk out with you and make sure you get off my property safely. I don't want to find you in the skip in the morning.'

I could hear the smile in his voice and felt my own lips curve, but just told him sternly, 'You should get a light out here before someone breaks their neck,' as we stumbled back down the path and squeezed past the skip.

'I'll get on to it tomorrow,' he promised, adding, 'Thanks for a great evening, Ellen.'

'But Miles did the cooking, I didn't do anything.' I paused with a hand on my front gate.

'Oh, yes, you did. I would say you were the sweet antidote to Miles' sour. Good night, Ellen.'

It took me a very long time to fall asleep when I finally climbed into bed and I put that down to Miles' complicated recipe. Obviously all those herbs and spices must be playing hell with my digestive system, not to mention all that champagne swilling around on top of it.

'Enough with the partying,' I told myself severely, giving the pillows a good thump. 'It's back to the quiet life for you, my girl. Early nights and quietly industrious days or you're never going to pay the bills, never mind make your fortune.'

The rain fell like stair rods the following morning helping to firm up my resolve and, after taking paracetamol for another persistent headache, I unplugged the house phone, turned off my mobile, and worked steadily through my order book.

Some cards were less complicated and relatively easy to make, these were often the more popular ones because I could keep the price down. At the end of the morning, I had cleared the orders for those, and had only short verses to produce for one or two of them. The majority of customers were more than happy to come up with their own words if it was going to save them money.

I can honestly say that I didn't give a thought to Bruce Redman or the bizarre evening we had spent at Miles' house. Well, I *could* have said that, but it wouldn't have been very honest of me, because he actually popped up in my thoughts far more often that I'd have liked. The fact that he popped up at all annoyed the hell out of me, because he had no business disturbing my work and I bet he thought he had won me over.

Of course, I mused, I had given him completely the wrong impression by drinking too much and behaving badly at Miles' house with him. I had no idea what on earth had come over me and I would certainly need to make my apologies to Miles, who had actually deserved better from the pair of us after he had gone to all the trouble of cooking us a meal. What on earth I had been thinking to go home with Bruce to drink even more champagne, I really had no idea at all.

I looked down at the undeniably handsome paper bridegroom I was holding in my hand and tried to ignore the fact that he reminded me of my neighbour with his smooth dark hair and immaculate suit. I threw a look of intense dislike at the simpering bride I was about to affix beside him and had to fight the urge to confine them both to the bin.

'Oh, for God's sake,' I stood up and walked away from my work table, 'get a grip, girl. What, exactly, is your bloody problem?'

It seemed a long time since breakfast and the fact that I was starving probably accounted for my strange thoughts and mood. I heated a tin of soup and lavishly buttered two thick slices of toast to go with it. Feeling better after some lunch, I dealt with a few emails and went back to the table in a determined frame of mind. Carefully not thinking too much about anything at all I completed the wedding card and put it to one side, realising I was still not in the frame of mind to come up with yet another romantic verse.

Working on a complicated leaving card, with lots of folds and lots of surfaces to fill with raised plates of delicious looking cup-cakes, was ideal for focusing my mind and I was getting on splendidly when the doorbell rang, breaking my concentration and making me curse furiously.

I could have ignored it, but the damage was done now. It would have been difficult to raise a smile whoever was disturbing me and it proved impossible when I found my sister, Alma, on the doorstep.

'What on earth are you doing here?' The words slipped out before I could do anything to stop them – even had I felt inclined to do so.

'Well, that's a nice way to greet your sister, I must say. Anyone would think I'd never visited you before.'

In truth, I couldn't even recall the last time, but as I preferred to keep visits from my family to a minimum I felt it would be unfair of me to mention it.

'Aren't you going to ask me in?' Alma said, and without waiting for the invitation that hadn't been forthcoming, she pushed past me and made her way to the kitchen. People seemed to be making a habit of doing that to me lately, I realised.

By the time I caught up with her she was already filling the kettle, and I muttered feebly, 'I *was* working.'

'And you can't stop for a little chat with a member of your own family?' She flicked the switch on the kettle, took two mugs from a mug tree and started going through the cupboards, probably looking for tea bags. 'I don't know why you can't keep them on the side in a pot marked tea like everyone else,' she said, when she finally found them still in the box they came in.

I couldn't be bothered to point out that having little chats with members of my own family was one thing I least liked to stop work for. They were often irritating, rarely productive and mostly seemed to follow similar lines – but perhaps today would be different.

I made a determined effort, putting sugar into a bowl and poking around until I found sweeteners – because I remembered that Alma was usually on a diet. I brought out a packet of biscuits as well – because her diets rarely lasted very long and she swore they didn't work anyway.

'Sitting room, or dining table?' I asked, and smiled as if nothing would please me more than sharing tea and a little chat with my eldest sister.

She seemed mollified and poured boiling water over the tea bags without slopping it everywhere. 'I usually prefer the kitchen, as you know, but yours is a bit tight for space.'

'Sitting room, then?'

I popped everything on to a tray and carrying it through put it on the oblong coffee table that stood adjacent to the sofa and then we sat down, one at each end. I sat on the edge, trying to give the impression that I should really be elsewhere, but Alma settled back against the cushions, folded her hands across her ample stomach, and looked settled in for a lengthy chat.

'This is a nice house,' my sister commented, looking around as if she'd never seen it before, 'surprisingly roomy, apart from the kitchen – and the fact that you only have the one bedroom.'

'I like it,' I said, watching her lean forward and add two sweeteners to her tea and then reach for a biscuit – and then another – wondering when she was going to get to the point of her visit.

'I've went to see Mum and Dad this morning.'

'Oh, yes, I saw them yesterday. Did Dad seem all right to you?'

'Don't change the subject,' she gave me a look that I had difficulty interpreting.

'I wasn't aware that I had.'

'They told me you'd met the guy responsible for the building works in the high street. Someone we all used to know. Why didn't you tell me when I phoned after the party?'

'Well,' I shrugged, wondering where this was going, 'for one thing I hadn't met him then, and for another I didn't think you'd be especially interested.'

'Didn't. . .' words seemed to fail her and she heaved her bulk round to stare at me, tea and biscuits temporarily forgotten. 'You do know who he is, don't you?'

'Of course I do.' I didn't add that it had taken me a while to work it out. 'He went to the same school as the boys.'

'He didn't just go to school with our brothers,' Alma was quick to remind me. 'They were the best of friends and went everywhere together. He was always at our house.'

I waited for her to remind me that I had used to follow him everywhere but, thankfully, she had either forgotten, or she had never noticed in the first place.

Alma was looking at me expectantly.

'What?' I asked.

'Oh, for goodness' sake, Ellen,' she huffed. 'He's Bruce Redman of Redman Construction, worth a fortune probably, and we all know him.'

'And?' I didn't need to ask really because it was becoming crystal clear where this was heading.

'He's probably the most eligible bachelor you could ever hope to meet – *and you already know him.*'

Alma sounded as if she had been running and she was obviously excited by what she saw as her big chance to present me with a potential husband whom even I wouldn't screw my nose up at.

I was momentarily lost for words and was actually relieved when the phone began to ring.

'Excuse me,' I said, and went to pick up the receiver.

It took me a moment or two to work out who was on the line and what they were trying to say, and then my blood literally ran cold.

'It's me,' my mother sobbed. 'I'm at the hospital with your Dad. Will you come?'

Chapter Six

Parking at Brankstone Hospital was a nightmare at the best of times. Despite the multi-storey car park there were never enough parking spaces during daylight hours to accommodate all those with out-patient appointments, *and* those visiting in-patients.

Of course, there were no special facilities at all provided for members of the public who had been called urgently to the hospital. No thought at all appeared to have been given to anyone who might be in a state of total panic about the welfare of a relative or friend brought in suddenly – no appreciation that you might not be of the mind to drive aimlessly round and round all the car park levels in search of a non-existent space while someone you loved dearly could be breathing their last.

I was ready to scream and about to park wherever the car would fit without causing an obstruction when the reversing lights on a four-by-four suddenly came on.

'There, there,' Alma, who had been sitting beside me tense and silent, shouted and pointed, as if I couldn't possibly have noticed a vehicle the size of a small bus that was reversing out right in front of me.

I didn't react to her bossiness as I normally would recognizing that she was as desperate as I was to get into the Emergency Department and find out what was going on. I had already been through a number of scenarios on the drive across town, so everything from a heart attack to a trapped nerve and anything in between were what I was expecting to find. The one thing I had refused steadfastly to contemplate was that our beloved Dad might already be dead.

We scrambled from the car and both ran, hand in hand, along the walkway leading into the hospital. For her size my sister was amazingly fleet of foot and she appeared to have no trouble keeping up with me. Fear had given wings to our heels, but it also slowed us down and made us drag our feet when we came to the sliding doors at the entrance to the Emergency Department and the truth we were going to find waiting behind them.

In fact, when we were directed behind the scenes and towards one of the many curtained off cubicles it was to find Dad sitting up, supported by pillows, looking very much alive despite the wires attached to his chest and the machine blipping next to him. Mum was sitting in a chair beside him holding his hand.

'What happened?' Alma and I said in unison.

'He was in such pain,' Mum told us, and Dad nodded and indicated his chest area. 'I thought he was going,' she said, gripping his hand even tighter. 'I was so afraid. We both were.' Dad nodded again.

'What exactly does that mean – "Keeping him in for observation"?' Alma asked the same question or a variation of it on the journey home for the umpteenth time.

'It means they are keeping an eye on him – which is what we should expect given his age.' I kept my tone soft and patient with difficulty, because she had been party to the same conversations and explanations from the medical staff as I had. 'It's pretty certain Dad hasn't had a heart attack. At least we know that much, but he will need to undergo further tests to discover the cause of the pains in his chest.'

'I think we should have stayed longer,' she said, 'it doesn't feel right that we're going home and just leaving them there.'

'I think we were all starting to get under the nurse's feet, what with everyone else turning up with their other halves. Mum has plenty of company now and once Dad is up on the ward they will all be sent home anyway.'

I felt as if I was stating the obvious, and suppressed a sigh when Alma said, very predictably, 'Yes, but I'm the eldest and I think I should have stayed.'

It was on the tip of my tongue to demand sharply why she hadn't done just that in that case, but I guessed she would tell me anyway, and I was right.

'Of course, I would have stayed, but I can't leave Les to manage on his own for too long.'

I couldn't even be bothered to ask why a perfectly healthy man in his fifties couldn't 'manage on his own', and so I said nothing.

When we reached her house the chaos I had come to expect from her family reigned. It would appear that Alma's husband, plus the grown-up children and various grandchildren who didn't even live with her, had all been waiting helplessly for her arrival. You'd think she had been away for weeks instead of just a few hours. My one overwhelming desire was to drop her off and drive off at speed as soon as I saw the size of the welcome committee gathered at her front gate. Alma must have read my mind and she over-ruled me, insisting I come inside and put everyone's mind at rest about Dad's health because 'You're much better at that sort of thing than I am.'

To my intense irritation I had to go through the whole scenario twice – once for those who'd crowded into the kitchen behind us, and then again for the helpless Les in the sitting room. It was obviously too much of an effort to get out of his chair either to greet his wife or to hear any news and, after listening to me in silence, his only comment was to remind me he hadn't had a cup of tea for hours.

I felt no compunction about asking straight-faced if the lack of refreshment was a result of paralysis of his limbs or a power cut. He looked at me as if I was talking some alien language and I wondered how it was that Alma hadn't strangled him long ago.

'I'll be off then,' I said, popping my head round the kitchen door.

'Stay and have a cup of tea,' Alma pleaded, looking up from pouring tea into numerous mis-matched mugs and handing them out to the eagerly waiting family members.

'No, thanks, really, I should be getting home.' I tried to say it as if there was something urgent waiting there for me.

I could tell she was torn between arguing and sorting out her family. In the end she settled for the latter and, after making sure everyone had their tea, she said, 'I'll walk to the gate with you,' and took Les a cup of tea on the way.

'No biscuits?' I heard him whine, and instead of advising him to get off his lardy arse and get them himself, she promised, 'I'll bring them in just a minute. Our Ellen is just leaving.'

How on earth did she stand it?

'How on earth do you stand it?' For a minute I thought she had read my mind and was parroting my own words back to me, and then she continued, 'Going home to an empty house must be just dreadful. No one to be pleased to see you,' she said and then, unbelievably, 'no one waiting to make you a cup of tea.'

I caught myself gawping at her and when I realised she was perfectly serious I managed feebly, 'Oh, I get by.' When she looked as if she was revving up for an in-depth chat at the kerbside I reminded her about Les waiting for his biscuit and that, thankfully, did the trick and she scuttled back indoors.

Home in no time, I stepped through my own front door, closed it behind me and leaned back against it with a huge sigh of real relief, letting the peace of my house envelope me. I hadn't even moved away from the door when the bell rang and I had to really grit my teeth and try to bury my frustration and annoyance before I could bring myself to open it.

To say I wasn't best pleased to find Bruce on my step holding his plans was an understatement of mammoth proportions and judging by his greeting I wasn't hiding it very well.

'Oh, dear,' he said, pulling a rueful face, 'have I called at a bad time?'

I forced a smile, saying, 'It's definitely not the best,' and willed him to go away.

'Anything I can help with,' he even sounded as if he meant it, and added, 'I'm offering practical help or a sympathetic ear or,' he took a good look at my face, 'I can make you a cup of tea.'

'The very last thing I want is for *anyone* to make me a cup of tea,' I assured him, but relenting for some reason that I was too tired to fathom, I found myself offering, 'but I'll make you one.'

We drank the tea, hot and strong and just the way I liked it, standing opposite one another in my small kitchen leaning against the worktops. Bruce was immaculately dressed in one of his, probably, numerous suits – this one black with a charcoal stripe – with the inevitable snowy shirt but no tie. I was still wearing the ancient jeans and t-shirt I had donned to work in that morning. I was sure I looked grubby, I certainly felt it, and was cross for minding.

'Rough day?'

'My dad collapsed and was taken into hospital this afternoon.' The explanation was blunt and totally without expression and the reason for that was that if I'd allowed any emotion to show I would have bawled and I was saving my tears for if – when – they might be needed.

'Is he all right?' His question was equally brief.

'He seems to be. We'll know once they've completed their tests, but I feel convinced by the information we've been given so far that it almost certainly wasn't a heart-attack.'

'That must be a relief, though you must also still be worried.'

'Mmm.'

'Of course you are. That was a stupid thing to say. Why wouldn't you let me make you a cup of tea?'

I told him about the visit from my sister – though not the reason for it, of course, bearing in mind that it had been all about him – just that we had ended up at the hospital and then the chaotic scenario when she'd arrived home and her misplaced sympathy for me.

Bruce threw back his head and laughed at my descriptive and sometimes pretty blunt language, but even as I found myself laughing with him, I was saying, 'It's really not funny. My family can't bear the fact that I'm very happily single with absolutely no plans to settle down. Happily single is a complex and foreign idea to them. They don't believe such a state even exists. Is your family OK with the fact that you're not married? Or are you? Married, I mean.'

He shook his head, still smiling. 'Like you, I'm extremely happily single. I chose to focus on building up a business, so you could say I'm married to that. There's just Dad and me now – Mum died several years ago – and he's too astute to venture an opinion.'

Despite the fact he'd spent so much time at our house when I was a child, I had never met his parents, though I didn't doubt that my brothers had. I remembered as he spoke that he'd been an only child, and wanted to sympathize about his losing his mum, but refrained from making any comment in case I gave away the fact that I had known him in the past.

'Wise Dad,' I said. 'Mine doesn't exactly interfere really, but he gets caught up in the efforts of the others desperately trying to fulfil their own dream of seeing me live their idea of happy ever after. Anyway,' I changed the subject quickly before he could start asking questions about my family and put two and two together from the answers, 'what did you actually call round for?'

'Besides wanting your opinion of my plans, pure nosiness, really,' he admitted. 'I wanted to get a look at the layout of your house – if you don't mind. I obviously have my own ideas, but thought it would be interesting to see what you've had done, but only if you don't mind. Feel free to tell me to get lost because I know I've got a bit of a nerve.'

'Well, since you admit it.' I found myself grinning at his honesty and recognized that I was warming to him yet again despite my determination not to. He seemed to have a habit of slipping under my guard. 'The story is that I liked the house and the location straight away, but there wasn't enough space for what I wanted.' I walked back into the sitting room we had walked through to reach the kitchen and Bruce followed, 'but my dad knew a semi-retired builder who was happy to turn the place into something that worked for me and he did just that.'

Bruce nodded. 'These old builders are worth their weight in gold and know tricks that no amount of college courses can teach you.' Then, changing the subject he said, 'I quite like the fact there is no hallway to these houses, just a porch.'

'Oh, me, too,' I agreed, 'and I've favoured archways between the downstairs rooms instead of doors to add to that illusion of space.'

He looked around. 'This is a decent-sized room, but the cream walls really help to keep it light and airy.'

I smiled, pleased with the compliment. 'That's what I thought. The one patterned wall,' I indicated the long wall behind the three-seater sofa, 'still has a cream background and, together with the blue-grey suite and carpet, was intentional to save the room from seeming bland or boring.' I moved through a slightly bigger arch and, with Bruce still on my heels, stepped from carpet on to laminated wood floor. 'My dining room and work space.' I waved an airy hand around the long room that took up the whole of the extension I'd had built on to the side of the property soon after moving in.

The dining end with its light oak table and leather chairs looked out through French doors on to the wilderness of the garden and under the window at the other end was my long work table, next to a computer desk, a filing cabinet and book case. A large pin-board on one wall showcased some of my work for the benefit of customers who called in person rather than looking on the website.

Bruce stood looking around, nodding his head. He eventually admitted, 'I think without this addition the house would feel a *lot* smaller.' He indicated the table with its seating for six, 'Do you do much entertaining?'

'Oh, God no,' I said without thinking. 'As Greg and Jasper will soon tell you – if they haven't already – I'm no cook and I happily leave the production of culinary delights to those who enjoy the process. I can barely boil an egg to be honest. In fact, the last one blew up when it boiled dry after I came in here to work and forgot all about it.'

His lips twitched as if he was trying hard not to laugh, but he merely asked, 'How do you manage for meals then? You are slim,' he looked me up and down and I shifted uncomfortably and rued the scruffy clothes all over again, 'but hardly emaciated.'

'Salad, soup, ready meals,' I ticked them off on my fingers, 'an omelette or jacket potato if I'm feeling confident and a bit creative. I also have friends who enjoy cooking and are generous with their invitations – like Jasper and Greg and Miles, of course.'

'Mmm,' he turned his attention to the cards displayed on the pin board, and said, 'These are quite beautiful.'

'Thank you. Do you want to look upstairs?'

'That would be great if you don't mind.'

It was only as he followed me up the stairs that I realised I should have sent him up on his own to view my sleeping arrangements. I was very conscious of him close behind me. The landing was miniscule, with just two doors off it and two people standing together made if feel crowded. I almost rushed into the bathroom and he stepped in right behind me.

'This is different,' he said looking round. 'The layout of my house is nothing like this upstairs.'

'Two bedrooms, though?'

He nodded.

'I couldn't bear such tiny rooms, they gave me claustrophobia, so I sacrificed one bedroom altogether and had it turned into a decent sized bathroom.' A sweep of my hand indicated a corner bath, sink with vanity, a toilet and shower stall and there was still room for a floor standing cupboard and an airing cupboard.

Stepping back out on to the landing, I made a joke of showing him the bedroom, with a 'ta-da,' as I opened the door.

Again he followed me in, but at least there was plenty of room for me to keep out of his way.

'That's amazing.'

Bruce looked round at the spacious room, taking in the wall of fitted wardrobes, double bed with matching bedside cupboards and chests of drawers. Again the walls were cream, apart from the wall behind the bed with its bold pattern of terracotta flowers on a cream background. The carpet was also terracotta, the curtains and bedding were cream.

'This area used to be the old bathroom,' I indicated the space I was standing in. 'It means, with the work I've had done, that I still live in a small house, but with decent-sized rooms.'

'The renovations have completely changed the place. I'm impressed.'

'I'm surprised that you are,' I admitted, forgetting about my embarrassment – though the thought did creep unwanted into my mind that he was the first guy to be invited into my bedroom – or any bedroom of mine – in longer than I cared to remember. 'You must manage building projects all the time.'

'My construction work is more of the industrial variety and new builds. I haven't knocked around and altered any existing houses since I first started out. I'd forgotten how satisfying that can be. You've made this house into a real home, Ellen.'

I was ridiculously pleased, but reminded myself I only felt that way because he was a builder who would have an eye for what worked and what didn't better than any lay person.

My pleasure was short-lived when we both made for the door at the same time and became jammed. An undignified struggle ensued and then I suddenly shot on to the landing at such a speed that I would have pitched head over heels down the narrow stairs if Bruce hadn't been swift enough to catch me and drag me back. For a long moment I was so shocked at what had so nearly happened that I could only stand in the circle of his arms and listen to the frantic hammering of my heart.

'Are you OK?'

His deep voice in my ear brought me to my senses and I had to fight the urge not to pull away from him, aware that a struggle in the very small space could cause a repeat of the very near miss. To my embarrassment, I remembered it wasn't the first time he had saved me from a fall.

'I'm fine,' I said, keeping my voice very, very steady and my mind off the way his breath was lifting tendrils of hair at the back of my neck in the most disconcerting way. 'You can let me go now,' adding when he didn't do so right away, 'please.'

Releasing me slowly was only a sensible move on his part, given the fright I'd just had, but all I could think about was putting some immediate space between us without it looking as if I was running away. Thankfully, the phone ringing gave me the excuse I needed and ignoring the fact there was a receiver in the bedroom right behind us I hurried down the stairs to the one in the sitting room.

'Hello,' I said breathlessly and then felt the blood in my veins freeze when all I could hear on the other end of the line was sobbing.

Chapter Seven

'WHO IS THIS? What's happened?'

Already imagining a scenario that involved my dad, intensive care, a fight for his life that might not be won, and even possibly his funeral, it was all I could do to keep a grip of my swiftly shredding nerves and say calmly, 'Take a deep breath, blow your nose, and then tell me what the matter is.'

I could hear the rustling of tissues and then a honking blow, and began to prepare myself for what was to come. My knuckles gleamed white as my grip tightened on the receiver, and I looked up to find Bruce frowning a query at me. I shrugged my shoulders, wished he would go away, and turned my back on him.

'James is back.'

As I realised who was providing this piece of information, along with a lot of sniffing and more rustling, two things happened. First of all my racing pulse and imagination settled down very quickly but, at the same time, my temper went through the roof.

'What do you mean by "back"?' I asked, making a good effort to rein the temper back a little, at least until I knew all the facts. 'Back as in, the country, the area, your house – please tell me he's not back in your bed?'

Bruce leaned round me and raised his eyebrows right up into his hairline. At any other time I might have found his expression funny, but I just scowled fiercely at him and turning away again, walked away from him and into the kitchen.

'Not exactly.'

I groaned loudly and demanded, 'Fiona, where exactly are you? And what on earth have you done?'

'I'm at home,' she whimpered, and then pleaded in a small voice very unlike her usual bossy tone, 'Can you come over?'

'Of course,' I said immediately, 'I'll be right there. You'll have to go, I'm afraid.' I told Bruce, as I grabbed jacket and bag and dropped the phone onto its charger, 'it's an emergency.'

'Sounds like it. Anything I can do?'

By this time we were standing on my front path, and I didn't even try to hide the fact that I was seething as I said through gritted teeth, 'Not unless you can supply me with the name of a contract killer to deal with Fiona's ex.'

'That bad, huh?'

'Worse,' I told him, and leaving him standing I made my way up the close to rap sharply on my friend's front door.

Fiona was a beautiful, confident lady. She was ten years older than me, but she certainly didn't look it. Her hair and make-up were never less than perfect and – as the owner of possibly the best boutique in town – she was never less than stylishly dressed.

The woman who opened the door to me bore no resemblance to the Fiona that I knew and loved. I couldn't believe the state she was in, but then when I thought of the cause of the state she was in, I found that I could believe it only too well.

I wanted to demand, 'What the hell has he done now?' but first I took her into my arms and gave her a massive hug, and then I said it.

'You won't believe it,' she began.

'Oh, trust me,' I said sourly as I followed her inside, 'I will.'

James was the ex-husband and the reason Fiona was living in a small house almost identical to mine and not in the large detached property she'd used to own before he'd come along and swindled her out of almost everything she had built up from the very successful business she'd been running long before she ever met him. Basically, he had broken her heart and all but ruined her, before disappearing out of her life without so much as a backward glance, taking with him what was left in their joint bank account and leaving behind a house re-mortgaged to the hilt.

'Shall I put the kettle on?' By this time we were seated side by side on the couch and preparing for a heart to heart.

'We might need a bit more than tea,' Fiona admitted, and then we both stared at each other as the doorbell rang and said at the same time, 'Who on earth is that?'

'It's him, isn't it?' I was already on my feet, ready to do battle on her account.

'No,' she said, quite emphatically, 'it won't be James,' before her face crumbled again and fresh tears began to flow.

'I'll get it and tell whoever it is to go away.'

Fiona didn't argue and I stepped into the tiny porch and reached for the door catch. If it had been James on the step, I wouldn't have been responsible for my actions, but being faced with Bruce bearing very welcome gifts was something I hadn't been expecting.

'Who is it?' Fiona's voice, still thick with tears filtered through from the room behind me.

'I do believe it's Redman Construction delivering pizza and wine,' I told her wryly, finding it hard to believe it myself. 'Whatever next? Pizza Hut erecting houses?' I added sarcastically. 'Shall I tell him to go away?'

My rumbling stomach was the main cause of the overwhelming feeling of relief I felt when she called out, 'No, it's OK. Let him in,' and then raced for the stairs, if I interpreted the sounds I could hear behind me correctly.

I wasn't surprised when there was no sign of Fiona in the sitting room. 'I think she's just popped upstairs,' I told Bruce. 'Come on through to the kitchen. Nice thought, by the way.'

'I realised you'd be starving after the day you've had, and the chances are that Fiona hasn't eaten either. Trying to set the world to rights on an empty stomach is usually a very bad idea, I find.'

'That doesn't account for the wine,' I nodded at the pair of bottles he was setting on the work top – chilled to perfection if the condensation running down the outside of the bottles was anything to go by.

'In my experience nothing ever seems as bad with a glass of decent wine in your hand.'

'And that's your philosophy, is it?' I asked, and then turned when I realised Fiona had come in behind us – and did a double-take. 'You're looking – mmm – much better.'

In no time at all she'd removed all sign of tears and was back looking so close to her usual immaculate self that I couldn't believe it. A make-over like that would have taken me hours and my eyes would still have been swollen to puffy slits. She'd even changed her crumpled outfit for a black silky lounging suit and teamed it with high heeled sandals. What with Fiona's make-over and Bruce still dressed in his suit and pristine shirt I felt very much like the poor relation. I'd have taken myself off home to change if I hadn't been far too hungry to waste the time.

'I only called in to bring refreshments,' Bruce smiled down at her. 'I was with Ellen when she got your call and I was pretty certain she hadn't eaten, for various reasons. Since I was one of the reasons for that, I thought this was the least I could do. I'll be off now, just make sure you eat the pizza while it's hot and drink the wine while it's cold.'

'Oh, you don't have to go, do you?'

The change in Fiona wasn't all in her appearance, I noticed. No one would have guessed she had been sobbing her heart out only moments earlier. The coquettish smile and fluttering eyelashes made me feel more than a little perplexed, and I was quite sure Bruce must have been wondering what had happened to the emergency that had brought me tearing up the road.

I realised he was looking at me, and said, 'Oh, don't leave on my account. Just get that pizza sliced and on to plates before I eat it through the box and, yes, I did say *through* the box and not *from* it.'

I left them to it, seeing as they seemed to be doing so well without my help and wondered why I suddenly seemed to be the odd man – or woman – out. There they both were dressed up to the nines and getting cosy together in the kitchen. For two pins I'd have just up and left the pair of them to it, but that would have meant going home and finding something to eat there, and that pizza did smell really good.

I was glad I'd stayed when my patience and goodwill was rewarded with a slice of pizza trailing melted cheese in one hand and chilled glass of Pinot Grigio in the other. Ignoring the pair of them I gave the food and drink the attention it deserved.

'So what do you think?'

Several long minutes had elapsed and, busily working my way through yet another slice I was actually becoming too full to think, so I simply ignored the question until it was repeated.

I stared at them, sitting close together on the sofa, and said, 'Oh, were you speaking to me?' with my mouth full.

'We've been speaking to you all along,' Fiona told me looking disgruntled. 'You just haven't been listening. Bruce has been kind enough to give me his opinion on the James situation. I thought you came here to do the same.'

My last slice of pizza suddenly didn't look so appealing, but I drained my glass before I asked, 'Would you have listened if I had?' It came out a bit more sharply than I had intended, but all of a sudden I didn't care. Standing up, I said, 'I'm really tired, so I'll leave you both to it if you don't mind. Thanks for the pizza, Bruce,' and then I left, closing the door behind me far more gently than I would have liked.

For the second time in just a few hours I went into my house, leaned back against the door and dared anyone else to press my doorbell and, in fact, it didn't go again until early the next morning.

'Fiona,' I greeted her with very little enthusiasm, 'to what do I owe this pleasure?' She would have got much shorter shrift had I not just rung the hospital and been told that my dad had spent a very comfortable night and that they would be running tests on him during the day with a view to coming up with some answers that should definitely dispel the heart attack theory.

'I came to say sorry,' she said in a small voice.

'You have?'

'Bruce told me about your day yesterday – he's really very nice, isn't he? I'm so sorry about your dad. Is he going to be OK?'

I nodded, 'I think so.'

'And then there was my asking you to drop everything, which you did, and then I had a go at you. I'm such a selfish cow sometimes.'

I didn't feel like disagreeing with that, but I loved her anyway and she was a lovely friend, as was proved when she went on. 'Look, let me make it up to you. Come down to the shop and pick out something stunning. You never treat yourself, so let me do it instead.'

I smiled. That was Fiona all over, self-centred at times, but generous to a fault at others.

'Thank you, that's so lovely of you to offer, but I never go to the sort of places where I'd be able to wear something stunning.'

'Then I'd say it was time you did. Get yourself down to the shop and leave the rest to me.' She had turned away before I could reply, and then said over her shoulder when she got to the gate, 'Trust me, I will not take no for an answer and I *am* still waiting for your opinion on what I should do about James.'

She must have known my answer to that would be short and very much to the point, but she didn't hang around to hear it, so I went back indoors.

It was a day of constant interruptions, from the lorry pulling up outside and very noisily unloading pallets of bricks, to my sister Alma ringing to request a lift to the hospital, 'because you know I don't like driving when the roads are busy,' – which since we lived in a lively town somehow seemed to me to negate the whole point of her owning a car – other calls brought various customer requests, and Simon turned up to make a start on the garden. His assurance that he wouldn't make a sound had a hollow ring to it, but as the morning was already almost over and the afternoon would be spent visiting the hospital, I saw no point in objecting.

The day got immeasurably better when I got the call from my mother saying my dad was being allowed home as soon as they had the test results, and could I go and fetch them later. I could have done without Alma's insistence on coming with us, which meant going out of my way but, as she so correctly pointed out yet again, she *was* the eldest. Being the eldest, however, obviously didn't mean that she could do the pick-up instead of me, for the reason she'd given me earlier. In truth, I was more than happy to do it, even if I did have to put up with Alma's unwanted opinion of my sad life. Simon benefitted from my improved mood when I took cheese on toast out to him when I went out to share the good news.

'Looking good,' I said looking around, impressed by what he'd already achieved; he purposely got the wrong end of the stick and took the praise far more personally.

'Do, don't I?' he agreed, nodding enthusiastically and indicating his tall scruffily clad form, he explained, 'It is, of course, the casual look. Overalls donated by my MOT specialist because he wasn't keen on the burgundy colour, boots courtesy of Oxfam, t-shirt half price in the Matalan sale – and lunch graciously provided by the proprietor of Ellen Carson's Cards if I'm not mistaken.'

I laughed. 'Are you ever serious?'

'Of course,' he said, 'when the occasion demands it.' He sat down and bit into a slice of cheese on toast, closing his eyes as if in ecstasy. 'I thought you told me you couldn't cook. This is superb.' He laughed at my exasperated expression. 'You're looking happier than you did.'

I told him about my dad coming home. Pleased to have someone to share the news with. 'Not sure what's wrong with him, but I'm banking on it being something that can be treated. We should know more later. I'll leave the house open for you and trust you not to have a party while I'm gone.'

That set us reminiscing about a girl from our school who'd had a party while her parents were away and how the kids had all but trashed the place by the end of the night.

'Cigarette burns everywhere, every drop of drink in the house gone and the bedrooms being used for illicit purposes. A couple of pregnancies even resulted from that night, so I was told,' Simon said knowledgeably.

'I know,' I could still feel my teenage shock when I'd heard. 'Where were we when all of that was going on?'

'Well, I seem to remember you had to be home by nine, and I didn't see the point of going back once I'd walked you to your door. Just as well, really, because I could be very easily lead in those days and would probably have got into all kinds of trouble. It must have all kicked off after we left.'

Once the cheese on toast was gone I left him to it and battled through the homecoming school traffic to Alma's. Predictably, she was busy getting everything ready for Les's homecoming, just in case she wasn't back. This was despite her house, as ever, being full of able-bodied people quite capable of making him a cup of tea and the sandwich he would apparently require to tide him over until it was time for his evening meal.

By the time she had held us up further in order to make a pot of tea for those expectantly waiting, I was practically beside myself and couldn't help demanding, 'Are none of you competent to make tea for yourselves?'

Everyone stopped what they were doing, although in fairness that hadn't been very much, and Alma stopped pouring. They all stared at me as if I had just spoken in a foreign language and one they definitely didn't understand.

'But she likes to do it,' someone said. 'I like to do it,' Alma echoed, 'it doesn't take a minute.'

With difficulty I managed not to yell, 'That's not the point,' at the top of my voice, and just gave up.

Even when I thought we were finally on our way, Alma paused at the door to enquire worriedly of the room generally, 'Now, you do know how Les likes his tea?'

'Two sugars, not too strong?' someone asked doubtfully.

'Two and a half and medium to strong,' my sister fussed, 'and wait until he's sitting down before you pour it.'

'I'll wait in the car,' I said tersely and before I lost it totally, 'but hurry up or we won't get parked at all.'

Alma finally climbed in the passenger side, looking immensely pleased with herself. 'I wrote it all down for them.'

I just swore quietly under my breath, reminded her to fasten the seatbelt and pulled out into the traffic. At least concentrating on the busy roads meant I could shut out much of her chuntering on, mainly about my not knowing what I was missing by having no family around me to keep me company and make sure I was all right.

We made the normal tour of the levels of the car park and then stopped as I spotted reversing lights ahead. As with last time, it was a four-by-four but this one looked familiar. It pulled out in front of us and then stopped and Bruce climbed out.

'Ellen? It is you.'

What I wanted to know was where was the queue there would normally be building up behind me that would have prevented this tete-a-tete?

'Here to see your dad, are you?'

'Hopefully to pick him up,' I said abruptly and then felt obliged to ask, 'You?'

'My dad, too,' he said chattily. 'He's had a bit of a fall and hurt his leg. We weren't sure if something was broken, but it turned out to be a sprained ankle. He's waiting at the front.'

'You'd better get on then, and so had we.' I could feel Alma breathing down my neck as she leaned over and waited for the introduction I was determined wouldn't be forthcoming.

Thankfully, a car appeared in my rear view mirror at that moment turning at the top of the ramp onto this floor and moving towards us.

'Hope your dad is OK,' Bruce went to get into his vehicle, and then called out, 'Simon's made a good start on our gardens already, hasn't he?'

'Wonderful,' I agreed, watching him pull away and wondering how long it was going to take for the pennies to start dropping, and for Alma to start getting even more excited about all the possibilities she could see in store for me.

Chapter Eight

A LMA DIDN'T HAVE much to say for herself as I parked and we made our way into the hospital. We had found Mum and Dad without too much trouble, and settled ourselves in the day room with them to wait for someone to come and tell us what was going on, when she suddenly sat up straight and stared at me. I did my best to ignore her, but I could almost hear the cogs in her brain whirring.

'That was him, wasn't it?' she said finally.

'That was who?' I said deliberately feigning ignorance.

'Bruce Redman,' she sounded so pleased to have worked that out.

'Bruno?' My mother immediately pounced. 'Where?'

Right on cue a nurse walked into the room. I could have kissed her – and even more so when she delivered some good news about my father's health.

The tests showed, she told us, that Dad had a hiatus hernia and then she went into a lengthy explanation of what that was and how the symptoms might be treated. As she also provided a booklet which would no doubt supply similar information and even more detail, the only thing I really took in was the fact that people with this type of hernia may experience chest pain that could easily be confused with the pain of a heart attack. That's why it had been so important for Dad to undergo the appropriate testing and get properly diagnosed.

We all nodded wisely, and I had already decided to read the booklet from cover to cover and to find out what I could from the internet as soon as I got home. I was already wondering whether Dad eating what was probably the hearty breakfast Mum always insisted upon, and then bending about in the garden straight after, might have brought on the attack. I mentioned this as soon as we'd got them back home and settled indoors and we'd had a chance to talk about the diagnosis and how best to help Dad to deal with it.

'I'm almost certain you can help yourself by not eating foods that can aggravate it and avoiding any strenuous exercise straight after a meal.' I went on, 'Probably help to keep some antacid treatment handy, as well.'

'How come you know all this?' Alma demanded, probably thinking it was her job to know – what with her being the eldest and all.

'My customers often tell me about their ailments or those of family members while they're choosing card designs,' I said, 'and I think this particular one came up quite recently. It's surprising what you find that you can remember. I seem to recall this lady kept a food diary, so that if she had another attack she would have a better idea of what to avoid.'

'That's a good idea,' Mum said, seeming quite taken with the idea. 'I'll start one right away.'

'Did you want me to pop to the shop for some indigestion remedies – just to be on the safe side?'

Unfortunately, she remembered she had some in the cupboard and Alma immediately took it upon herself to start fussing around checking what was available. My slim hope of escaping before she again recalled the chance meeting with Bruce Redman in the hospital car park disappeared entirely when my brother, Richard, walked through the back door.

The minute Alma pulled her head out of the cupboard she was investigating and saw him, she became so excited that she almost fell off the kitchen stool she was standing on.

'We saw an old friend of yours today, Rich. Didn't we, Ellen?' She looked at me for confirmation and climbed down to give the matter her full attention.

I managed a barely audible, 'Mmm,' when I realised the whole Bruce thing, with all its implications, was about to be dragged out into the daylight and examined minutely for possibilities where I was concerned.

'Oh, who was that?' Rich said with very little interest. Having always lived in Brankstone he probably had more old friends than he knew what to do with already.

'Well,' Mum got in first, 'apparently it was that Bruno, the one who spent so much time round our house when Ellen was a little girl. She had quite a crush on him, I seem to remember.'

I cringed, went to protest, but then thought better of it. Best ignore the whole thing and let them talk themselves out, just in case by opening my mouth I ended up making matters a whole lot worse. I made a point of fussing round Dad, whom everybody else seemed to have forgotten in the excitement that the thought of a new love interest for me always gave them.

'God, yes, she did – followed him everywhere. Still fancy him, do you, Ellen?' Rich teased. 'If he's back in town you could do worse than hang your hat up there, you know.'

I showed that remark the contempt it deserved by acting as if my brother hadn't spoken. It didn't stop them discussing me and my prospects as far as Bruce Redman was concerned for a minute, of course.

They debated how much money he was probably making, the fact that he was – very handily – an old family friend, hopefully still unmarried and therefore eligible, just about the right age and good-looking enough even for someone as fussy as I obviously was.

'Well, when you've all quite finished matchmaking on my behalf, I would quite like to be getting home so that I can get some work done.' I made it sound as if I wasn't bothered that they were up to their old tricks, in truth I was absolutely fuming. 'Anyway,'

I flourished the trump card I knew would be sure to make Alma recall her obligations at home, 'Les will be waiting for his tea,' and then very foolishly added, 'and I left Simon working in the garden.' I could have bitten off my tongue.

'Oh, yes,' Alma wasn't about to be distracted until she had all the facts, 'I heard Bruce say something about his making a good job of both your gardens.'

'So?' I said in a brittle tone, feeling the net closing in on me. 'Simon's a gardener. He works on lots of gardens.'

'Is Bruno actually living next door to you, Ellen?' My mother asked the question and my heart sank. I would never manage to fob my mother off and knew I would never get away with lying to her either, not even a half-truth.

'Yes,' I said, and watched a speculative look appear on everyone's face but my dad's. He had apparently had enough, too.

'Now leave the girl alone,' he ordered, tetchily. 'I can see what you're all thinking, but she's happy on her own – and so she keeps telling you. If I know you've been interfering again I won't be best pleased, I can tell you. Now, isn't it time we thought about getting something to eat, Lydia? I don't think letting me starve will do this hernia any good.'

'Thank you, Dad,' I hugged him and told the rest of them shortly, 'He's the one you should be taking care of – especially after the scare he's given us. I'm big enough to take care of myself, *and* to make my own decision and my own choices. Now, are you coming, Alma, or not?'

They all flushed at the implied criticism and we left Mum fussing over the ingredients for Dad's favourite meal, and Rich settling down for a man to man chat with Dad. Slightly shamefaced, Alma followed me out and she remained subdued all the way back to her place. She was welcomed into the bosom of her waiting family as if she'd been away for months and left them to starve.

'Come and eat with us?' she pleaded over her shoulder as they hustled her away. 'You can't enjoy eating alone, surely?'

This time no amount of entreaties could convince me to go inside, so I just laughed and said, 'I actually enjoy my own company, Alma, hard as that may be for you to believe,' before I climbed back into the car and drove off tooting the horn cheerfully.

However, I was well aware that though she might have given up for now, I hadn't heard the end of this as far as my sister was concerned, and the thought made me feel very uneasy.

In spite of my qualms, when I arrived home and went to see how Simon had been getting on in the garden I found my spirits soaring the minute I walked through the house and stepped outside.

'That,' I said admiringly, 'is amazing. If I hadn't just walked through my own door, I would think I'd come to the wrong place. You *have* been busy.'

He looked pleased. 'Not cut it back too much for you?'

'God, no, you've almost doubled the space – but where did the slabs come from?' I was gazing at a paved section he'd created that stretched right across the back of the house, so that either the back door or French doors gave access to a patio area that definitely hadn't been there when I went out earlier.

'Well, I guess your old next door neighbour had intended laying a path or something similar to this at some time in the dim and distant past,' he explained, 'because we kept finding these paving stones plonked down randomly, and there were loads stacked behind the shed.'

'We?' I asked, not sure I liked the sound of something that smacked of unwanted charity.

'Yeah, Bruce turned up when I was clearing over there. I've been dividing my time fairly between your gardens,' he was careful to point out. 'Though most of the work over there involves getting rid of seemingly endless iron bedsteads, bed springs, bike frames and pram wheels – I've already filled a second skip because it's like a scrapyard over there. Yours has been much easier, just a lot of cutting back and a bit of mowing has made a hell of a difference, which is why you can see such a change in such a short space of time. I'll need to come back and set the slabs properly, but you can see how it will look.'

'I can't accept them,' I told him flatly.

'Why ever not?' Simon was looking at me as if I'd lost my senses.

'Because,' I said, preparing to count the reasons off on my fingers and then only finding two, which was a bit disappointing, but better than nothing, 'Bruce can use them himself in his own garden, or he can sell them, but he can't simply get his unwanted rubbish moved into my garden.' I knew I sounded petty and child-ish, but I also knew what my family would make of this, along with everything else, if they ever got to hear of it.

'Now you're just being silly.'

'That's as maybe, but I'm not a charity case, Simon. If I want slabs I can afford to go and buy them.'

'Why on earth would you want to do that when these are going begging? We're doing the guy a good turn by taking them off his hands since he just basically wants the site cleared ready for the work on the house. It will cost him if I have to load them into yet another skip. Honestly, he was pleased to see the back of them. He even gave me a hand to bring them round.'

'Well, he can just damn well give you a hand to take them back, because I don't want them.' I didn't stamp my foot – I didn't really need to because I was aware I was being childish in the extreme now. The back door slammed very satisfyingly behind me as I marched indoors and I knew I had finally lost it when I burst into tears.

I eventually looked up to find Simon standing in front of me holding out a mug of tea. He set it on the coffee table in front of me and then sat on the sofa beside me.

'So,' he said, 'what's this really all about, because it's more than just a bunch of mouldy old slabs, isn't it? Have you had bad news about your dad? Is that it?'

I shook my head and sniffed. 'No, and I know you'll think I'm being silly but. . .' and then it all came pouring out, everything that had happened that day and what I expected to happen in the future regarding the family's determined plans for Bruce and me – or me and any even half-eligible man, really.

'Ellen, you just can't let them keep getting to you like this. You're a grown woman with a mind of your own. Have you tried telling them that?'

I nodded, and a tear trickled down my cheek, 'But they never listen – they never have.'

'Then you have to treat it as the joke it really is, you know,' he said seriously. 'You managed to laugh it all off on the night of your party.'

'That's because *you* did, and made it easy for me, but believe me, most guys don't find their interference a laughing matter and they either run for the hills or, like Miles they take it far too seriously and start planning the wedding. I would be mortified if they got carried away with the Bruce-and-me-as-a-couple idea and I will just die if they remind him about my following him around when I was a kid.'

'Exactly,' he said triumphantly, 'you've just said it yourself. You were a kid, Ellen, and now you're a forty-year-old woman. No one is going to take a child's crush seriously – unless you do.'

'Really?' I peeped at him from under my fringe.

'Really,' Simon assured me. 'Laughing at the very idea will make your family look far more foolish than you, and please don't throw the slabs back in Bruce's face just because *they've* upset you. The guy was just making a friendly gesture that actually cost him nothing more than about an hour of his time and helped me to clear his garden much more quickly into the bargain.'

'I'm being very silly, aren't I?' I raised a weak smile from somewhere.

'Not really,' he pulled a rueful face, 'I can see that their constant meddling would be bloody annoying.'

'The garden does look great.'

'Thank you.'

'I expect a bill, when you've finished,' I warned.

'You'll get one,' Simon promised.

'I'd like to take you out for a meal meanwhile,' I said, 'for being so logical about everything and making me see sense at last. Perhaps not tonight, since it's already late, but maybe tomorrow?'

'Great,' he accepted. 'It'll be Friday night, too, and a nice way to start the weekend – it's not often my clients treat me to a meal. What about tonight, though? Fancy fish and chips?'

It didn't take a lot of thought. 'I do, especially as the second choice is cheese on toast again. I'll pay.'

'You will not, it was my idea. Won't be long.'

With that, Simon was gone. I drank my tea and then a glimpse of myself in the mirror I passed on my way to put the plates to warm sent me rushing up the stairs to get rid of all traces of my earlier tears. I had reason to be thankful for that and the fact I'd even run a brush through my hair when Simon came in, bringing with him the delicious aroma of fish and chips – and my next door neighbour.

'Look who I found outside,' Simon said easily, 'he hasn't eaten either and is following the scent. There's plenty for all of us.'

'He actually invited me, Ellen,' Bruce corrected. 'I hope that's OK with you?'

'Of course,' I said, trying to mimic Simon's careless tone and mindful of his earlier advice. Despite my family and what could only be their transparent attempts to match me up with Bruce, only my reactions to it all could make it into a big deal, just as Simon had said. Start as I meant to go on, I reminded myself.

'She might be no cook,' Simon called from the kitchen, 'but she's great at warming plates and buttering bread for the butties.'

'He has a nerve maligning my catering skills when his own attempts probably don't go much further than the regular use of a can opener,' I said loud enough for Simon to hear, and then I requested, 'Put another plate in to warm, Simon, if you can manage it. Laps or dining table?'

'Laps,' said Bruce and 'Dining table,' came from Simon.

Before we could ask why the formality, he reminded us, 'We can admire my handiwork outside if we sit at the table and I can bask in the glow of your approval.'

I rolled my eyes at Bruce and, as I collected place mats, cutlery and glasses to carry through, I said, 'I must thank you for the slabs, too, and I must pay you for them.'

I could see he was going to refuse, and got ready to insist, but he was there with an answer that I couldn't really argue with. 'Technically they're not even my slabs, they belong to the previous owner – Ivy, is it? – and I'm sure she would be happy for you to have them. They're no earthly use to me, I assure you.'

'What is it with you men?' I demanded, but I was laughing as I reached into the fridge for the wine I'd put there earlier to get a bit of a chill. 'You have an answer for just about everything. Not sure what I can do for you in return, though.'

Bruce wasn't looking at me as he answered, 'Oh, I'm sure we'll think of something.'

I refused to look for a hidden meaning as I thrust the bottle in his direction and said, 'Go and get pouring, then. It's not champagne, is probably not up to your usual vintage, but it might be just a little more chilled than the stuff we got into trouble with at Miles'.'

Of course, Simon picked up on that as he helped me carry the loaded plates through and the whole sad story had to be told and we ended up laughing a lot.

'You see,' I told Simon, pointing at Bruce, 'he has a habit of inviting himself round for meals with the neighbours.'

'That's a bit harsh,' Simon teased adding, 'though I have to say he did make sure I was carrying take-away food before he crossed your threshold, Ellen.'

I looked up from arranging chips on to thickly buttered bread and, refusing to rise to the bait, merely said, 'Obviously more sensible than he looks then, isn't he?'

'And I'm sensible enough to recognise that you make much

better butties than I do, Ellen. Any chance of you making me one?'

Bruce was smiling at me winningly as he made the cheeky request and I joked, 'It's like being back at home with my brothers.'

'You have brothers?' he asked, looking interested, 'Any chance I might know them?'

Chapter Nine

THERE IT WAS – the question I had been waiting for and dreading ever since Bruce Redman had reappeared in my life. I forced myself to concentrate on the butty I was making placing the chips with a steady hand, but out of the corner of my eye I caught the quick glance Simon threw my way. He knew, just as I did, that this was when the history between my family and Bruce was going to be revealed. Unless I lied which really wasn't a sensible option.

'Depends how old you are,' I said, playing dumb. 'Simon and I were at St Barts together, but I don't remember you being in our year. My brothers are both a few years older than me.'

'I'm forty-eight and I did go to St Barts.'

'I'd be surprised if you didn't know them then,' I said in an easy tone that belied the fact that my heart was thumping at the thought of what was about to be revealed. 'Richard is the same age as you and Jonathon just a bit younger.'

'Not Richo and Jono Carson?' he looked astounded. 'They were my best friends through school. I was always round at their house – your house.'

'Oh,' I said, as if it had only just occurred to me, 'you must be Bruno, then. Fancy that. I had no idea.'

Simon smiled approvingly at me across the table and that made me believe I was making quite a good job of what I had expected to be a really difficult situation.

Bruce looked even more amazed and exclaimed, 'You must be little Ellie. She was just the sweetest little thing,' he told Simon, 'but of course you must remember that if you were at school with her.'

He hadn't even mentioned the fact that I'd followed him everywhere and I couldn't believe he'd actually thought me "the sweetest little thing," back then. I found myself warming to him all over again – and it was without the aid of alcohol this time since I hadn't even sipped my wine yet.

We ate the chip butties I had generously prepared for us all, enjoyed the crisply battered fish liberally showered with salt and vinegar and toasted our younger selves with a sip or two of wine. I enjoyed the reminiscing and the light-hearted teasing and, probably for the first time in many years, really understood what it felt like to enjoy the companionship of male friends without any pressure or reservations.

Thank goodness for Simon, I thought, and his common sense approach to my family and the pressure they always put on me to marry. A pressure that it was clear now I should have been simply ridiculing all these years instead of taking it so seriously.

I woke to a watery October sun and a great feeling of well-being which set me to work in an excellent frame of mind. Funny how a mood could have an effect on your productivity because quite intricate cards just seemed to evolve from my fingers with very little effort throughout the morning, and verses popped into my head with an ease that surprised and pleased me.

I made a bit of lunch for myself, and for Simon, who had been setting the patio slabs permanently in place at the back of the house with so little fuss or noise that I'd scarcely been aware that he was there.

'Good morning?' he asked, tucking in as if the food in front of him was something wonderful and not just plain old beans on toast.

'Actually, yes,' I smiled at him. 'It was a good evening, too, wasn't it? And that's thanks to you, really.'

He looked pleased, but rather taken aback, 'Thanks to me?'

'Mmm.' I nodded. 'That could have been a very awkward moment, when the subject of my brothers came up, but because of the advice you'd given me earlier it was easier than I thought – and I'm sure I can deal with my family in a more rational way now, as well, and again that's thanks to you. Please feel free to choose anything from the menu tonight,' I encouraged, 'because you've more than earned it and I'll come and pick you up so that you can have a drink.'

I followed him outside to admire the patio and also the neat, tidy area that he'd rescued from the overgrown jungle that had been there before.

'It doesn't take long once you get stuck in,' he assured me, when I said again how impressed I was by what he'd achieved in so short a time. 'That's what I like about gardening – you can really see results quite quickly. You might want to pop some spring bulbs in if you get a minute.'

'I might just do that, and even plant a tub or two up to stand on the patio,' I said before I went back inside.

I worked steadily through the afternoon, trying to make up for the time I had lost for various reasons through the week, and was reasonable pleased with what I'd achieved. When I stopped I noticed Simon had already left and, looking at the time, thought I'd better do something about getting ready.

Simon lived in a flat on the other side of town and he'd obviously been looking out for me because he answered the door before my finger had even left the bell. We looked each other up and down and both burst out laughing.

'Scrub up pretty well, don't we?' he grinned, taking in the freshly shampooed and straightened dark hair that fell sleekly to my shoulders and the carefully applied make-up.

I was dressed all in black, and so was he. I was wearing trousers, as I invariably did, with high-heeled boots, and a lacy long-sleeved top under a bum-skimming leather jacket. Simon wore black shirt, jeans and a bomber-style suede jacket. He was freshly shaved and had managed to fit in a haircut since leaving my house.

'We look like serious devotees of the late Roy Orbison,' I noted.

'I like black,' he said emphatically.

'Me, too,' I agreed. 'Let's go, the table is booked for eight and I'm starving.'

This time, instead of the local Italian restaurant, I had opted for one in Poole situated right on the quay. There was no awkward hand holding as we walked from the car park and no awkward silences, either. I just knew I was going to enjoy the evening – with no wrangling over the fact that I would be paying the bill at the end of it. To reach the eatery we had to climb steps and I guessed the view across the water was going to be spectacular.

I saw them the minute I stepped into the restaurant, though they were tucked cosily away at a table for two in the corner. My stomach dropped and my appetite fled – though I had absolutely no grounds for feeling so . . . confused, unsettled – and all sorts of other mixed up, unexplainable emotions.

There was no reason in the world why Bruce and Fiona shouldn't be enjoying a meal together, I reminded myself harshly. It was a free country, after all.

They hadn't seen us, Simon hadn't seen them and, to my immense relief the waiter led us to a table on the opposite side of what was, thankfully, a very large restaurant. I made sure I took the chair with my back towards them and hoped the large pillar in the centre of the room would block Simon's view.

Becoming very animated, I selected my favourite things from the menu and encouraged Simon to do the same, discovering as we made our choices that we both still loved mushrooms, and that he favoured a tomato-based sauce with his pasta while I preferred the rich, creamy variety. I drank sparkling water, but encouraged him to indulge in a glass or three of his favourite red wine.

I laughed a lot at Simon's – not always very funny – jokes and had him chuckling as we reminisced – and all the time I was wondering what my friend and my next door neighbour were doing out together. Were they already an item, even though she had been weeping bitter tears over her ex-husband only days ago? It was possible, because Fiona was renowned for being a fast worker where the opposite sex was concerned.

Well, of course, I told myself firmly, as the first course arrived, it has absolutely *nothing* to do with me, because either of them can eat where they like, when they like and with whom they like. With that I speared a deep fried mushroom savagely with my fork, coated it liberally with garlic dip and tucked in with an appearance of enjoyment that was completely deceptive.

'That must be good, because I've spoken to you twice now and got no response at all.' I looked up to find Simon looking at me quizzically.

'I'm sorry but this food is just gorgeous and that, together with the fabulous view across the water is making it difficult to concentrate on everything at once. What did you say?'

'I was saying,' he laughed and shook his head at me, 'it's a good job this isn't a date or I would be mortally offended that you weren't finding my company and conversation more riveting – and isn't that your sister over there?'

'Alma?' I screwed my head round in surprise because I knew for a fact she rarely went anywhere in the evening, and I would have been amazed to see Les in a decent restaurant – never mind a foreign one. 'Here?'

'No, not Alma – the other one – what's her name – I can't remember?'

'*Molly*? Really?' I screwed my head round, commenting at the same time, 'She and Gordon must be going through a good patch in their marriage for once if they're out for a meal together.'

Then I spotted them and realised immediately that the man with Molly was definitely not my brother-in-law Gordon. I was also forced to acknowledge this was no innocent meeting and they were clearly more than friends since they were holding hands over the table and gazing adoringly into each other's eyes over what looked like generous portions of spaghetti carbonnara.

I wasn't sure what surprised me most – seeing Molly openly sitting there with another man or the fact that she was eating spaghetti which she'd always detested. Well, I'd known for a long time she had marriage problems because she was always going home to Mum and Dad – even at her age – but I'd have sworn that cheating wasn't her style.

Now I was in a real quandary. Did I acknowledge that I'd seen her and embarrass us both? Or did I ignore yet another couple?

'Aren't you going to speak to your sister?' Simon was looking at me oddly, and he hadn't even seen my neighbours yet.

'Shhh,' I warned, 'I'm thinking.'

Simon obviously knew when not to push things and began to chat inconsequentially as the main course arrived. It seemed like no time at all before we were near the end of our meal. I would have loved to simply brazen the whole thing out, greeting both couples briefly as we left but, unfortunately, there was the little matter of the bill to be requested and paid before that could happen. I was just debating how I could manage that without drawing attention to myself, when the restaurant door was thrown open with force hitting the wall behind it with a resounding crash, and a man who definitely *was* my brother-in-law Gordon came steaming in.

It took him only seconds to spot his wife. 'I knew it,' he roared, 'I bloody well knew it.'

'Oh, sh. . .' I murmured, cringing at the thought of the scene that was about to develop, and feeling quite sure that this was not the moment to announce my presence.

'The man she's with is not her husband, and the one who's just come in is?' Simon hazarded a guess.

'Well worked out, Sherlock,' I muttered, wishing I could pull the tablecloth over my head or even place the napkin strategically, anything that would shield me from the embarrassment of yet another of my family's domestic affairs being played out in public. I'd seen far too much of it over the years. The irony in the fact that they all honestly thought this was what my life lacked wasn't lost on me.

To start with there were just angry words being exchanged, with anxious waiters hovering and doing their best to cool the situation down. It was when Gordon, perhaps unwisely, tried to force Molly to leave with him that it all started to get a bit nasty and the two men squared up to each other threatening violence.

Realising that feigned disinterest was no longer a viable option, I finally leapt up out of my seat, but Simon had already beaten me to it and by the time I got there, he was holding my brother-in-law back. When I saw it was Bruce who had the other man's arms pinned behind him I could, quite literally, have died on the spot.

'What are you doing here?' Molly demanded, glaring at me as if I was the one who had no business being there.

'I *was* enjoying a quiet meal until this all kicked off,' I pointed out.

'Who with?' she was looking from Bruce to Simon and back again.

'That is none of your business,' I said flatly, 'but what you're doing here with a man who isn't your husband has suddenly become mine and that of every other person in the restaurant who simply wants to enjoy their meal in peace.'

I think it was only at that moment that Molly appreciated the attention of the whole place was upon her, as other customers, the waiting and even the kitchen staff looked on – the two men prepared to compete for her affection, clearly ready to use violence if necessary.

'Oh, pack it in,' she told them severely, as if they were just a couple of naughty boys. 'I'm going home,' she turned to the man she'd been gazing across the table at only minutes earlier, 'with Gordon. I hate spaghetti anyway,' she added, as if that were reason enough for her sudden change of heart.

With that, pushing Gordon in front of her she left the restaurant with her head held high, leaving her paramour to pay the bill – which he did with indecent haste, almost falling over himself in his eagerness to quit the scene of his humiliation. I would have done anything to have been able to do the same.

I suddenly realised Fiona was standing behind me. 'What was that all about?' she asked, looking at each of us in turn.

'I think it was Molly being caught with her knickers down,' Simon said bluntly, 'though not literally, of course.'

'*That* was Molly?' Bruce exclaimed, his dark brows almost meeting his hair line.

'Who the hell is Molly?' Fiona demanded in a mystified tone.

'You might well ask,' I said, realising I was actually shaking and that we were still the focus of far too much attention. 'Can we pay the bill, please, Simon, and get the hell out of here?'

'Gentlemen,' the manager was coming towards us, and I groaned inwardly at the thought of Simon and Bruce taking the blame for my family's disgraceful behaviour, 'we would like to offer the drinks of your choice for yourselves and your ladies – on the house, of course – for defusing what could have been a very awkward situation and with the minimum of fuss.'

'Oh, no, not for us – really,' I pleaded, hot with renewed embarrassment. 'We were just about to leave.'

It was Bruce who coaxed, 'Come and join us, Ellen. Look, you're shaking like a leaf. Simon, Fiona, take her over to our table while I go and see about these drinks.'

My protests were ignored as I was practically manhandled to a seat at the table for two in the corner and then watched while two extra chairs were squeezed around it.

'Don't take it to heart,' Simon cajoled, crouching down to take my cold hands into his and trying to rub some warmth into them. 'Look, Fiona's brought your jacket and handbag over and all's well that ends well. There was no real trouble, after all. A storm in a teacup really.'

'Would someone mind telling me what just happened – please?

And why Ellen is so upset over a bit of a domestic?' Fiona said plaintively.

I sighed deeply and pulling my hands free of Simon's I turned to face her. 'The lady involved was my sister.'

'You're kidding, right?' Fiona's face was an absolute picture. 'One of the sisters who are always giving you a hard time for not being married, and this one is apparently in the process of screwing up her own marriage by playing away from home?'

I gave a deep nod, while making excuses about my family 'meaning well' when they interfered in my life and tried to bulldoze me into accepting that their way was the right way. 'That's about the size of it, yes. Obviously, in their eyes, a poor marriage is far better that no marriage.'

I could tell by the look in her own eyes that she kind of sympathized with that sentiment and I knew she was thinking of James and how hard she had fought to keep her marriage intact against all the odds and despite their frequent rows. Whatever her own views were, however, Fiona did at least keep them to herself and wouldn't have dreamed of trying to influence me.

'Champagne?' I heard Simon say, 'How on earth did you manage that?' and I realised that Bruce had returned.

'Feeling better, Ellen?' he asked, looking down at me with what seemed like genuine concern.

'Yes, sorry about that. If it didn't bother Molly to be shown up like that, I'm not sure why I let it upset me so much. My family grows older – she is in her fifties, after all – but not wiser, is seems.'

He poured drinks into the fluted glasses provided with the sparkling wine and held one out to me.

''Not for me,' I shook my head, 'I'm driving.'

'Just a sip,' he coaxed, 'it will help you to relax.'

I took the glass to please him, but had no intention of even tasting the liquid in it and soon placed it on the table out of temptation's way.

'Where were you two sitting?' Fiona asked nosily. 'How odd

that we were all in the same restaurant without seeing each other – hadn't you even spotted your sister, or she, you?'

I wanted to say that it wasn't that odd that they'd not spotted me, since both couples were totally wrapped up in each other, with eyes for no one else. I didn't say it, of course, merely pointed out the size of the place and that I'd only realised Molly was there just before her husband had stormed in – which was close enough to the truth.

'Anyway,' I said, 'we must be off. I'll just go and pay the bill and we can leave you to enjoy what's left of your evening.'

I might have known Fiona would pick up on that. She might give the impression of being a very modern woman, but she still had some very old-fashioned ideas.

'Not even going Dutch,' she commented, 'how very emancipated you are, Ellen.'

'She's saying thank you,' Simon pointed out, 'for services rendered.'

'Oooh,' Fiona said, widening her eyes and looking from him to me, 'you must have done something *very* well.' I gave her a look, but before I could tell her, quite mildly, to grow up, Bruce stepped in and did it for me, but in a far more forceful manner.

'Don't be so ridiculous, Fiona,' he said, sounding extremely annoyed. 'You're acting as badly as Ellen's family now – looking for hidden agendas where there are none.'

It was nice of him to stick up for me, though I did wonder why he was so cross on my behalf over something that was little more than a joke. Feeling sorry for Fiona, who was looking thoroughly chastised, I explained, 'For gardening services – for which he will also be paid the going rate, I hasten to add – and for some excellent advice that I was sorely in need of.'

'Oh, what was that?' Fiona looked interested.

'None of your business, I suspect.' It was Bruce once again putting her in her place, even though I could sense he was curious himself.

'Exactly,' I managed a light laugh. And turning to Simon I said, 'We should be off. I have some orders to complete in the morning.'

'Tomorrow is Saturday,' he pointed out.

'Yes,' I agreed, 'and, as I keep saying, when you're self-employed it's like any other day, especially when you're running behind because of various interruptions. Fiona works Saturdays.'

'Yes, but I run a shop and Saturday is my busiest day,' she suddenly stopped and then reminded me, 'and you haven't taken me up on my offer yet. When are you coming down to find an outfit?'

I laughed, 'When you can tell me where I would go to wear something as dressy as I would find in your boutique?'

I could have wished I'd thought before I'd spoken when she said immediately, 'The four of us could go out, to somewhere a little more up-market than this place – not that the meal wasn't very good,' she added, suddenly mindful that she was criticizing what might have been Bruce's choice of venue. 'What do you say to a double-date, guys?'

The silence that greeted this suggestion was absolute.

Chapter Ten

I<small>N THE END</small>, bearing in mind Simon's suggestion about not taking my family so seriously, I decided friends should be treated in the same way and burst out laughing. 'A double-date, Fiona?' I chortled, 'How very twee.'

Bruce had been looking a bit starchy, I thought, up to that point, and then his expression lightened into one of relief and he even grinned. 'My sentiments exactly, Ellen. Makes it sound as if we're all "going steady," to coin another old fashioned phrase when actually, Fiona, I think you'll find Ellen was merely treating Simon to a meal by way of a thank you tonight and *we* were here to talk business.'

Well, that had told Fiona – and me – exactly how things stood between them. If I had been wondering – which, of course, I hadn't been, I reminded myself sternly. I had no interest in Bruce Redman – he was simply a friend and could see whoever he chose. He didn't have to give a reason for my benefit.

'It was a joke,' Fiona said quickly, but she was pink and flustered with embarrassment. I thought she also looked more than a little disappointed.

'No reason we shouldn't all go out for an evening, though, is there?' Simon asked, adding, 'Just as friends.'

'I suppose not,' I agreed, thinking of the night before and how much I'd enjoyed sitting down to eat fish and chips with two male friends – and how relaxed it had been. 'What do you think, Bruce?'

'No reason at all. What about a week tomorrow. You girls sort out your outfits and we'll organise the venue,' he said including Simon.

'Happy to leave that to you, Bruce,' Simon shrugged. 'I've been out of the area too long to know anything about the coolest eating places in Brankstone or the surrounding area, but I'd imagine you get wined and dined regularly in your line of work. Tonight is a first for me.'

'And we split the bill four ways,' I said firmly, as if it was a foregone conclusion, and turning to Bruce I reminded him, 'and when you're deciding on the venue, bear in mind that at least two of us are not high-powered business people, so it needs to be somewhere affordable.'

'Three of us,' Fiona chipped in, 'the recession's had an effect on most of us – among other things,' she added darkly.

'Cheap and cheerful, in other words,' Bruce said with a resigned expression on his face that didn't actually look very convincing. 'So what's it to be – fish and chips again, or would you prefer burgers next time?'

'Fish and chips *again*?' Fiona pounced on the word. 'Have I missed something?'

'Yeah, I bumped into Bruce on my way back to Ellen's last evening,' Simon told her carelessly. 'He got a whiff of what I was carrying and invited himself inside to share our supper.'

'It wasn't quite like that,' Bruce protested, 'best chip butties I've ever tasted though, so I'm glad I happened to be passing at just the right moment.'

'You should have given me a shout,' Fiona said lightly, but it was clear she was miffed. I wouldn't have thought her taste ran to fish and chips, but I guessed it did run to Bruce Redman and I judged it was time for us to leave her to work her magic on him.

'Come on, Simon Weller, time to go. I've got work tomorrow even if you haven't. I'll get the bill on the way out.'

106

'Why don't you let me get that along with ours?' Bruce offered, but I gave him a look and he held up his hands and said, 'OK, OK.'

'Flash devil,' I said as we made our way down the steps outside.

'Oh, I don't think he is,' Simon said, shaking his head, 'just a generous kind of guy.'

In my heart I knew he was probably right, but I wasn't about to say so.

An early and hangover-free start in the morning saw the orders continuing to stack up into a very promising pile. I'd have liked to keep going all day, and really get ahead of myself. However, a number of cards had to be posted to the recipients, so I felt I'd just as well pop those into their 'do not bend' stiffened envelopes, catch the Saturday post and know they were dealt with and would arrive in plenty of time. I was also aware that it would do me good to get out into the fresh air. It was an unhealthy habit to stay bent over the cards for too long at a time, as I often knew to my cost and paid with aching shoulders and sore eyes.

Perhaps after I'd done that it would be a good time to pop into Fiona's shop and choose this outfit that so much was being made of. I was rather more enthusiastic than I normally would have been since I had inadvertently begun to enjoy some kind of a real social life in recent days.

There'd been little of that nature going on in my life since the short time I'd spent with Miles – and he had hardly been what I would call a party animal. 'Happier in my own four walls', was how he described himself, and 'set in his ways' were the words I would have used. He was only forty-four and all ready to settle for being a pipe-and-slipper's man. I'd begun to feel the walls of his pristine house closing in on me and to see matching slippers waiting for me on the polished hearth in my mind's eye by the time I realised it was time to call it a day.

I still hadn't quite decided whether to do both errands while I was out or to be sensible and return and take care of more card orders having gone to the post office when the phone rang.

'Oh, Mum, I was going to pop round with the stuff I printed up about hiatus hernia from the internet for you,' I said as soon as I heard her voice. 'Is everything all right?'

'Well, your dad's fine, if that's what you mean.' She sounded a bit disgruntled, I thought.

'But you're not,' I guessed, purely from the tone of her voice.

'The boy's are both here, watching football with your dad, but that's not much fun for me. I thought Molly was calling in today, but there's been no sign of her.'

'Really?' I hoped my voice was non-committal, 'She's probably just busy. Hey,' I had a sudden thought, 'Why don't I come and pick you up? I was thinking of going into town to look for a new outfit and you could help me choose. You have a much better eye for clothes than I have. If we go now, we can have lunch first.'

'Oh, that would be *lovely*,' Mum brightened immediately and sounded thrilled by the idea. 'I haven't been shopping properly since I don't know when. Your sisters always seem to have too much else going on in their lives to do more than pop in. What with Alma being so wrapped up in her family and Molly and her marriage problems, I barely get a look in.'

I wanted to ask her how much she knew about Molly's marriage problems, but thought better of it. I had always tried not to get involved and had managed it – until last night – and even then my involvement wasn't intentional. Should I see Molly reneging on her wedding vows at any time in the future I fully intended to put some distance between us – fast – and stay right out of it.

'I won't be long,' I promised, 'just have to stop off at the post office on the way.'

I put on my coat and gathered up the pile of envelopes, leaving my work table littered with the various tools I'd used – scissors lay by the side of a folder and rulers, a paper trimmer nudged various marker pens – and in the middle of it all were cards in various stages of completion. I told myself I could come back to it later.

Mum was obviously keen to get going. She was hovering on the front doorstep in her best coat and shoes and barely gave me a minute to pass the time of day with the football fans, each of whom barely looked away from the TV where the game was being discussed at great length by the experts even before it had been played.

I have to say we had the loveliest time, which made me question why I didn't take Mum out more often. My only excuse was that she always seemed so wrapped up with Dad and the lives of her married children and grandchildren, added to which I carried the feeling – real or imagined – that she must be very disappointed in me and my determination to remain single despite all of the family's best efforts to marry me off.

We only had a light lunch of jacket potatoes, because – as she reminded me – Mum had to cook for Dad when she got home, but the delicious fillings and fresh side salad more than made up for the simple fare.

'It looked as if you left them well provided for,' I smiled, enjoying the way she was tucking in, 'those plates of sandwiches were piled so high they were positively teetering.'

My mother laughed and I thought it was a while since I'd seen her look so happy. 'Don't you worry, they'll all have been eaten long before there was any chance of any of them slipping off the plate.'

'You're probably right.' Changing the subject I offered, 'What about a pudding? I hear they're very good here.'

'Ooh, not for me,' she said immediately, 'especially if we're going to be trying clothes on. I'm not as lucky as you with your slim figure. Every calorie I eat goes straight to my waist.'

'And there's me thinking I got my excellent metabolism from you,' I joked, refusing to get into a discussion about weight and diets which had always been a favourite topic with the women in my family. 'Let's go and see what Fiona has to tempt us with,' I encouraged, helping my mother on with her coat.

'She's that friend of yours who owns the dress shop, isn't she?'

I nodded, and took Mum's arm as we stepped out on to the

street. The precinct was as busy as you would expect for a Saturday afternoon.

'I thought it was a bit up-market for my taste when I popped in there once with Alma,' she said doubtfully. 'Perhaps we could go to M & S when you've chosen your outfit?'

'If you like,' I agreed, rather thinking that Alma's opinion on that visit might have influenced my mother's judgement – as proved to be the case when she found something she liked practically the minute she entered Fiona's exclusive emporium.

'You made it, Ellen,' Fiona's greeting couldn't have been more effusive, 'and you've brought your mum.'

'Hello, dear,' my mother looked up from checking the quality of a rather eye-catching animal-print skirt.

'Nice isn't it, Mrs Carson?' Fiona went over and whipped the skirt from the rail and spread it out, showing all the panache of a matador laying his cloak temptingly before the bull.

'But a bit young for me, though.'

'What nonsense,' Fiona contradicted, 'according to Ellen you're very young in your outlook with a sensible refusal to be dictated to by your calendar years – and you have a wonderful figure.'

My mother positively beamed and was persuaded to go and try the skirt on.

'I bet you say that to all the elderly customers,' I accused, with a grin.

'Yes, but with some of them I do mean it,' Fiona said, and then turning as my mother came out of the changing room she cried, 'Now doesn't that look fabulous?'

I had to admit that it did, and my mum preened in front of the mirror, swishing the skirt that fell in soft folds to mid-calf, this way and that.

'I would team it with a black top or sweater, a nice pair of black knee-length boots, and finally a black fitted jacket to set it off.' Fiona was in full sales mode. 'I don't often advocate black, but there is already enough pattern and colour in the animal print of the skirt and the slight touches of black in it will pull the outfit together. The whole thing will look absolutely marvellous with your silver hair.'

Of course, she had just the right items on her rails, and the boots could be purchased in the shoe shop just a few doors down.

'Fabulous,' we both said when my mother appeared from behind the fitting room curtain for the second time looking very pleased with herself as she preened in front of the mirror.

'But when will I get the chance to wear it?'

'Christmas is just around the corner,' I pointed out, 'and we always go out for a family meal then.'

I watched her expression droop obviously at the thought of the long wait from mid-October to late December.

Fiona must have seen the same thing and interpreted it correctly, because she said suddenly, looking at me, 'Why don't we bring your mum and dad out on our double-date and make it a treble?'

It was a lovely spontaneous gesture but, knowing my family as she did from our many conversations, I wondered what had made Fiona make it – and in just the sort of terms that would send my mother's unrealistic expectations into overdrive, as indeed proved to be the case.

My mother's reaction was entirely predictable. 'A date? You're going on a date, Ellen? Why didn't you say something?'

'Because I'm not – we're not,' I protested and, glaring at Fiona, added, 'you know it's no such thing.'

'I was only joking,' she said unconvincingly, and then repeated that for my mother's benefit. 'I was only joking – really.'

'It's just four of us going out for a *friendly* meal, that's *all* there is to it,' I said with probably far too much emphasis and felt honour bound to add, 'but, of course, you and Dad are more than welcome to join us, and it will give you a chance to wear your lovely new outfit.'

'Oh,' Mum clasped her hands to her new top, 'how exciting. It's not often we get to socialise with Ellen's friends. Who else is going?'

'Just Bruce Redman and Simon Weller – Ellen's known them

forever, apparently, so I suppose you must know them, too,' Fiona provided the information blithely and I could feel my heart sink lower and lower towards the carpeted floor.

'Oh, how *lovely*.' I could almost hear the hysterical delight in my mother's voice at the thought of my spending an evening with not one, but two such eligible men, though she was doing her best to hide it. In fact, she became brisk. 'Well, we'd better get to work on this outfit Ellen's going to be wearing then, hadn't we, Fiona?'

The pair of them went into raptures as they pushed and pulled me into and out of one smart frock after another until I quite literally felt I'd lost the will to live. I allowed them both to make my choices for me, simply paying up and receiving the shiny bags emblazoned with Fiona's name with little idea of – or interest in – the contents. I took far more pleasure in helping my mother to choose her new boots.

I knew there were going to be repercussions and I didn't have very long to wait, because we were scarcely through my parents' front door before my mother was sharing details of the proposed evening out with my father. My brothers, predictably, were all ears and immediately invited themselves along, eager to reacquaint themselves with their old school friend.

It was obviously too much to hope for that my sisters would let this pass and by mid-week they had also inveigled invitations to come along with their husbands. I was amazed by Molly's nerve and also that of her husband, given that the people they would be sitting at a table with had only very recently been involved in their very public mêlée. I was even more amazed that Alma was going to be able to get the charmless Les to vacate his armchair and to go out for the evening – that was twice within a month if you counted my birthday celebration.

I realised I had no choice but to go round and advise Bruce of the sudden increase in the number of diners. I felt obliged to apologize and try to explain away the fact that a simple meal for four people had suddenly turned into something quite different.

'It's fine,' he said, hiding his surprise well, considering that suddenly my whole family were foisting themselves upon us without as much as a by-your-leave.

'Well, it's quite obviously *not* fine,' I insisted, following him inside a house that was still a complete shambles, 'but once Fiona had invited my parents to come along the whole thing just got completely out of hand. I suppose we can count ourselves lucky that the grandchildren haven't been included.' Bruce laughed and his merriment drew a rueful grin from me. 'You should bring your dad along – even things up a little bit. How is his sprained ankle by the way?'

'Not bad,' Bruce replied, 'given his age, and the fact that he refuses to rest.' He's hobbling quite badly, but being as stubborn as a mule, he insists he knows best.'

A familiar voice filtered through from the kitchen. 'Who are you calling stubborn?'

'Is that. . . ?' I began.

'My dad,' Bruce nodded his head and then stared at me as I pushed past.

I stood in the kitchen doorway and could feel the smile growing bigger by the minute. 'Jack,' I said, 'it *is* you.'

Bruce walked in and found us beaming at each other. 'How do you two know each other, then?' he demanded, looking from one to the other of us.

'Erm,' I admitted reluctantly, 'I have to confess that history seems to have repeated itself because I had a go at Jack outside. It was about keeping the noise down when he was demolishing the front wall. I didn't realize he was your father.'

'Would it have made any difference if you had?' Bruce asked, without rancour.

'Probably not, I do have a habit of speaking my mind, as you must have noticed.'

'Nothing mambypamby about Ellen,' Jack said in an admiring

tone, 'not like some of the lily-livered females you come across these days.'

'I did provide him with a tray of tea *after* I'd told him off,' I said, in my own defence.

'Have you come to join us?' Jack queried, going back to give the big pot on the ancient cooker hob a brisk stir. 'It's beef stew made from my own recipe and there's plenty to go round.'

'Oh, no, I couldn't,' I said immediately, though the gorgeous smell of stewing meat and vegetables was making my stomach rumble and it suddenly seemed a very long time since my lunch-time jacket potato. 'I just came to explain to Bruce how a meal for four friends has turned into a massive family gathering – to which you must come, as I was saying to Bruce. Of course, I didn't know his father was you, then, but now I'd be even more delighted if you would come.'

'Well,' Jack said, 'I would love to, but only on one condition.'

I guessed what was coming and found myself sitting with the two of them at the rickety little kitchen table, watching as he ladled generous helpings of the stew and amazing fluffy dumplings into bowls and placed one in front of each of us. I was too hungry to be self-conscious and tucked right in.

Jack remembered my brothers and was keen to see them again. 'I don't think I ever met you, did I?' he asked, 'though I believe I met your sisters a time or two.'

Bruce grinned and told his dad, 'Ellen is the baby of the family by a few years, so she wouldn't have been allowed to hang out with the rest of us.'

'Yes,' I agreed, with my mouth full, 'I was mostly beneath their notice, though I have to say that Bruce was always very kind to me – even when I hung around them like a bad smell, annoying them with my presence.'

'I don't remember you being annoying,' he said. 'In fact, I always thought you were a sweet little thing.'

'There,' I chewed thoughtfully before swallowing and then

continued, 'he's still being kind to me.'

'She still seems like a sweet little thing to me,' Jack said with a smile.

'There again,' I smiled right back at him, 'it's a case of like father like son, obviously. Have you decided where we're all going?' I turned back to Bruce. 'You've ended up with a mammoth task now that there are so many of us to fit in and I feel bad about leaving it all to you. Is there anything I can do?'

'All sorted,' he said lightly, 'a friend of mine has just taken over a pub with a good-sized restaurant and he's still trying to build up his clientele and a reputation for good food at reasonable prices. We'll be doing him a favour by bringing in a crowd and he'll do us a good deal if we'll allow him to use photos of the packed restaurant for his website. I didn't think anyone would object to that.'

'Ever the business man doing his deals,' Jack said with a wry look in my direction.

'I have to take some of the blame,' I found myself defending Bruce, though I was sure he didn't need me to, 'since I asked him to keep it cheap and cheerful in the first place – and then landed the whole of my family into the middle of his plans.'

'It'll be no problem – and it might even be fun. It'll be great to see the Carsons again after all this time.'

'If you think that, Bruce, then you've obviously got a very short memory where my family are concerned,' I said, and though I was laughing I did feel a real a trickle of unease crawling along my spine that was difficult to ignore.

Chapter Eleven

Sometimes the week could be long, but not this one. Saturday seemed to race around far too quickly. A last minute rush of card orders meant that the colour I had intended to use on my hair to hide any creeping grey sat unused and still in the packet on the bathroom shelf, and the trim I'd intended to book myself in for to rid myself of visibly split ends went right out of my head. I looked at my short, unvarnished nails on Saturday morning and knew I'd be lucky if I found time for a single coat of nail colour, but still I couldn't bring myself to stop.

By ignoring the phone and concentrating on the matter in hand, I managed to catch the post with the most urgent batch of the recently completed cards and, after a couple of slices of swiftly buttered toast to combat the hunger pangs, I was soon lost again in creating verses to complement the cards waiting for this final creative touch.

'Ellen.' I almost jumped right out of my skin when a deep voice spoke suddenly from behind me. I swore like the proverbial navvy, loud and long, before turning to say savagely, 'Are you trying to give me a heart attack?'

'I'm so sorry, but I did knock, several times at the front *and* the back door. When I realised the door was unlocked I let myself in. I was actually getting a bit concerned about you.' Bruce came to stand beside my table. If he was shocked at my language he hid it well, and he did look quite contrite. 'Only I did say that I would be picking you up tonight. You *are* still coming?'

'I can hardly wriggle out of it, with my whole family turning up en masse, can I?' I'd calmed down by then, enough to realize he was looking at me and the work piled in front of me rather strangely – and that he was dressed to go out. 'Why? What time is it?'

I almost shrieked when he told me and I realised any chance I'd had of making myself look remotely presentable for the evening ahead was long gone. Forget the hair colour, forget the haircut and forget the nail varnish, I'd be lucky to get a quick shower and find the time to drag a comb through my hair. For a moment I contemplated going as I was and looked down at my frayed jeans and long sleeved t-shirt helplessly.

'What can I do to help?' He said it quite sweetly, but I could tell he had already accepted that getting me out of the door on time was a lost cause.

'Any chance you can pick the others up first?' I pleaded. 'A half an hour might just about do it.'

He left without arguing, or saying anything at all apart from advising me: 'Lock the door behind me, I could have been anybody walking in.'

Leaving everything as it was, I raced for the stairs, telling myself as I went, 'No one's going to be looking at me anyway,' but realised my family would automatically make the assumption that I'd made little effort on purpose just to prove I wasn't trying to attract anybody. I shrugged and reminded myself they were free to think what the hell they liked – just as they usually did.

I found it was amazing how quickly you could actually clean teeth, shower, whisk your hair up into a messy pile on top of your head and dab make-up on, all with scarcely a glance in the mirror. Now, where was the damn dress? I finally discovered it – still in the bag – in the bottom of the wardrobe. Despite the hurry I was in, even I couldn't ignore the fact that it was badly creased. A flick among the clothes along the rail told me what I already knew, that I didn't have another suitable thing to wear since the dress I'd worn to my surprise party was still awaiting collection at the dry-cleaners and my only pair of smart trousers were in the laundry basket.

I pulled the dress on, fastened the zip with the difficulties that long back zips invariably cause, and knelt to drag shoes and bags from the bottom of the wardrobe. The dress was in shades of blue, and the only high-heeled shoes I had were black, likewise the only suitable bag and they would have to do. I didn't know anyone who matched everything up except Fiona, anyway. I'd just snatched up a light jacket also in black when the doorbell went so I hurried down the stairs and opened the door.

I'd been about to issue a ta-da to indicate that I was actually ready when Bruce whistled and said, 'Wow.'

'What?' I said, peering at him to see if he was being sarcastic and then down at myself to see if I'd missed something crucial. 'What?' I said again.

'Half an hour,' he said, shaking his head, 'I confess I never thought you'd manage it and I'm impressed. You look gorgeous.'

He was being kind, of course, and one look at Fiona confirmed that impression because even in the dim light of the car's interior I could see that she'd pulled all the stops out. Glossy hair, meticulous make-up and even with her jacket on I could see that her assets were being displayed to the best advantage. I didn't even bother to look at her nails.

Simon was already in the back beside Fiona, and Jack was in the front passenger seat, which was probably irking Fiona, who would have seen that as her spot, overlooking the fact that clambering in and out of the back would not have been great for a man of advanced years with a sprained ankle.

'You did give everyone directions, didn't you, Ellen?' Bruce asked, as he held the back door open for me to climb in on Simon's other side.

I rolled my eyes at him. 'Honestly, anyone would think I was unreliable – just because I forgot to get ready for tonight. You really shouldn't be so quick to judge. Of course I gave them directions

– at least, I think I did.'

He laughed down at me and I realised I was warming to him a little more each time we met. I wondered briefly if that should be a cause for concern.

'Look at me,' Simon gloated, putting a careless arm around Fiona and me as we sat back for the ride to the restaurant, 'a rose between two thorns.'

'That should have been my seat if it hadn't been for this damned ankle,' Jack complained bitterly, making us all giggle.

'Sit next to me in the restaurant, Jack,' I pleaded, 'and let's see if my family turn their valiant efforts to find me a husband into trying to marry the two of us off.'

'They won't have to try very hard as far as I'm concerned,' he assured me, 'but you're probably joking.'

'I only wish I was,' I muttered gloomily, until Simon gave me a sharp nudge in the ribs and reminded me of his previous advice to treat all their efforts as a hilarious joke.

'They can't make you do anything you don't want to do,' he said, 'and should have accepted that by now. After all, none of their schemes have worked so far, have they?'

'I don't know why it bothers you so much to be honest,' Fiona muttered, 'they obviously just want you to be happy.'

'They want me to be married,' I pointed out, 'and that's not necessarily the same thing, as you should know, but don't let's get into all that now. Oh, is this the place, Bruce? It looks really nice.'

We had pulled up in front of a mock Tudor building that had obviously had a recent make-over with its white painted walls gleaming in the headlights of the car, the retouched black of the woodwork standing out sharply. Lights shone a welcome from every room.

Bruce walked round the car, obviously with the intention of helping his father to alight. Before he could reach for the front passenger door handle Fiona had exited the car in a flash and attached herself to his side. Grinning at the thought of the chagrin on my family's faces when they realised they'd already been out-manoeuvred by an expert, I went to open the door for Jack myself, and Simon helped me to get him out of the car.

By the time we'd ignored Jack's mutters that he really could manage, and he'd given in ungracefully – telling us bluntly that we were making him feel old – Bruce and Fiona were already inside and had been engulfed by my family who appeared to have arrived en masse. All of their efforts to oust Fiona from her place at Bruce's side made no impression and she continued to cling to Bruce's arm with commendable tenacity.

We were greeted warmly by the publican, a big, bluff, bearded individual who obviously knew Bruce well judging by the easy familiarity between them. I noticed him throwing curious glances Fiona's way, but if he was expecting an introduction from Bruce he was destined to be disappointed.

There were other diners, but ours was by far the largest group and heads turned as we began to make our way across the sizeable room towards a large round table reserved for us in the centre of the room.

Alma stayed me with a hand on my arm. 'Isn't that woman with Bruce Redman the one from the dress shop in the precinct?' she demanded, throwing a sour look Fiona's way. Without waiting for an answer she continued, 'Stolen a march on you, hasn't she? You obviously had the advantage with knowing him for so long but while you were dithering she's seized the opportunity, raced after the most eligible bachelor this town's ever had like a rat up a drain-pipe and left you standing – on your own as usual.'

'What a charming way you do have with words, Alma,' I laughed, adding, 'I have no compunction about wishing them both very happy,' before pulling away from her to make my way back to Jack's side.

There was a lot of pushing and shoving around the table and it became obvious that Bruce would have won any popularity contest for the evening by a mile. With sheer grit and determination Fiona managed to hold on to her place beside him in the face of stiff competition from the brother who hadn't gained the seat on Bruce's other side and the efforts of my two sisters to evict her and put me in her place.

I rather thought I had come off best placed, as I ended up being between Simon on my one side and Jack on the other. As far away as possible from the teasing that would surely have been my lot had I been sitting within range of the raking over of ancient reminiscences that was going on at the opposite side of the table. Knowing my brothers once they got going I was surprised that Fiona wasn't bored to tears, but her smile of enjoyment was firmly in place every time I glanced across.

On our side of the table, Jack and Simon paid me outrageous compliments between courses and vied to top each other's tall stories until I was helpless with laughter.

'What's going on over there?' Bruce raised his voice above the hub-bub, 'Is Ellen leading you astray, Dad?'

'I wish she would,' Jack said without a pause, 'if I was ten years younger and didn't have a gammy leg, I'd have been well on my way to whisking her up the aisle by now I can tell you.'

'You could try,' Fiona said firmly without a hint of humour apart from a glittering smile that didn't reach her eyes, 'but Ellen prefers the single life, always has and always will. Isn't that right, Ellen?'

That was nothing I hadn't said myself in the past. However, I wondered if I was alone in thinking there was something faintly malicious in the way she broadcast what was, essentially, my business and if, in fact, she wasn't actually issuing a warning to *me* to stay away from a man she had clearly set her sights on. The ex she'd recently been distraught over had conveniently been forgotten now that she had bigger fish to fry.

'Nothing wrong with that,' Bruce said, looking straight at me, '*some* of us actually like living alone.'

'Nonsense,' Alma said emphatically. 'It's obviously just a case of meeting the right one – for both of you.'

'If it was really that easy to meet the right one,' he told her flatly, 'there would be no second marriages.'

I watched my sister's face flame and wanted to yell, 'Touché.' Then I felt sorry for her and said instead, 'It's simply a matter of choice, Alma, and not everyone chooses to be one half of a couple whether it be marriage or co-habiting. Some of us just need our own space.'

'Exactly,' my brother Jonathon suddenly said bitterly. 'I grew up, just like Ellen, having the whole idea of marriage thrust down my throat – as if that was the only way to live. It never worked for me and the effort of trying again and again has cost me dearly both financially and emotionally over the years. From now on I'm going to take a leaf out of our Ellen's book and remain happily single.'

'I'll drink to that.' Simon raised his glass. I raised mine and watched Jonathon doing the same. The smile on Fiona's face began to look more and more as if it had been frozen into place during the course of the conversation, and it finally disappeared altogether as Bruce followed suit. I couldn't help noticing that she was glaring at me as if the whole of this conversation had been my fault.

I expected my mum and dad would have had something to express in support of marriage with all their years of matrimony behind them, but my mother surprised me by making quite a speech on the subject.

'I never meant to thrust my values on to anyone,' she said, looking quite serious, 'but I'm beginning to see that we may have been guilty of promoting an old-fashioned attitude among our children and in doing so put some of them under pressure to follow our example, which was quite wrong of us.'

Dad nodded and agreed, 'It was very different in our day. We grew up knowing we would be married and have a family. Divorce was far less common, and we married expecting to stay together for life.' He took my mother's hand and said, 'I wouldn't change a thing about my life, but it's a whole different world now and it's time we embraced it and changed with the times.' My mum was nodding and smiling.

'Exactly right,' Jack spoke up. 'I wouldn't change my life either, for all that I've ended up on my own, but that doesn't mean I think Bruce should feel obliged to follow my example. However,' he looked at my sister, 'in a way you are right – Alma, isn't it? – none of these single people have met the right one, because if they do this conversation will become elementary.'

'*When* they do,' Alma was determined to have the last word.

'And that,' Jack said with emphasis, not allowing her that pleasure, 'is something only they can decide. No one can force anyone else to fall in love, Alma, not even you, and no matter how much you would like it to happen. For my part, I just want my son to be happy – whether he is married or single makes no difference to me.'

'Well, of course,' Alma said huffily, 'that's what I want for Ellen – and Jonathon, too, but I can't bear the thought of their being lonely.'

'You can be lonelier in a bad relationship than you ever could be living on your own,' Simon said firmly and I just knew he was speaking from bitter experience.

'And isn't that the truth?' my brother-in-law, Gordon, said looking at my sister Molly in a way that I couldn't interpret and I noticed she refused to meet his gaze.

The party atmosphere we had started with was rapidly slipping away and I probably wasn't the only one who was relieved when our host bowled over to ask how we had enjoyed the meal. Without exception we were effusive in our praise, because no fault could have been found with the excellent cuisine or the service.

He was equally grateful in his appreciation of our comments. 'That's very good to hear,' he said, 'but I would really welcome any suggestions on how things might be improved. Sometimes it's the little things that make a difference.'

'You should get our Ellen to come up with something special for your menus.'

I was amazed to hear my brother Richard speak up because he'd always seemed to be the one person in the family with the least interest in what I did. 'Yours are a bit, you know, plain, and though there's nothing wrong with that – because the food is, of course, the most important thing – a beautifully presented menu would really complement the candles and flowers on the table to give a great first impression when people arrive.'

Everyone seemed to have an opinion on whether this was a good idea or a complete waste of time and money. My embarrassment kept me quiet and I felt sorry for Bruce's friend who was being put under pressure to consider something that was hardly likely to make a scrap of difference to the success of his business.

In the end I just said, 'For heaven's sake leave the poor man alone.'

'You must be Ellen, I'm Ray,' the big man turned to me with a smile, his deep voice cut across the theories and advice being bandied around the table as he thrust out his hand. 'I've heard about your cards from Bruce and had a quick look at your website. Your work is impressive and with Christmas around the corner I might well be in the market for something special for my menus. I'd be happy to see any ideas you have and an idea of the cost.'

'You're going to be busy,' Simon said, as Ray walked away. 'I might have a word with him, too, about sprucing up his garden and hanging a few winter baskets out the front. Even a car park can be made to look more welcoming. Your brother is right – finishing touches can make all the difference, however small they are.'

'At this rate,' Alma said crossly, 'Ellen is going to be so busy that she'll never meet anyone.'

'Alma,' I said warningly, 'you're doing it again. Your persistence would be funny if it wasn't so irritating. Haven't you listened to a word that's been said tonight?'

'Yes, but . . .' she began.

'I would rather have a successful business than be married – end of story.'

'Me, too,' said Jonathon, looking happier than I'd seen him for months.

'That leaves those of us who already have successful businesses, who might be looking for more out of life,' Fiona said with a sly look in Bruce's direction and a blatant disregard for both the fact he'd already clearly stated his desire to remain single and that she had told us only the week before that her business wasn't doing so well in the face of the current economic climate. I wondered briefly whether money could be the attraction where Bruce was concerned, especially given the mess her failed marriage had left her in, and then I mentally berated myself for being so cynical.

It had been a different kind of an evening, but agreeable enough for all that, especially because a lot of misconceptions had been dealt with as far as my family were concerned. At forty years old I finally felt that my views and decisions had been listened to and even accepted and I had high hopes, that being the case, for a simpler life of my own choosing in the future.

The extra work, if it materialized, was going to see me becoming extremely busy in the next few weeks. However, I did know what I was capable of when I knuckled down and made work my priority, so I wasn't daunted and went to bed promising myself that tomorrow would be another day of concentrated effort. The fact that it was Sunday had nothing to do with anything and I couldn't wait to start.

It was still very dark when the doorbell went and it didn't feel as if I'd been in bed very long at all. The chill when I threw back the covers told me the heating hadn't yet come on, the digital clock showing 3.30 a.m. provided the reason why.

I had barely found one sleeve of my dressing gown before the bell was pressed again – long and hard, and I shouted, 'All right, all right, keep your hair on. I'm coming as fast as I can.'

It was only as I approached the door, that I thought to wonder who the hell was ringing my bell at that time of the morning. The hand I had already stretched out towards the lock was immediately withdrawn and I hovered indecisively,

Common sense told me that a potential burglar wouldn't be

foolish enough to announce their arrival, but then only a fool would open their front door in the early hours without first checking the identity of the caller first.

'Who is it?' I called and, horrified to hear the way my voice wobbled, I said again much more firmly, 'Who is it? Who's there?'

'Ellen, it's me, Bruce. I need your help urgently. Please hurry.'

My hands were cold and I fumbled with the lock, but finally it turned. I opened the door and Bruce practically fell inside.

'What. . . ?'

'It's Dad,' he said hoarsely. 'He's in a lot of pain from that ankle – far more than would be normal from a simple sprain. I'm taking him to the hospital but I think I'm going to need help getting him into the car. Can you come over?'

Suddenly, I was wide awake. 'Give me a few minutes to pull on some clothes and I'll be there,' I said. 'You'd better get back to him.'

He disappeared back through the door and slamming it behind him, I fell over my dressing gown hem several times in my hurry to get up the stairs. Pulling on jeans, a thick sweater, socks and boots and snatching up a warm jacket and my bag, I hurtled back down the stairs and out into the street. From the light falling through the open door of Bruce's house I managed to pick my way past the skip still taking up most of the path and hurried inside wondering what I was going to find.

Chapter Twelve

'H<small>E HASN'T SLEPT</small> at all,' Bruce told me, leading the way into the house. 'In fact neither of us have.'

Jack was in the kitchen. 'It's just a sprain,' he muttered, but you could see he was in pain and I remembered noticing that he could barely put his foot to the ground at the restaurant, 'perhaps frozen peas will help.'

'Putting on a brave face isn't the answer any more, Dad. This is something that needs sorting out now – I'm not happy to leave you in that much pain until the morning. You should have said something before and I should have noticed the ankle wasn't getting any better.'

'Bruce is right on both counts,' I told Jack firmly. 'A sprain shouldn't need frozen peas after all this time,' and turning to Bruce I said, 'You should have called an ambulance.'

'We can get there quicker in the car,' Bruce said tersely, 'most of the emergency service vehicles will be out dealing with drunks at this hour.'

'One of us each side of you then, Jack,' I told him, lifting his arm around my neck as Bruce did the same on the other side. He wasn't exactly light, and the path was like an obstacle course. I staggered a time or two, but somehow we manhandled Jack between us sideways past the skip and out to the car. With some groaning from him and some huffing from us, Bruce and I heaved him inside.

The minute we pulled up outside of the emergency department, I jumped out of the car and managed to find an abandoned wheelchair almost immediately. In minutes Bruce was wheeling his father inside.

The ankle was, of course, broken – it didn't even need the x-ray to tell us that – but somehow this hadn't been picked up on the earlier visit. The fact that Jack had been walking on the injury probably wasn't going to help matters at all. He remained stoic, in spite of suffering days of pain, merely saying through gritted teeth that these things happened and he dismissed his son's offer to be treated privately with the derision he obviously felt it deserved.

To be fair, Jack's case was treated as a priority, probably the fact that his face had lost every vestige of colour, and that he had clearly been misdiagnosed the first time around had something to do with that. If anyone waiting with their Saturday night alcohol-fuelled war wounds had a problem with that, one look at Bruce's face was enough to keep them silent.

When we finally left, the painkillers had begun to work and Jack was being prepared for admission to a ward. We walked outside like a pair of zombies, to be greeted by unexpectedly bright sunshine. Climbing wearily into the four-by-four, we made the journey home in complete silence.

I didn't think twice when the car pulled up at the kerbside before saying, 'Come in with me, Bruce. It's been a hell of a night, neither of us have had much sleep, and – not to put too fine a point on it – your house is a mess, and probably freezing cold as well. I'm surprised you allowed your Dad to stay there – though with hindsight it's just as well that you did.'

The warmth that greeted us as we stepped inside my house was very welcome and we drank tea, sipping it as hot as we could stand it. After that I brought him a blanket and a pillow and left him to bed down on the couch before making my way to my own bed. In seconds I was sound asleep.

It must have been hours later that I woke because the sun had gone, the sky had darkened and the room was dim. I lay quite still for a moment, trying to work out why I was in bed so late in the day. After a few moments the earlier events began to come back to me. I made a move to get up, but the quilt seemed to lie heavily on me and when I reached out to see why that was, I encountered an arm. I fought the instinct to yell and thrash about and took a peep over my shoulder to find a peacefully sleeping Bruce Redman tucked up behind my back with his arm around my waist. He was, at least, lying on top of the quilt and not underneath it with me.

I lay still for a moment or two, assessing the situation, and eventually accepted in my mind that it was all quite innocent. He must have come up to use the bathroom, become confused in the darkness and simply laid down on the nearest bed – which was, in fact, the only bed up here. He was going to be as horrified as I had been initially when he opened his eyes.

Bruce moved suddenly and I held my breath, but he settled again with a deep sigh, pulling me closer against him. I found I was in no hurry to move and, indeed, was even quite enjoying the novelty of being held in a pair of masculine arms. It *had* been a very long time.

I was going to have to wake him, of course but, recalling that I was only wearing my underwear – entirely due to my haste to get beneath the covers on my return from the hospital – I realised that leaping out of his arms and out of bed wasn't going to be an option if we weren't both going to be acutely embarrassed.

I was still pondering, when his voice murmured sleepily in my ear, 'Mmm, this is nice, Ellen, but how – exactly – did we get here?'

I don't know what came over me, but I burst out laughing. I just couldn't seem to help myself, and rolled over to face him.

'I was here all along,' I told him with a smirk, 'at what point you came and joined me I have no bloody idea at all. I left you bedding down on my couch and only woke up myself about a minute ago to find you tucked right in there behind me. You're damn lucky I didn't scream the house down.'

'Why didn't you?' he asked in an interested voice.

'You don't scare me,' I told him, with more confidence than I was actually feeling now that some of my bravado was beginning to leak away. 'If you'd had designs on my person you would have leapt on me in the night and found yourself kicked off the bed for your pains.'

'Nice to know that I don't scare you,' Bruce murmured, the warmth of his tone and his close proximity sending unexpected heat trickling through my veins.

I wanted to turn away, but his gaze held mine steadily and I found that I couldn't look away – and that I really didn't want to.

I couldn't have said later exactly who moved first, but then it wasn't only our gazes meeting, but our lips, tongues, and eventually our bodies. Slowly and unhurriedly we made love and it was better than anything I had ever known, better than anything I could have imagined.

At some point he left me to phone the hospital and then – satisfied that his Dad was in safe hands and all that was needed was being done for him – joined me in the shower and eventually carried me back to bed.

I was in love with Bruce, of course, I probably had been since I was in my teens, I realised. He was the hero of my childhood and everything that had been missing from my life all these years. Being in his arms was all that I had ever dreamed of in my youthful infatuation and I knew I would never regret a single moment of these precious hours together no matter what the future held for us. If this was all there was going to be, I could live with that, because I, of all people, shouldn't be looking for a happy ever after.

We hadn't eaten since the meal in the restaurant over twenty-four hours previously and suddenly discovered we were ravenous in the early hours of Monday morning. Watching Bruce rustle up cheese omelettes from the meagre contents of my fridge gave me a lot of pleasure, particularly as he was only wearing boxer shorts at the time.

We laughed a lot, but at one point he looked serious and went to say something to me. I guessed it was probably something I wouldn't want to hear and put my fingers to his lips, and then kissed him to make sure I had silenced him.

'Don't,' I said, when I finally drew away. 'Don't say a word.'

We went back to bed, but I made sure I didn't sleep again after we had made love, wanting to savour every moment of a time that was all the more precious because I was well aware these few hours might be all I ever had.

I was up early in the morning, despite the lack of sleep and busy working by the time Bruce put in an appearance.

'Mmm,' he said, kissing my neck gently, 'I was hoping I could tempt you back to bed, but you're putting me to shame and I'm already late for a meeting.'

I smiled up at him, fighting the urge to jump into his arms and make him forget all about the meeting. 'There's fresh tea in the pot and bread by the toaster,' I told him. 'A few more minutes won't make much difference.'

He brought me tea, and asked, 'Will I see you later?'

'Bound to,' I replied lightly, 'you only live next door.'

I bent over the card I was working on, giving it all my attention, but I could feel his gaze on me and he didn't make a move for what felt like several long minutes. I thought he was going to say something else, but in the end he just left and closed the door behind him very quietly.

The card fluttered from my fingers and leaning forward I put my elbows on the table, covered my face with my hands and, taking a deep breath, I fought hard to get my emotions under control. I wanted to cry and I wanted to laugh at just how neatly the tables had been turned on me, because suddenly all my arguments against marriage and commitment counted for nothing at all. Everything had changed because after all these years I had met the one man I knew I could spend my life with. The problem was he was also the one man who shared my views on relationships and was, therefore, the one man who was as dead set against marriage as I had always been – the irony of the situation didn't escape me.

Discarding the card I'd been working on I began another. It was made up of all the hearts and flowers I had always secretly despised and was dedicated 'To The One I Love'. It took most of the day and I poured my heart into the making of it and into a verse in which I gave full rein to all the feelings I would never be able to express. When I had finished I held it in my hands and cried and cried as if my heart was broken – and one day soon I knew that it surely would be – because whatever Bruce and I had started certainly wasn't meant to last.

Strangely, once I had cried myself to a standstill and dried my tears I realised I felt better for getting my feelings out and down on paper and, if I said it myself, the card was one of the most beautiful I had ever made, the words all the more poignant for being so completely true.

The doorbell ringing made me jump, as it always did. I was really going to have to invest in one a little more nerve-friendly at some point before mine were completely shattered. On my way to the door I realised the blanket and pillow I'd provided for Bruce two nights before were still there in a pile on the couch. I hesitated, made a move to collect them up, and then left them when the bell went again.

'Fiona, what time is it?'

'Well, it's obviously home time, if I'm standing here at the end of a working day.' She stared at me. 'You look terrible, are you all right?'

Realising my eyes and nose would be red from the tears I had shed, I dismissed, 'Oh, a bit of a cold coming, I think, so don't come too close. What's up?'

'Well,' she said, 'if you let me in, I'll tell you, though you might know more than me, with you and Bruce being next door neighbours and all that.' She pushed past me saying, 'Apparently Jack ended up back in the hospital in the middle of the night where he was in so much pain from that ankle of his. It was after we went for the meal.' She pulled up short at the sight of the makeshift bed on my sofa. 'Lodger?' she asked.

I had no idea how much she knew, or how much would become common knowledge in the near future, so made the swift decision to simply brazen it out with my own version of the truth.

'Oh, yes, Bruce knocked me up in the early hours to give him a hand getting Jack into his car.'

'Why you?' she demanded looking most put out. 'I know you're his closest neighbour, but surely another man would have been more sensible and there's Greg, Jasper and Miles all close at hand. Did you go with them?'

'Yes, and then Bruce slept on the couch when we finally got back. Least I could do was to offer – you know what a state his house is in.'

'Actually, no I don't,' she said coldly, 'because *I've* never been invited inside.'

'Probably didn't think you'd make it past the skip in those heels,' I tried making a joke of it.

'Anyway,' she said sounding deeply suspicious, 'that was two days ago. Why is the bedding still there? Did he sleep on the couch last night as well?'

'No,' I was able to answer truthfully, hoping I wasn't blushing, 'Bruce didn't sleep there last night and I'm not quite sure why I'm getting the third degree here. I was just helping out a neighbour because he asked me to and it didn't seem appropriate to send him round the houses under the circumstances. If you have a problem with that you really should speak to him.'

'No problem,' Fiona adopted a breezy tone. 'Just getting the facts right. So, what's happening now?'

'How should I know?' I matched her light tone. 'Jack's probably being plastered up – or whatever it is they do with broken ankles these days – as we speak, and will be home in no time.'

'Oh, my God, he actually had a fracture?' Fiona sounded genuinely horrified, and then added a bit sheepishly, 'I confess I thought he was making a fuss over nothing that night when you and Simon were carrying him around. You know what men are like – but then, of course, *you* don't do you?'

Usually I found Fiona funny, but I was fast losing my sense of humour where she was concerned. 'I do have a father, and brothers, Fiona,' I said sharply, 'and I have had boyfriends from time to time – even if I chose not to make any of them a permanent fixture.'

'Or even semi-permanent,' she laughed. I didn't laugh with her but she didn't appear to notice. 'Well, he's not going to be able to manage in his own home with a leg in plaster and, if you're right about Bruce's house, he's not going to be able to stay there. I wonder if there's anything I can do to help?' she mused. 'I'm not sure what, but the least I can do is offer – just to be neighbourly, you know,' and with that she was gone.

I took the bedding upstairs, and found myself staring dreamily at the rumpled bed and wondering if I'd dreamed the whole thing. I started guiltily when the doorbell went again, but was relieved not to have to make an immediate decision over whether or not to wash the scent of Bruce from the sheets sooner rather than later.

'You've heard about Bruce's father, I expect?' It was Jasper on the step and he got straight to the point.

'Yes.' I didn't waste any words, either.

'Fiona seems to think we should put our heads together, as a community, and decide how best we can help,' he went on.

'Right,' I said, still keeping it brief.

'Everyone's coming to ours in about an hour.'

I nodded, noticing that Fiona's helpful thoughts didn't include our using her house for the meeting she'd decided we should have.

'You'll come then? Greg and I can rustle up a bite to eat for those who haven't had time, with it being a working night. Oh, look, there's Miles,' and with that he was gone.

I went back to tidy away my work for the day, when I heard the back door open. I didn't know whether to be glad or sorry when Simon came through the arch.

'Just thought I'd pop in before I went off for the day,' he smiled,

'I haven't seen sight or sound of you all day.'

'Mmm, I've been busy.'

'So I see.' He went across to the card table and to my horror he picked up the hearts and flowers card and stood studying it for quite a while. 'This is something special,' he said.

'Well,' I launched into a totally unnecessary explanation, 'I wanted a break from the sudden run on Christmas cards, so I thought I'd see what I could come up with for Valentine's Day. It will be here before we know it,' I added, as if to justify something that really needed no justification.

'You'll want that on display,' he pointed out, and I watched help-lessly as he attached it in pride of place on to my show board. 'How someone without a romantic bone in her body can come up with such a thing is beyond me.'

'It's no different than any author writing novels,' I pointed out, 'they don't have to have experienced everything they write about.'

'True,' he nodded. 'Bit of a bugger about poor old Jack's ankle, isn't it?' He went on, changing the subject.

'Who told you? Fiona, I suppose?' I kept my tone carefully neutral, and wondered why I was allowing her involvement – inter-ference, call it what you like – to bug me so much. She probably meant well, even if she did have an ulterior motive.

'No, it was Bruce. I bumped into him this morning – coming out of your gate as a matter of fact. He told me what had happened and what a great help you'd been.' There wasn't a trace of sarcasm or suspicion in his voice. 'I wonder what he'll do now? I shouldn't think his dad will be able to manage on his own, and there's no way Bruce can have him to stay in his house, even if it wasn't for the stairs. The place is a health hazard and needs gutting.'

'Oh, Fiona has that all in hand,' I said ruefully. 'She's called a meeting to see how best we can all be of help.'

'Oh,' Simon said, raising an eyebrow, 'Nice of her, isn't it?'

'Very,' I agreed, and for the first time that day I felt like laughing – and did.

Chapter Thirteen

The meeting was already in full swing by the time I arrived, having spent time making myself look as if I hadn't spent a sleepless night or been crying. Fiona opened the door to me – she appeared to be dressed for a night out in a figure-hugging black dress and killer heels.

'You're looking better,' she almost sounded disappointed. 'I thought we'd have to manage without you. After all, you won't want to be passing germs on to Jack.'

'Yes, I'm feeling better,' I agreed blithely. 'It was obviously nothing more than a sniffle that has no intention of turning into a full blown cold. Just as well, really, because I've got a lot on at the moment.'

'Well, you're not going to be much help then, are you? But then,' she went on, 'you've already done your bit, haven't you? Oh, look,' she said peering over my shoulder, 'there's Miles,' and before I could say that Jasper had already spoken to him, she'd pushed me to one side and sprinted out to meet him.

I hung my coat up and made my way towards the sound of voices, musing as I went that Fiona seemed to have developed a real problem with me lately. I was almost certain it was since Bruce had appeared on the scene because prior to that we had always got along famously. She had obviously decided he was perfect for the position of the second Mr Fiona Watkins, but that I might have designs on him myself. To say she would have a problem if she discovered recent developments was an understatement. She would probably kill me.

'Good gracious,' I said, coming to an abrupt halt on the threshold of Greg and Jasper's lounge. 'I wasn't expecting such a crowd.'

'Well, Bruce is very popular and we're all keen to help out. Come on in, darling,' Jasper urged, 'and share with me your preference – tea, coffee, or something stronger?'

He rushed off to fetch the cup of tea I'd requested and everyone started to speak at once. It all became a mish-mash of advice, suggestions and offers with each person promoting their own ideas.

I'd only taken the first sip of my tea when Fiona heralded her return, calling in a pleased voice from the hallway, 'Look who I found outside.'

I was expecting Miles, but it was Bruce she was ushering into the room, immediately taking her place by his side.

'What is this? What's going on?' he asked, looking bewildered, as well he might.

'It was my idea to get everyone together,' Fiona said, quickly taking the credit. 'We all wanted to help.'

'Help?'

'With Jack's care, you're both going to need some support.'

Everyone started to speak at once again, and Bruce looked across the room at me. I shrugged, indicating that this had nothing to do with me.

He didn't look pleased – in fact, he looked furious, I thought – but I could see he was making a clear effort to control his reaction to something that was obviously over the top, but kindly meant nevertheless.

'Well, that's very good – erm – of you all,' he raised a smile that definitely didn't reach his eyes, 'but my father has broken his ankle – not his neck. I think we can manage very well between the two of us.'

'Oh, but . . .' Fiona began to protest. 'How will he manage for his meals, for example with you working?'

'We can manage,' he replied tersely, 'but thank you for the offers,' he looked around the room. 'I do appreciate them, and realize that they were well intended.'

I could see that Fiona had more she wanted to say but, thankfully, Greg got in first. 'Well, now that you're here, Bruce, stay and have a bite to eat. Everyone else has eaten, so they can get back to whatever they were doing before Fiona rounded them up.'

'Ellen thought it was a good idea,' she said sulkily and without any basis in truth.

Bruce disappeared into the kitchen with Greg, and Jasper began to usher the rest of us out, but he caught my arm when I reached the front door. 'You've only just arrived,' he said, 'so you can stay.'

Fiona almost skidded to a halt from her position about two steps in front of me. 'Oh, but I . . .' she began.

'Have already eaten, just like everyone else who came earlier,' Jasper pointed out shortly, 'and Ellen hasn't. We've done what you wanted, and do realise that you meant well, but Bruce doesn't want our help, Fiona, you heard the man. He's made that quite clear. Best leave it.' With that he closed the door leaving her, still protesting, on the step. 'Sometimes,' he said crossly, 'that girl doesn't know how to take no for an answer – and you *didn't* know anything about this, did you – not until I called round?'

I shook my head. 'She means well,' I said, 'and I should go.'

'Go and do what?' Jasper demanded, 'carry on working on an empty stomach? Treat yourself to beans on toast? No you don't, not when we have more than enough Stroganoff made to feed an army.' With that he pushed me in front of him in the direction of the kitchen.

I hadn't planned on seeing Bruce so soon, if I could help it, but making the best of it, I asked how Jack was doing, when Bruce thought he would be home, and whether there would be any permanent damage to the ankle – given the fact the fracture had originally been overlooked and factoring in Jack's age. The answers I received were so brief as to be monosyllabic and I was glad when

Greg and Jasper took over, chatting easily and urging us both to tuck into the healthy portions ladled on to the plates in front of us. I had no trouble doing justice to mine.

I put Bruce's cool manner towards me as a sign that he was having serious second thoughts about the wisdom of what had happened between us. He probably had grave concerns about what my expectations might be, and would be absolutely mortified if he realised I'd been foolish enough to fall head over heels in love with him as a result of what would have been little more than pure lust on his part.

Well, he need have no worries that I would be imitating Fiona and pursuing him relentlessly, either now or at any time in the future, I thought sourly, accepting another helping of Stroganoff from Greg and tucking in again as the conversation drifted on around me.

'It's as Ellen said,' I looked up, fork poised, as Jasper mentioned my name and he continued, 'Fiona does mean well.'

'I'm sure she does,' Bruce replied evenly turning to me, 'but, even so, I'm surprised that you went along with it without checking with me first, Ellen. I thought you would have known me better than to suppose I would welcome that sort of interference – however well intentioned.'

I stared at him for a long moment, and then got slowly to my feet, dropping my fork onto my plate as I did so. 'And I,' I said, 'am surprised that you couldn't accept that something was well meant – if a little heavy-handed – and just politely decline the offers of help and leave it at that. Thank you for the food, Greg, Jasper, it was delicious. I have work to do, so I'll wish you goodnight.' With that I turned on my heel and, once I was out in the hall snatched up my jacket and practically ran out of the front door.

I bumped into Miles coming up the drive and striding past him, advised briskly, 'I wouldn't bother if you were thinking of making an offer of help to Bruce Redman. I can assure you the offer will *not* be well received.'

I found my legs were shaking when I closed my own front door behind me and leaned back against it. 'Bloody man,' I fumed, 'bloody insufferable man. Just who the hell does he think he is?'

I went straight to my work table and hadn't realised I'd been expecting the doorbell to ring until it did, but I already knew I was going to ignore it. Despite the fact a finger kept pressure on the bell for long moments I turned a deaf ear and gave a good impression of concentrating on the card I was holding. Bruce Redman could take a long walk off a short pier as far as I was concerned and I for one wouldn't be throwing him a lifeline.

I was still sitting staring sightlessly at the incomplete card in my hands when I heard the back door open and someone walk in. I listened to the footsteps getting closer and eventually stop behind my chair.

'Get out,' I ordered, and didn't even turn around as I added tonelessly, 'You have absolutely no right to walk into my house without an invitation.'

'You should learn to lock your door if you don't want people walking in uninvited,' Bruce said sharply.

'And you,' I said furiously, as my temper rose, 'should learn some bloody manners.'

'I know, *and* stop jumping to conclusions,' he agreed, sounding contrite. 'You didn't know what Fiona was planning, did you? Why didn't you say something when I started having a go at you?'

'Because,' I turned to face him, 'whether I knew or not is neither here nor there, and it shouldn't have made any difference. You were rude to everyone, not just me. Your neighbours offered friendship and support and you threw it back in their faces. If that's going to be your attitude, I can tell you now that you're setting up home in the wrong place. We try to be community-minded around here.'

'I know. You're right, I behaved like an idiot and I'm very sorry. There was no excuse for my behaviour.'

'Oh.' With the wind taken right out of my sails I sat and stared silently at Bruce.

'Yes,' he continued, hanging his head like a little boy who has just received a scolding from a parent, 'I know I will have to apologize to everyone – including Fiona – and I will, but a meeting, Ellen, a bloody meeting. An offer to do some shopping or cook Dad a meal would have been more than enough.'

I could feel my lips beginning to twitch, because it couldn't be denied that Fiona had gone ridiculously overboard, but then I pressed them firmly together. I wasn't ready to forgive Bruce for his disgraceful conduct just yet.

'So how are you and Jack going to manage then?' I asked, keeping my tone carefully impersonal and only faintly curious. 'You can hardly bring him back to your place. That would be another accident waiting to happen. If I wasn't afraid you would bite my head off, I would offer to have him here, but I'm well aware it wouldn't serve anyway, because of the stairs and the lack of sleeping accommodation.'

'You're not, are you – afraid to make an offer of help to me?' He looked dismayed.

I shook my head and managed a hint of a grin. 'No, not really, I can give as good as I get, as you've probably realised by now but, all joking aside, how will you manage?'

'Well, Dad lives in a warden-controlled flat, so he could probably cope after a fashion and with me helping out, but he's really too independent to leave to his own devices and would be getting himself into mischief in no time. Greg and Jasper have kindly offered to take him in – and despite my being so stiff-necked about accepting help – that was one offer I couldn't refuse. They've got a guest room with en-suite facilities downstairs that he can use, and they've assured me that one of them can manage in the shop so that the other can be at home to keep an eye on Dad.'

'Bless them,' I said fondly, knowing the offer was just like Greg and Jasper. 'If they both need to go to the shop, I'd be quite happy to go and sit with Jack. I love him, and I'm sure he'd be no trouble.'

'Unlike his son, eh?' he quipped.

'Well, you said it.' We were silent for a moment and I wondered what Bruce was waiting for, since he'd obviously said what he'd come to say.

It was clear he hadn't, and there was something else on his mind when he said, 'Ellen, are you all right with what happened between us?'

I wasn't stupid enough to try and pretend I didn't know what he was talking about. I thought it best to just make light of something that was supposed to be nothing more than a pleasurable interlude for both of us.

As far as I was aware, I didn't even blush as I said airily, 'Of course. We're both consenting adults, aren't we? These things happen in the heat of the moment. Though it's no one else's business and I wouldn't want it to become common knowledge – especially where my family are concerned.' I laughed, and he would never know the effort it took for me to ask, 'Oh, were you worried I'd be anticipating an offer of marriage, Bruce, or expecting my family coming after you with a shot gun? No, of course you weren't. We both clearly know where we stand on matters of matrimony.'

'Yes, of course we do.' His tone was strangely colourless and I thought he was probably sagging with relief, but I had already turned back to pick up the card I was supposed to be working on.

'Well,' I said lightly staring, unseeing, at the unassembled pieces in front of me, 'if there's nothing else, I'd better get on.'

'Of course, don't let me keep you. I'll go out of the back door and lock it behind me, though. I can post the key through your letterbox. You really shouldn't sit in here with the door unlocked. Anyone could walk in.'

'But you're not just anyone, are you?' I said aloud, as I heard the back door close and the key turn in the lock. 'And that's the problem.'

The flowers arrived mid-morning, and I suspected that I wasn't the only recipient, which turned out to be true when Fiona phoned soon after.

'I got flowers,' she said, excitedly, 'with a card saying thank you and sorry.'

There was no point in lying, I thought, or pretending I hadn't. 'Oh, yes,' I laughed, 'so did I and I suspect the rest of the close did as well.'

'But you didn't do anything,' she sounded outraged.

'Well, in theory, neither did you,' I reminded her, 'apart from suggesting a meeting and leaving it to Greg and Jasper to arrange.'

'Mmm, fair enough,' she muttered, 'but the intention was there and I suppose you did help Bruce get Jack to hospital.' She suddenly sounded contrite. 'I've been a bit unbearable to you lately, haven't I?'

'A bit,' I agreed, surprised that she would admit it. 'Was it something I said, or something I did?'

'Neither,' she admitted. 'It's just . . .'

'Just?' I prompted.

'It's Bruce.'

'Bruce? What about him?'

'Oh come on, Ellen, you must have noticed how close we've become.'

Close? No, to be honest I hadn't noticed they were close – unless there was something they both weren't telling me. There had been the pizza night when Fiona was upset about her ex – yes, and what about her ex? She seemed to have forgotten all about him – the meal that Bruce had made clear was about business and the family meal when she had clung to Bruce like a limpet all evening.

'You must have guessed that I'm mad about him,' she giggled girlishly.

I didn't agree or disagree, just asked carefully, 'And does he feel the same about you?'

'Oh, I'm sure he really likes me,' she said confidently, 'but you know what these confirmed bachelors are like.'

'Actually, I don't, given my lack of experience with men.' The sarcastic words were prompted by her previous comment, made on the night of the meal, but that obviously went over her head.

'Well, they just need a bit of encouragement. Give him time and he'll come to see that we'd be ideal together. With my business acumen I would be a real asset to him, exactly the sort of lady he should have on his arm.'

'I see that you have it all worked out, but what has this to do with your being snippy with me?'

'You're competition,' she said flatly, 'and you live right next door to him, *and* you knew him before, which gives you an unfair advantage.'

'You make us sound like predators stalking the same prey,' I tittered, 'or a couple of teenagers after a spotty boy. Doesn't Bruce have any say in this? I thought he made his feelings about settling down very clear on the night of the family meal.'

'Oh, they all say they have no intention of settling down,' Fiona said airily, 'but they don't mean it. James said the same and in the end he couldn't wait to marry me.'

Mmm, probably when he got a look at her bank statement, I thought, and then told myself not to be so unkind. I was sure he must have loved her in the beginning – before the money went to his head.

'I know what you're going to say,' she went on.

'You do?'

'Yeah, about to remind me what happened to James and me – but, Ellen, this would be quite different. I'm older now – old enough to know what I really want.'

But what about what Bruce wants? The question was on my lips, but it was never uttered because Fiona said suddenly, 'Oh, customer – got to go. I feel so much better now we've had this conversation and we both know where we stand,' and then she was gone.

I slowly replaced the receiver on the stand to charge, listened to it bleep and stood staring at the red light for a very long while.

There was no doubt about it, I had been warned off. Not that Fiona thought I was interested in Bruce, obviously, given my well aired views on the subject of relationships, but her cards had been well and truly laid on the table. Hands off, he's mine, had been the very clear message and, of course, she was welcome to him.

Chapter Fourteen

Over the next few days everything settled down, and Jack moved in with his temporary carers and professed himself very well suited. I popped along to see him regularly, sitting with him when required, and accompanying him when he felt like a hop on his crutches around the close.

My visits were timed with meticulous precision to avoid coming face to face with Bruce. The less I saw of him the better for both of us. That way there would be less chance of misunderstandings by either of us or anyone else. My infatuation with him had been, I decided, just that – an infatuation. No more than a continuation of my childhood crush inflamed by an ill-advised intimate incident that couldn't, by any stretch of the imagination, be described as a meaningful affair. The sooner I accepted that was the case the better for us all. I was an adult now, and had been for a very long time. Fiona was welcome to him.

The clocks changed soon after that and the weather deteriorated, bringing darkness each day by late afternoon. October moved swiftly into November, ensuring I was kept busy producing a record number of bespoke Christmas cards. It seemed that people were deciding that only a really special card could justify the cost of postage these days. I never tired of making those with traditional greetings enhanced by Christmas trees on the front covered in realistic lights or fat robins on snowy branches. The more modern

Winter Wishes variety never held the same appeal. Still, it was whatever the customer wanted since they were paying the asking price that eventually paid my bills, so I could hardly complain.

I took time out to visit Mum and Dad, bumping into assorted siblings from time to time. There were often veiled queries about how I was spending my time and who with, but a stern look from Dad ensured it never went further than that. I mostly drove over, picking up shopping for my parents and for myself as well on the way. The few times I walked I made sure to avoid the high street like the plague.

I was kept in the picture though with regular up-dates and according to Mum it was 'coming along a treat', especially now that money had apparently been invested in the project. I'd already been told by Greg that he and Jasper intended to shut up shop and enjoy a rare and very welcome holiday for the duration of their own shop's major renovation. A spring unveiling of the whole area was anticipated because the work to be done was mainly cosmetic and involved very little actual rebuilding.

My garden make-over had been completed and paid for, and I'd even taken an hour or two to thrust daffodil bulbs carelessly into borders and pots. It was so dark when I was out there that I could scarcely see what I was doing, but that lessened the chance of coming face to face with my neighbour through hedges that had been so ruthlessly pruned that they would give very little privacy until they bushed out again in the spring.

Work next door was also moving steadily forward, judging by the to-ing and fro-ing as materials were delivered, but I steadfastly averted my eyes whenever I walked up or down my path. There wasn't enough noise to get in the way of my working, what with the double-glazed windows shut tight as the temperature began to drop outside.

I hadn't seen Simon for a week or two when he suddenly turned up on my front doorstep and said accusingly, 'Your back door is locked.'

'Yes,' I agreed, 'and your point is? You've warned me enough times about my lack of security awareness.'

He put his head on one side and smirked. 'I have, haven't I? I suppose I should be pleased, but I was hoping not to disturb you until it was ready.' He brought a bag from behind his back which was, judging by the delicious aroma wafting from it, holding parcels of fish and chips. 'I come bearing gifts because I guessed you be working flat out.'

'And I have to eat.' Knowing what was coming, I said the words for him.

'Exactly.'

I stood back to let him inside and he made his way through to the kitchen. 'You carry on,' he advised airily, 'I know where everything is.'

I was happy to leave him to it and went back to my work table, concentrating on the 3D effect of the Christmas tree taking shape on the card in my hands and ignoring the faint sounds behind me as Simon moved back and forth setting cutlery out on the table at the other end of the room. I had far more difficulty trying to ignore my mouth watering in greedy anticipation of the treat to come.

'Haven't seen much of you,' Simon said, once we were seated at the table and tucking in.

'Well, I've been really busy,' I shrugged, 'and I haven't seen much of you. I just assumed you were busy, too.'

'I am,' he said, shaking vinegar liberally over his chips, and then – after tasting one – followed that with more salt, 'mostly around the close. Lots of little tidy-up jobs that will certainly keep the wolf from the door. Working for you and Bruce has certainly paid off for me. Funny how people see you working and it reminds them of all the jobs they have outstanding, even at this time of the year.'

'I'm glad you talked me into letting you re-organize and clear my back yard,' I said, 'it's almost doubled in size, but are you sure you didn't go a bit mad on cutting back those shrubs along the boundary. I'll have no privacy when the days warm up and I want to sit outside.'

'Oh, they'll grow back thicker than ever,' he assured me, and then gave me a straight look. 'Not fallen out with the neighbour again, have you?'

'Which neighbour?' I asked, though I knew perfectly well which one he meant.

''Well, I don't mean Alan and Shirley, do I?' he said, giving me another look. 'They're not known as "the quiet couple" around here for nothing, according to the other residents, and take keeping themselves to themselves to a whole new level. Come on, what's Bruce done to upset you now?'

'Nothing,' I said quickly, probably far too quickly, because Simon raised a quizzical eyebrow and his look became searching, as he queried, 'Nothing?'

'I just like my privacy, and over-looking a building site isn't my idea of an interesting view either.'

'I think you'll find it will be finished – or the bulk of the building work anyway – by the time you want to go out there. One of the perks of owing your own construction company is obviously that you can give your own jobs priority.'

'All right for some,' I said sourly.

'I'm sure he would do the same for his friends,' Simon said, in Bruce's defence.

'Yes, of course.' I kept my voice even and wished we could talk about something or even *someone* else and, to my relief Simon did change the subject, but not exactly as I would have wished.

'Hey,' he said, looking across at the pin board with my samples on it, 'I see the card is still on the board. I must say I'm surprised that one of your customers hasn't snapped it up yet.'

'Which card?'

'The one you were making when I came in the other day. It's still where I pinned it on the board.'

'Oh, yes, so it is,' I said as if I'd just noticed. 'Well, that's hardly surprising with Christmas just around the corner, is it? Most people can only think about one celebration at a time and that card would be more appropriate for Valentine's Day.'

Simon got up from the table and walking over removed the card from the board to look at it more closely even though he'd seen it before. 'Mmm, I suppose so. Wouldn't it be amazing to receive something like that in the post? I can tell you, I'd be made up. I don't think anyone has ever felt like that about me – certainly not the ex-wife.'

He stood there for a moment or two, evidently lost in admiration, and then looked at me as the doorbell rang.

'If you're going to say, who's that?' I joked, 'I can only say I've yet to discover a way to see through walls and doors and I'm not psychic. Probably Greg or Jasper at a guess, because they were desperate for more bookmarks for the shop and said they would come and collect to save me going into town tomorrow.'

I went to get up, but Simon ordered, 'You stay there and finish your meal. I'll go.'

I could hear the murmur of voices, then the front door closing and two sets of footsteps coming my way. 'They're over there on the filing cabinet,' I said, 'all parcelled up and ready to go,' and then I turned round to find it was Bruce standing in the archway.

'Look who I found on the doorstep,' Simon smirked from behind him. 'A bit slow off the mark this time, mate, or you could have shared the fish and chips again.'

'I'll be sure to make more effort to call in earlier next time,' Bruce smiled, but he was looking at me, and the smile didn't reach his eyes. I think he knew he wasn't welcome, but not why. How could he when I wasn't sure myself?

Caught off guard, I was aware of the juvenile feeling of butterflies in my stomach and the way my pulse had speeded up. I really should be over him I reminded myself crossly. It was a very long time since I was that teenager with a massive crush on my brothers' good-looking friend.

'I was only joking. There's actually plenty left that I can heat up in the microwave,' Simon offered, 'if you fancy it.'

'Thanks, that would be great,' Bruce accepted the offer to my surprise and Simon went off to the kitchen taking our plates with him.

'You don't really want warmed up fish and chips, do you?' I said, as we listened to the ping of the microwave starting up.

Bruce shrugged, 'Not really, just wanted to make sure you weren't avoiding me – you know after what happened between us.'

'We've already spoken about this and I told you there wasn't a problem. I haven't seen Simon either for a while either, because I've actually been busy.'

'You've seen plenty of my dad,' his tone sounded accusing, but I wasn't sure why since who I did or didn't see was obviously none of his business.

'That's because Jack's in the close twenty-four-seven and I can fit him in when I stop for a brief break. Anyway, he obviously needs the company at the moment and you don't.' Even as I explained I was cross with myself for feeling the need to do so.

'I still think you're avoiding me.'

'Oh and why do you think I would go to all that trouble?'

'After what happened between us, I'm pretty sure you think I'm going to read too much into it and try to sweep you off your feet and into marriage.'

I almost gasped out loud because that was almost exactly what I'd been thinking he was expecting from me.

'But,' he continued, 'I can assure you that nothing could be further from my mind.' He stopped then because Simon came back with a steaming plate of re-heated fish and chips and he sat down and tucked in with every appearance of enjoyment.

Well, that told me how it was, didn't it, loud and clear? Instead of the relief I should have been feeling, though, I just felt as if he had slapped me hard across the face. He didn't have to be so bloody brutal about the fact he wouldn't marry me if I were the last woman on earth. I was surprised how much that hurt, which of course was totally unreasonable because he had made very clear at the family and friends' meal the fact that he wasn't the marrying kind.

'What's that you've got there?' Bruce watched Simon pick up the card again and move towards the display board, apparently to put it back.

Simon held it out, and said, 'It's one of Ellen's latest creations. Rather beautiful, isn't it? The words are wonderful and I'm not normally a sentimental man.'

Bruce took it, after carefully wiping his hands on a paper napkin. I held my breath as he took his time, first examining the carefully built up picture of a faceless man and woman waltzing beneath a starry sky, and then turning to read the words inside. It felt very weird seeing him giving all his attention to a card that might – under different circumstances – have been made just for him.

'Whoever the recipient is will treasure this forever,' he said slowly.

'What a sentimental pair you are,' I said, keeping my voice light, 'I thought it was only women who enjoyed the romantic stuff.'

'That's a very sexist remark, Ellen Carson,' Simon told me sternly.

'Well, I make and sell the cards and I can tell you that three quarters of those of the starry-eyed variety are ordered by women for men. I prefer the jokey variety myself,' I lied, 'but don't get much call at all for those.'

'Did you think any more about opening a card shop in the high street when it's been refurbished?' Bruce asked suddenly, out of nowhere and without looking up. 'With cards of this quality on show you could probably treble or even quadruple your turnover.'

'I have trouble keeping up with the orders I already have,' I said shortly. 'Expanding the business would mean I'd have no life at all and I'd be back to the stressful existence I used to *enjoy* – and I use the word loosely – in my previous employment.'

'You could employ staff to do the selling,' he pointed out in the sort of reasonable tone that got right up my nose.

'Life isn't all about money, you know,' I said furiously, 'and I actually like my life just the way it is, thank you very much.'

He looked up then, a faintly shocked expression on his face, and he held up his hands. 'OK,' he said, 'it was only a suggestion. I'm sorry if I spoke out of turn.'

I felt foolish then, and noticed that even Simon was looking a bit surprised. 'No,' I said, 'I'm sorry I snapped at you. I just get a bit fed-up sometimes with everyone thinking they know what's best for me. I'm a big girl now – and I do know my own mind.' Except where you're concerned, I could have added, and found myself actually grateful when the doorbell announced another unexpected caller.

'You're popular,' Simon took the words out of my mouth.

'Aren't I?' I agreed lightly as I made my way through the arch to get the door, 'It's getting like Clapham Junction in here.'

'Oh, hi, Fiona, come—' I didn't get the chance to complete the invitation before Fiona pushed past me, saying, 'Is. . . ?'

'Fiona,' Simon greeted her from where he stood in the archway, but she barely acknowledged his greeting before she pushed past him as well and then stopped short at the sight of Bruce spearing chips on to a fork with one hand and still holding the card in the other. He didn't look up until Fiona actually spoke to him, though he would have heard both my greeting and then Simon's.

'So here you are, Bruce,' Fiona's tone was sharp – almost accusing.

I watched Bruce turn slowly and almost reluctantly in his chair and look up at her with a quizzical expression on his face. 'Yes,' he said, 'here I am. Something I can do for you?'

She didn't answer the question immediately, but posed one of her own. 'Do you two make a habit of eating fish and chips with Ellen?'

I thought that was a bit over the top, since it had been all of twice and Bruce had been around each time by pure chance, but I remained silent.

'Every chance we get, eh?' Simon directed his jokey question at Bruce, who rose to the challenge with a quip of his own, 'Must be something about the way she warms her plates or the vintage of her vinegar,' he grinned.

Simon sniggered and even I could feel myself smiling because it was so childish and so harmless.

Fiona obviously didn't find their wise-cracks remotely funny and, after treating Simon and me to a freezing glare, she turned back to Bruce and said, 'What about us?'

'Us?' he stared at her and, to me, appeared genuinely puzzled by her question. He had put his fork down, though he was still toying with the card, and I had to fight the urge to snatch it from his hand.

'Yes,' her tone was sharp, 'the modern art exhibition at my friend's gallery – you must remember my telling you about it. We were going to have supper together afterwards. Surely you can't have forgotten.'

It was only then that I realised she was all dressed up for what was obviously going to be a special occasion. I hadn't noticed before because Fiona was always very well dressed – as she would be in her line of work – but a closer look told me she had made an even greater effort for this event; I felt even more of a rag-bag than usual in comparison, dressed in my habitual working outfit of t-shirt and jeans. The ancient cardigan I was wearing over the top didn't help, either, or the fluffy boot slippers on my feet.

'I don't think it's a case of my forgetting, Fiona. I do vaguely remember you talking about it, but I had no idea you were issuing a firm invitation or I'd have told you that modern art is definitely not my thing. In fact, I'd go as far as to say that I detest it.' The latter was said in a flat tone that offered Fiona no opportunity to try and persuade Bruce to change his mind.

'Oh,' she said, obviously totally taken aback.

'Don't mind it, myself,' Simon said, with a shrug. 'In fact some of it is very cleverly done.' It was clearly an off-the-cuff remark, probably thrown in to fill the sudden silence, but Bruce immediately used it to his advantage.

'There you are, then,' he said, as if that solved everything. 'Take Simon with you, if you're in need an escort. He might enjoy it, I certainly wouldn't.'

Both Fiona and Simon looked so aghast that I had real difficulty keeping a straight face. I couldn't even look at Bruce, but could easily imagine the smug look on his face at the way he had so easily turned the tables.

'Erm, not dressed for it,' Simon indicated his leather jacket and jeans.

'Oh, it'll be fine,' Bruce said, waving the hand holding the card airily. 'In my experience these arty types wear what the hell they like to these events.' When neither Fiona nor Simon looked like moving, Bruce encouraged, 'I'd get a move on, if I was you, or you'll miss the wine and canapés.'

Left with little choice – unless each flatly and very rudely refused the other's company – they moved reluctantly to the door and the next minute they were gone.

I couldn't help it. I spluttered and then burst out laughing. 'You – you're wicked, you are. You must know that Simon is going to hate every minute.'

The grey eyes gleamed, but Bruce's expression was all innocence. 'You heard him. The guy actually *likes* modern art.'

'But he didn't want to go with Fiona and she didn't want to go with him.'

'Then one or both of them should have said so. *I* did.'

'Did you?' I asked, giving him a straight look.

'Yes,' he said, meeting my gaze, 'I did. Fiona likes to get her own way, it seems, but she needs to learn that I never do *anything* that I don't want to do.' There was no doubting his meaning and I felt myself flush.

He took me by surprise when he suddenly changed the subject and, holding the card out, said, 'I'd like to buy this.'

I wanted to ask why, instead, snatching it from him, I said, 'It's not for sale.'

'Oh, already earmarked for someone?'

'That's right,' I nodded, glad to have the reason provided for me. 'It's a commission.'

Bruce stood up, but made no move to leave, just stood looking down at me until I was sure the air between us crackled. I turned away and fiddled around, taking my time to fix the card back on to the display board and felt myself gradually calming down – until I realised he had come to stand right behind me. I could feel his breath on my neck and felt the hairs at my nape stand on end.

It was all that I could do not to turn around and fling myself into his arms – and a pretty fool that would have made me – especially when he said carelessly, 'Fancy a stroll along to see Dad, or have you already visited today?'

'No, yes, that would be great. I'll just get my coat.' Anything to get him out of the house, it was far too tempting to be alone in his company – even though I was well aware there was no future for us outside the bedroom.

I almost pushed him out of the front door, snatching a jacket from the row of pegs in the porch as I passed.

I knew he had noticed my hurry – and probably guessed the reason for it, I thought, cringing – when he said with a touch of humour, 'No rush. Dad won't be going anywhere in a hurry. In fact, he's made himself so comfortable that I think Greg and Jasper might discover they have an elderly squatter on their hands when the time comes for him to leave.'

Jasper opened the door and ushered us inside to where Jack was holding court surrounded by a small circle of visitors. Jasper immediately went back to fussing around him with cushions and a footstool, and Greg appeared from the direction of the kitchen carrying a tray of steaming cups of coffee and what looked like home-made biscuits.

'See what I mean,' Bruce murmured, for my ears only, 'they'll have trouble shifting him with dynamite when his leg's healed.'

I acknowledged Miles, who gave me a hard stare when he saw whom I'd walked in with, and then did a double-take when I realised my own parents were sitting among neighbours who also included Alan and Shirley.

'Mum, Dad, fancy finding you here. I'd have come and collected you both if I'd known you were heading this way,' I told them, and Bruce added that he could have picked them up on his way across town earlier.

'Oh, Michael's quite well enough to drive now.' My mother beamed at us both and I felt sure her gaze rested fleetingly, but ever hopefully on my left hand. I almost shook my head because she was never going to give up on the expectation that I would surprise her one day with a sparkly ring on my engagement finger. 'Have you two been out?' she asked obviously anticipating a positive reply.

'Dressed like this?' I indicated my clothes. 'I've only just stopped work. We've just met outside,' I stretched the truth and threw a defiant glance in Bruce's direction that dared him to contradict me.

'Fiona was in earlier looking for you, Bruce,' Greg said, passing him some coffee and then offering the sugar bowl. 'She seemed to think you had an arrangement.'

'Did she?' There was no curiosity and very little interest in Bruce's response.

'Mmm,' Jasper joined in. 'Some kind of modern art exhibition.' He grimaced slightly, 'Not really *my* thing, I have to say.'

'Or mine either,' Bruce said, 'but we saw her going off quite happily with Simon, didn't we, Ellen?'

I obviously had to allow him the courtesy of stretching a bit of truth of his own, so I nodded and even found myself smiling conspiratorially at Bruce over the rim of my cup. He met my gaze and held it. The warmth in his grey eyes took my breath away and forced me to acknowledge a truth I wasn't ready to face. I loved him. Yes, I really did and I didn't know how much longer I was going to be able to pretend – to him and to everyone else – that I didn't.

Chapter Fifteen

THERE ENSUED A cosy debate among Jack's hosts and visitors concerning their preferences for modern or traditional art. There appeared to be two definite camps and, surprisingly I thought, the very quiet Alan and Shirley came out as devotees of the former and held quite definite views which they were eager to express. They'd never, to my knowledge, given the impression they might have held any strong opinions on any subject. Art was quite an individual thing to my mind and a lively debate ensued.

Personally, I preferred anything that was bright and cheerful for my own walls and whether it depicted unidentifiable splotches or the clearly recognizable was of no great matter. I was far more concerned currently with the huge resurgence of a childish crush that I should have grown out of long since.

I became very busy, which was always my solution when something was troubling me. I rushed around collecting cups, loading the dishwasher – knowing even as I was doing it that Greg would have a particular way of doing that task and would hate anyone interfering. I looked up to find him watching me.

'Something bothering you?' he asked in a mild tone.

'Sorry, I know you'll have your own way of doing this.' I pulled a face. 'I wanted to help and got a bit carried away.'

'Be my guest. It's fine. Something *is* bothering you, though, isn't it?'

I nodded, 'But I'm not ready yet to talk about it. If I were,' I added, 'I'm sure you know I would happily talk to you.'

'Thank you,' he said, 'and be sure that you do. Here you are, take these biscuits in. They're disappearing so fast in there that I wouldn't be surprised to find they're all filling their pockets.'

'Neither would I,' I agreed biting into one and enjoying the crisp, crumbly texture, 'these make the shop-bought varieties taste like cardboard.'

I carried the plate through and, ignoring the empty chair beside Bruce, squeezed in beside Miles on the sofa and found myself concurring that the old masters were the best and nothing was ever going to beat them. Whether I agreed or not was neither here nor there, as far as I was concerned. I was just trying to prove a point – to myself and to the room at large. The point was that Bruce and I were not a couple and we never ever would be. To press the point home I encouraged Miles to walk me home when the party broke up and the only men I kissed good night were Jack himself and my dad.

'Coming in for a coffee?' I offered when we'd reached my front door and I realised that Bruce had followed us out and was standing on the pavement watching us. I practically hauled Miles inside when he showed signs of hesitating and hurried to put the kettle on.

Carrying through cups of coffee that neither of us wanted, I found Miles standing in my work space looking at the display board.

'Thank you,' he said, taking the proffered cup and then, indicating the board with its selection of cards he added, 'you really are a very talented lady.'

'Thank you,' I replied and then burned my lip sipping a drink that had had no time to cool down.

'These are each pieces of art in their own right,' he assured me in his solemn tone, 'though this one,' he held out the card I had made after the discovery of my feelings for Bruce, 'while very beautiful would be far too sentimental for my taste.'

'Yes,' I agreed, 'I imagine that it would be. My customers are always very specific when they detail their requirements and no two choices are ever the same.'

When he moved to the sitting room and made himself comfortable, I began to regret bitterly inviting him inside, especially when he started chatting in that laboured and long-winded way of his about everything and nothing. I wondered, not for the first time, how I had put up with him for so long. I supposed looking at Miles as a handy escort and a safe option had had something to do with it. I was certainly never in any danger of falling head over heels in love with him even at the very beginning of what could only loosely have been termed a liaison.

I yawned and stretched several times, but he was completely oblivious to my hints that it was time for him to leave. I lamented the lack of a cat or even milk bottles to put out on the step and I had no alarm clock to wind pointedly. So desperate was I becoming that I even played briefly with the idea of just getting ready for bed. The thought that he might take that as an invitation stopped me. Somehow I held my patience, and settling deeper into the armchair, I tuned out and let his earnest words wash harmlessly over me.

'Ellen, Ellen,' a voice spoke softly and a hand shook my shoulder.

I forced up eyelids that felt like weighted roller blinds, 'Wha. . .' I began, and finding myself staring up into Miles' face with its concerned expression, I hauled myself upright with an effort. 'Did I fall asleep? Oh, how rude of me. I'm so sorry, Miles, but it has been a long day.'

'My fault,' he said stiffly, 'I've obviously outstayed my welcome.'

I was actually too tired to contradict Miles and was just relieved to see him leave. I didn't even get up to see him out and wasn't at all sure I could rouse myself enough to go up to bed. I was very tempted to remain exactly where I was and closed my eyes for a moment while I decided what to do. When I opened them Bruce was standing in front of me.

Wide awake in an instant, I sat bolt upright and demanded, 'How did you get in here?'

'Your idiot boyfriend didn't close the front door properly. It would have been swinging on its hinges all night if I hadn't spotted it.'

'Walking your dog, were you?' I asked, my tone thick with sarcasm, 'or did you just happen to be passing? And he's not my boyfriend,' I concluded.

'I notice you didn't say he's not an idiot,' he came right back. 'You could have been burgled or murdered in your bed because of his carelessness, Ellen, so this is no time to be flippant.'

Knowing he was right didn't help and I snapped, 'I'd have noticed before I went up to bed.'

'You looked like you were settled for the night in that chair to me. You need to take more care – and I'm being serious here. There's no point at all in remembering to keep the back door secure if you allow your late night visitors to waltz off leaving the front one wide open.'

'Do you regularly try the back door then?' I demanded. 'Since when, exactly, did my safety become any concern of yours?'

'Since. . .' he began, and then he stopped as if momentarily lost for words, before continuing in a less forceful tone, 'since we became neighbours.'

'Oh,' I glared at him, letting my disbelief show, 'and do you take the safety of *all* of your neighbours as seriously?'

'No,' he said crossly, 'just the ones who don't consider their own safety important.'

'So that would be me, in fact? The one who has lived here for a hell of a lot longer than you and, look, I've survived despite regularly neglecting to lock doors and windows. Now why don't you go and take care of someone who will appreciate your concern, Bruce. I'm a big girl now.'

'Yes, so I've noticed.' He looked me up and down in a way that made me burn with embarrassment, and continued, 'What a shame it is that along the way you seem to have lost the sweet nature and charming manners that once set you apart from your sisters.'

With that he turned on his heel and went out, slamming the front door behind him with all the force he could muster.

'Go to hell,' I said belatedly, and promptly burst into tears before stomping my way up to bed.

Even I recognized that the situation became ever more ridiculous after that. I could hardly fail to notice the lengths I'd go to in order to avoid a face to face confrontation with Bruce. Opening my front door to go out on an errand I would close it quickly if I caught sight of him even in the distance; if he came to visit his dad at Jasper and Greg's I would leave by the back door as he came in the front. It was only when I found myself practically crawling along next to the hedge and realised that he was on the other side that I decided it had to stop.

After all, what was I afraid of? It was quite clear he had also been avoiding me like the plague since Miles's unfortunate visit. Why I had been so cross with him that night was also a mystery to me if I was honest. Biting his head off for being a concerned neighbour was irrational to say the least. I could have just thanked him for his concern in a reasonable manner and made it clear I was quite able to take care of myself.

The truth was that despite my forty years of age and ever since sex had reared its ugly head and turned our friendship into something else entirely – on my part at least – I seemed to alternately turn into a quivering wreck or a vicious-tongued harridan whenever Bruce came near me. For the first time in my adult life I was letting my heart rule my head and out of the window had flown my carefully laid plans for an uncomplicated solo life.

It was a sobering thought that, after all the years of protesting that marriage was the very last thing on my mind, it was never far from the very same mind these days. Worse, the one person I would marry in a flash if he asked me was as against marriage as I had ever been – and far less likely to change his mind.

Well, something had to change and the only one I could change was myself. Trying to avoid Bruce clearly wasn't working because even a glimpse of him still made my heart beat faster – and I had wasted far too much time shutting myself away.

Actually though, I reminded myself with a satisfied nod, my time hadn't been wasted. I had been working solidly and, as a result, all my Christmas orders were completed, and the menus and extra book marks had been delivered long since, and here I was ready to make a start on the early Valentine's Day orders – in November. My order books had never looked so healthy and neither had my bank account.

The realization made me think about the idea of a card shop. Though I remained unconvinced that such a venture would be right for me, I thought I would kill two birds with one stone and go and check on the progress of the new look high street, and actually seek a meeting with Bruce instead of running a mile every time I saw him. Familiarity would surely breed contempt in his case, I decided.

I wrapped up warmly against the chill in the air with a cherry-red coat, wound a black wool scarf around my neck and pulled on knee-high black boots. To look good was to feel good, I assured myself, picking up my black bag and gloves and slamming the door behind me.

Progress was clearly being made, judging by the hammering and banging going on, but most of the improvements were well hidden behind hoardings and the unveiling wasn't going to take place until spring of the following year. There were a few hard-hat wearing individuals around writing on clip-boards but, annoyingly, after I had built myself up for a meeting with Bruce, there was absolutely no sign of him.

After I had walked the length of the street twice I gave up and went into the bookshop for a warm and a chat, only to find Bruce standing behind the counter looking very much at home. My intention was to be cool calm and collected in his company at all times but, taken completely by surprise, I became quite flustered and was furious that he had that effect on me.

Luckily a customer approached the till before I managed to behave badly yet again, and by the time he had taken the money and wrapped the book I had managed a few deep breaths and was once again in control of my emotions.

'Hi,' I said sweetly as the shopper left with his parcel, 'just thought I'd pop in and see how the book mark stocks were doing since I found myself coming this way when I nipped out for a bit of fresh air.'

'Good to see you getting out and about,' he said pleasantly. 'Jasper was only saying this morning that he thought you were working far too hard.'

'Well, Christmas is my busiest time,' I said, matching his tone. 'Where is Jasper? I take it he's on shop duty today.'

'Mmm,' Bruce assented with a nod of his head. 'He had to pop out, and it's easier for me to take over here than to go all the way back to relieve Greg so that he can relieve Jasper. It's the least I can do after everything they've done – and are still doing for Dad.'

'He's doing well – Jack – isn't he?' I was beginning to feel more normal by the minute and was exceptionally pleased with myself, but annoyed that it had taken me so long to realize that this was the way forward. 'He's looking forward to getting the plaster off.'

'He is, on both counts. He's always hated being inactive and can't wait to get back to work. He's made me leave the garden wall for him, so I'm sorry if it looks a bit unsightly. If I had my way it would have been back up weeks ago.'

'Hi, Ellen,' Jasper breezed in with his arms full of parcels and, spotting me, he launched into an explanation. 'I've taken advantage of Greg not being here to do a bit of Christmas shopping. I normally have the devil of a job because he always wants to know where I am and what I'm buying. It's a good thing you've popped in,' and turning to Bruce he said, 'have you asked her yet?'

For one very long moment my brain went into overdrive and arrived at the totally ridiculous conclusion that he was expecting

Bruce to ask me to marry him, and then I came back to planet earth with a thump. I had no idea what was wrong with me. I had never been of a fanciful nature, but lately my imagination seemed to have a mind of its own – especially just before I fell asleep at night, when anything seemed possible. I waited for Bruce to speak and for my stupid pulse to slow down.

'No,' he told Jasper, 'Ellen's only just got here.'

'Well, you see,' Jasper took over in his efficient way, 'we're nearly into December and business is starting to pick up, with people doing their Christmas shopping, and I can really do with Greg here so we were wondering . . .'

'It's not fair to put that on Ellen, though, is it – when it's her busiest time, too? We'll have to come up with another solution, or I can take care of Jack, myself. He is my father, and my responsibility.'

'She can work from our house just as easily as her own, if we get it all set up,' Jasper argued, even though they hadn't actually asked me anything that I could say yes, or no to.

'You want me to mind Jack?' It was an easy guess. 'Of course I will.'

'Only he doesn't get his plaster off for at least another two weeks,' Jasper said.

'And if he's not watched he's liable to do something stupid,' Bruce added.

Then they both stared at me. 'What did you say?' they said in unison.

'I said, of course I will.'

'But – your work, Ellen,' Bruce protested, and I was certain he had been expecting me to say no.

Probably even as recently as the day before I would have refused to get involved, but my present mind-set even thought it might be a good idea. I was very fond of Jack anyway, and the more I saw of his son the better were my chances of viewing him as no more attractive than any other man.

'I've put in a lot of hours lately so the Christmas rush is taken care of,' I said calmly, 'and, as Jasper said, I can just as easily work in their house. We can't do it any other way because Jack won't be able to manage the stairs in my house and, as you know, I have no downstairs loo.'

Still Bruce hesitated, and I began to forget my resolve to remain calm around him. 'Look,' my tone was sharp, 'I accepted your bloody concrete slabs against my better judgement, so now you can damn well accept my help when it's offered.'

'Well, if you put it like that,' he said with a wry grin.

'Have you got a better idea?' I demanded.

'There you are then,' Jasper didn't wait for a reply to a question he already knew the answer to, 'that's all sorted. Shall we say you'll start on Monday then? I could do with Greg here ASAP, to be honest, so that we can get the Christmas decorations up. He has a better eye for such things than I do, believe it or not. If we leave it any later we'll be into December. Come over for supper tonight and let us know what you need.'

I was so up to date with my orders that I could have had a break from my work for a couple of weeks with no harm done, or I could work in the evenings when I got home. However, I had only been planning to build up my standard stock and realised I could talk to Jack at the same time as long as I wasn't working on anything too elaborate. I was sure if he could see me getting on with something, it would make Jack feel less as if he were being a nuisance. So Monday, when it came, found me set up and ready to go at a different table in a different house.

I appreciated very quickly that Jack could probably have managed perfectly well without me there, because he had a steady stream of visitors throughout the day more than willing to make him cups of tea and bringing with them all manner of little treats.

'Honestly,' I said, on the second day, licking sugar from my fingers and jam from my lips, 'if I eat one more doughnut I won't have a stitch of clothing that fits.'

'Nonsense,' Jack looked me up and down, 'I've seen more fat on a wishbone. I'm the one who should be abstaining, because I'm not doing anything to work it off.'

'Come on then,' I said, 'I'll get our coats and we can take a turn around the close.'

'I don't want to take you away from your work,' he protested, but had his coat on and was waiting at the front door on his crutches in no time.

If anything it was even more sociable outside, where the world and most of the neighbours were coming and going. Alan and Shirley were the first to make an appearance on their way out to buy a living Christmas tree, they informed us.

'We won't bring it indoors until Christmas eve, though,' they said in their serious way, 'but we like to choose ours early to be sure of getting one with a really nice shape. Then on Boxing Day we'll take it out and plant it in the garden. We have quite a little collection out there now.'

'Their own little miniature forest at the bottom of the garden, by the sound of it,' Jack said wryly, 'but they're nice people who mean well.'

'They've certainly become more sociable since your accident,' I realised, 'they used not to say boo to a goose. Oh, look, there's Simon.'

'Oh, glad I didn't have to knock and disturb you at your work, Ellen,' he climbed out of his Land Rover and came across to where we were standing – we hadn't actually done very much walking at all. 'Hi, Jack, how are you doing?'

By the time they'd passed the time of day and discussed the progress of Jack's leg, my feet were freezing from standing in one spot.

'Something I can do for you, Simon?' I asked, eager to get Jack moving as well as myself.

'Nope,' he said cheerfully, 'something I can do for you. How're you fixed for a Christmas tree this year?'

'Well,' I grinned up at him, 'same as any other year. No tree, no bother. Christmas trees are for those who have kids, so I leave the decorations to my family.'

'No tree?' he looked dismayed.

'No tree?' Jack echoed, looking if anything, even more shocked, 'but even I have a tree in my little flat.'

'She must have a tree, mustn't she?' Simon appealed to Jack who backed him up all the way with an emphatic, 'She *must* have a tree.'

'Says who?'

'We do,' they chorused.

I shook my head. 'I don't know how we got into this pointless conversation or why you're even asking me about trees.'

'Because I have one with your name on it, Ellen, and it's free of charge. *Now,*' he looked immensely pleased with himself, 'isn't that an offer you simply can't refuse?'

'But I don't have anything to put on a tree,' I protested. 'It will be standing bare and unadorned in the corner.'

Simon rolled his eyes at Jack. 'Next she'll be expecting me to provide the blasted tinsel and baubles as well as the tree. Honestly, there's no pleasing some people. All right, all right,' when I just stared at him he threw up his hands, 'if that's what it takes to make you have a tree in your house, I'll supply the decorations, too.'

'But I don't *want* a tree,' I began again, and then found myself giving in with good grace after all. 'OK, if it makes you both happy, I'll have a tree – but I'll go out and choose my own decorations.' I actually began to feel unexpectedly excited at the prospect and was already deciding to make sure that I got some twinkling lights as well. 'I'll pay for the tree though. I don't expect you to buy it.'

'It won't cost me a thing,' Simon assured me, looking pleased with himself. 'I've bought a job lot from a local supplier and I expect to make a healthy profit. As a result of seeing what I've done in your garden your neighbours have kept me in work these past weeks, so you can take it as a thank you. I'll drop it off in your back garden in a week or two.'

'Well,' I said, 'if you put it like that I can hardly refuse. It might make a change to get into the Christmas spirit for once. Fancy a hot chocolate?'

I was glad I had invited him when Bruce turned up just a few minutes later unannounced. I left the three men chatting and went off to make the hot drinks and then almost jumped out of my skin when Bruce suddenly spoke behind me.

'I should have offered to do that,' he said, 'we're taking you away from your work.'

I forced myself to laugh, and clutching my chest dramatically, said, 'Oh, I didn't hear you coming, you could have given me a heart attack. Look at the mess I've made.'

He reached out and put his hands on my arms, and I almost stopped breathing. This was the moment I'd been waiting for, the moment he was going to pull me closer, he was going to kiss me and tell me that he loved me. I knew it, and knew that I couldn't do a thing about it and I knew that I didn't want to.

Chapter Sixteen

Bruce's hands were firm on my arms as he pulled me closer, and my lashes fluttered down over my eyes as I waited to feel his lips on mine.

And then, instead of drawing me into his arms and whispering words of love, he moved me firmly to one side and, laughing, said, 'What are you like?' before he let me go and started to wipe away the mess of powdered hot chocolate I'd scattered on the worktop.

To hide my confusion and embarrassment, not to mention a ridiculous feeling of disappointment, I became very efficient, rattling around with cups, saucers and teaspoons, arranging them on a tray as if my life depended upon it. I didn't think he had noticed, but I was well aware I'd very nearly made a complete idiot of myself and, worse, I actually felt like sobbing my heart out because he *hadn't* kissed me. I was relieved when he downed his hot drink and left, and Simon took himself off soon after.

'You're not getting very much done, are you?' Jack frowned, perhaps seeing that all wasn't well with me, but hopefully having no idea of the real reason. 'It makes me feel very guilty, taking up your time like this.'

I patted his hand. 'Honestly,' I said. 'It's fine. Without my usual procrastination I'm right on top of the Christmas orders and that's normally unheard of this side of December. Pity I can't say the same for my feeble attempts at Christmas shopping, but my family is so big that the very thought of even making a start fills me with fear. Half of my nieces' and nephews' likes and dislikes are a mystery to me.'

'I can understand your problem, but you're lucky to have that strong family circle.' I thought Jack looked sad as he continued. 'Bruce is the sum total of my family. Being only children ourselves, me and the missus would have liked a bigger family, but it just never happened for us. We always enjoyed it when your brothers came round because it was so much fun having a houseful. I'd kind of hoped I'd have grandchildren by now, but that shows no sign of happening either.'

'I suppose it's not likely to happen in the future either with Bruce being as dead set against marriage as I am,' I sympathized, thinking of my mum with the steady stream of family visitors she so looked forward to.

Jack looked at me in evident surprise. 'What makes you say that?' he asked.

'Well, that's more or less what he said at the meal we all went to.'

'Ah, yes, he did, didn't he?' Jack agreed nodding. 'Though I think you'll find he was actually dropping a strong hint to that pushy friend of yours, *and* possibly trying to show your family that you weren't alone in not wanting to leap into marriage. Some of them are quite bullying in their tactics, aren't they?'

'You noticed it too, did you?' I said ruefully. 'I do try to remember that they mean well, but it isn't always easy.'

'I wouldn't be surprised if all that pushing you towards marriage didn't have quite opposite to the desired effect. Probably made you dig your heels in even more – I'm right aren't I?'

Jack was looking at me shrewdly and I found myself giving a reluctant nod, perhaps realising for the first time how right that assumption was.

'Early marriage and a parcel of kids was never on the cards for me, even if I might have been eventually inclined,' I admitted. 'I had other plans and a life I wanted to live before I gave any thought to settling down, but my siblings never were the listening kind, and eligible men were shoved my way at every given opportunity. I kept saying I had no intention of getting married and the more I said it to convince them, the more I came to believe it myself. Mind you, their marital histories have been enough to reinforce my no-wedding bells vow over the years.

'So,' I said, feeling we'd talked enough about me. I changed the individual under discussion, if not the subject matter. 'Why do you think Bruce has never married?'

'Oh,' Jack pulled a face, 'too single-minded by half is that one. He saw me work hard as a bricklayer all my life – always for someone else – and that made him determined to be his own boss. He's done well, and I'm very proud of him, but I fear it's at the expense of his private life. He's mixed more socially since he came back to Brankstone than he's done in years.

'Come on,' he said suddenly, quickly and easily changing the subject, 'come and show me how to make one of those cards – one for a lady. I've had an eye on one for a while. She lives close to where I do, and we've been speaking on the phone while I've been here. It's being away that has made me ask myself what I'm waiting for. It's true what they say about absence making the heart grow fonder.'

If I was surprised by his confession and by getting such a request from someone advanced in years whom I was sure wouldn't have an artistic or romantic bone in his body, I was sure I hid it. Jack very soon became engrossed. In fact, I had a job to get him to stop for long enough to eat a sandwich. It was a wonderful piece he eventually created, with glitter spray liberally applied and realistic dew drops on his many roses. I was leaning over him, guiding his hand when a slight noise behind us made us both look round to find Jasper, Greg and Bruce lined up in the doorway, watching us with fascinated wonder.

Jack held up his card with all the pride of a child showing off his first school painting. 'Look what I've made,' he said, and watched with dismay as one of the roses became detached and fell on to the table.

'Brilliant first attempt,' I assured him, handing him the glue, 'don't you all think so?' I appealed to our audience.

'Marvellous.'

'Charming.'

'Fantastic.'

Jack beamed. 'Ellen has been amazing,' he said, 'and I've been telling her she should start classes.'

'If she can coax a crusty old bricklayer into producing something as special, I actually think she might have found a gap in the market. I've never seen Dad create a thing that didn't involve bricks.' Bruce smiled at me approvingly, and I could feel myself warming to him again. But then I'd come to realise that it didn't take much.

All these years I hadn't thought I had a type when it came to men but I was wrong because Bruce Redman was definitely my type of guy. The question was – what was I going to do about it?

'Mind you,' Bruce continued, 'it isn't all about the beauty of the card itself, but also what's inside.'

'What do you mean, son?' Jack opened his card and looked at the blank page.

'The thing that makes Ellen's cards so special are the words inside. If you're looking for the heart it's *in* the cards, otherwise it's just a pretty creation.' He grinned at Jack. 'I'm looking forward to seeing how good your poetry is, Dad?'

We all laughed, but I was more touched than I could say by Bruce's unexpectedly thoughtful view of the cards I made.

The weather grew colder as we crept into December and I was forced to accept that Christmas was just around the corner. Some effort would have to be made to embrace the festivities and that meant going shopping.

At least I had no concerns as far as money was concerned. My earlier efforts to avoid Bruce's company had seen my card output rocket, along with the contents of my bank account. Of course, it wasn't only the cards – the Christmas menus I had come up with for the restaurant had been eagerly accepted – and Valentine menus were already being planned – and Greg and Jasper couldn't get enough book marks for their shop. They swore their book sales had soared because of them, allowing them to compete with the big name bookshop in the precinct to their great delight.

I had found that diversifying in such a way helped my concentration and my enjoyment in what I was doing. Financially, I was also in better shape than at any time since I became self-employed.

Regarding the Christmas shopping – I had thought all along that one concerted effort would be better than several forays into town. Once Jack's plaster was removed and he had returned home – freeing me from my duties as far as he was concerned – I realised I could delay the inevitable no longer.

In fact, I missed his company more than I would have believed – even after such a short time – and was glad of an excuse to go out. Up earlier than usual, I dressed myself up warmly and picked up my list. As soon as I stepped outside I was aware of a flurry of activity out on the pavement and hurried to see what was happening.

'Are you sure you should be doing that?' I demanded, staring at Jack who stood there, trowel in hand, obviously ready to make a start at rebuilding the front wall to Bruce's property.

He beamed at me from under his thick woollen hat and assured me, 'Don't you worry about me, physio swears I'm as good as new and I can't spend another day doing nothing.'

Somehow, I doubted that, given Jack's age, but I supposed it wasn't up to me to argue with him. However, I hovered, undecided about what I could do without coming over as bossier beyond what was acceptable from someone who was a mere friend.

To my huge relief, Simon suddenly appeared pushing a wheelbarrow of freshly mixed cement down the path.

'Making a start on the wall, then?' I said casually, trying to indicate my concern about Jack with a nod of my head.

'That's it,' Simon said, adding with a wink, 'Jack's allowing me to labour for him, seeing as I'm at a loose end at the moment and have always wanted to try my hand at a bit of building work. Can't have too many strings to my bow and I'll be taking lessons from the master of brickwork.'

'Oh, absolutely,' I agreed, realising he'd have taken a day away from his Christmas tree sales, probably at Bruce's request, especially to keep an eye on Jack and make sure he didn't over do it.

I set off for the post office with a few last minute Christmas card orders to post along with late December and early January birthday card orders as well. From there I would make for the high street to deliver yet more book marks to the shop. I was looking forward to checking on the progress made. According to Jasper and Greg most of the shops had now been reserved by various retailers, but I still didn't feel inclined to make the huge step towards opening my own card shop. For one thing I didn't need the pressure and if that indicated a lack of ambition in me, I really wasn't bothered.

The hoardings were up along most of the high street but, through the gaps you could see boards had been replaced with the traditional windows of times gone by – some with the name of the new proprietor and business already in place. I could feel a frisson of excitement as I noted the wool shop, teashop and family butcher. It was a huge project and was the facelift the tired old street badly needed to breathe new life into it and encourage the shoppers back to this part of town. It clearly wasn't meant to compete with the modern precinct with its big name shops, but to offer an alternative with a return to the time-honoured and yes, old-fashioned way of trading.

The bookshop was busy, despite the fact that very few of the neighbouring shops were still trading. Of course, that couldn't be put down to my bookmarks, but was more likely the personal service that Jasper and Greg offered with gift-wrapping just one of them.

'Oh, good,' Jasper exclaimed, the minute I showed my face round the door, 'we only have a handful left.'

Even I was surprised by how eagerly they were received, with customers crowding round to make their selections, and taking time to match the bookmark to the personality or age of the recipient.

'It just finishes the gift of a book off so perfectly,' said one lady, choosing one covered in kittens to go with a children's book about a well-known cat. 'Now all I need is a greetings card and I'm done. You don't sell those in here, do you?' she asked Greg, and when he shook his head, she said, 'Pity.'

'She's not the first person to say that,' Greg told me when the shop had cleared apart from a couple of browsers perusing the shelves. 'Are you sure you're not interested in having your own card shop close by, you'd make a killing?'

I shook my head. 'I like my life the way it is, and there is more to life than work and money, you know.'

'My sentiments exactly, but it's taken me a bit longer than it has you to realise it.'

We both spun round as Bruce strolled in wearing a hard hat and high visibility jacket, with clip board very much in evidence.

'You're not helping,' Greg frowned, 'I was just trying to persuade Ellen to open the card shop we talked about before. I'm always getting asked if we stock cards to go with the books people buy as gifts.'

'So why don't you, then?'

'Why don't we what?' Greg looked confused.

'Why don't you stock Ellen's cards in your shop? She doesn't need a whole shop and the display needn't take up much more than a corner of yours. You'll have the space anyway with the redesigned layout we've planned.'

Jasper had obviously overheard because he stopped what he was doing immediately and rushed over to say, 'That's a brilliant idea.'

'Is it?' I said, suddenly feeling quite nervous about what was being thrust upon me.

'Let's put it this way,' Bruce said. 'You'd have no overheads. You would also have control over how much or how little you are prepared to put on display and you could work out between you what percentage of each sale could go to Jasper and Greg.'

'Ellen's cards would be a huge draw so we'd be happy to sell them here for nothing,' Greg said smartly.

'No, you wouldn't,' I said just as quickly. 'If you're going to sell my cards you must take a fair cut.'

'So you'll do it?' There was no mistaking the delight on the three faces staring at me.

I shrugged. 'I don't see why not – as long as the display isn't *too* big. It might mean less in the way of disruption with fewer local customers coming to call at the house. Do you think you could take orders for specific cards as well – if I provide some sort of a catalogue?'

'Absolutely,' Greg confirmed immediately, with Jasper adding, 'No problem at all.'

'Look,' Jasper said as several potential customers came through the door at once, 'we can't discuss this properly here. Come over for dinner tonight. You too, Bruce and bring Jack. We're missing having him around.'

'He must feel the same because he's back already,' I laughed. 'When I left home earlier he was hard at work on Bruce's front wall.'

'Is that wise?' Jasper looked horrified.

'I'd like to see you or anyone else try and stop him,' Bruce said flatly. 'I coerced Simon into labouring for him to limit the amount of work he had to do and keep an eye on him at the same time. I'm not sure what else I could have done. He's my dad and he's not going to take kindly to my giving him orders.'

'I think you'll find Simon has already persuaded Jack to give him lessons in bricklaying, thereby ensuring he gets to do some of the work,' I soothed, 'and I have to say they both looked as happy as Larry when I waved them goodbye. Anyway,' I looked at my watch, 'time I was on my way. There's Christmas shopping to be done.' I glanced round the shelves of books and said ruefully, 'What a pity none of my family are what you'd call readers, I could have done everything without moving a step.'

'Need a lift anywhere?'

I hadn't realised that Bruce had followed me from the shop until I heard his voice behind me.

'No, thanks, the walk to the precinct will do me good – and I wore comfortable boots especially. If you have any ideas about what interests a teenager these days, that would be helpful, though, because I haven't a clue.'

Bruce pulled a face and then suggested, 'I'd stick to vouchers if I were you. That works on two levels, because they weigh nothing and the recipient gets to choose whatever they like. Failing that, just give them money. I'm sure they never have enough cash if they're anything like we used to be.'

I laughed, 'I'm sure you're right. I must admit I'm usually all Christmassed out by the time the festivities get here because of all the cards I've been working on. You can't just get them all done early because the customers are mostly very specific and often very late with their requirements. I can't believe I allowed Simon to talk me into having one of his trees because I never bother.'

'I'd have had one like a shot if the house was finished,' he said, surprising me. 'It'll be the first real home I've had in years, so celebrating Christmas in it would be kind of appealing. Never mind, there's always next year.'

'Come and help me decorate my tree when it arrives,' I offered, before I could think twice and change my mind, adding, 'If you'd like,' just in case he needed a get out clause.

'I would,' he said, very quickly, as if he was afraid I *would* change my mind. 'I'd like that very much.'

'Good,' I said, perhaps a bit too heartily. 'Now I must get on.'

'See you later – for dinner at Greg and Jasper's,' he called, as I hurried away.

The first person I bumped into at the precinct was my sister,

Alma, and I couldn't help hoping we could just exchange greetings and go our separate ways. Sadly she was one of the last people I'd choose to spend time with. She was obviously on a Christmas shopping trip of her own but, unlike me, who had yet to make a start, Alma was already loaded down with parcels.

'What a pity I didn't bring the car,' I said rather insincerely, 'I could have offered you a lift home.'

She surprised me by saying, 'Oh, that's OK, I drove myself,' sounding quite proud and, to be fair, I supposed for her with her dread of busy roads it was quite a big deal.

'Well done,' I told her, and she positively beamed.

'Hey,' she said, 'if I pack this lot into the boot I can come and help you with your shopping. That is what you're here for, isn't it?'

It would have been churlish to refuse so, giving in with fairly good grace, I walked with her to the car park. On the way back we popped into a cafe for a cup of tea and then made a start on my list.

It was the longest time I'd ever spent with Alma without her managing to remind me of my single state even once, or tell me in tedious detail about at least one eligible man she'd met recently who'd be just right for me. I began to warm to her as, true to her word, she really was helpful; by the end I was amazed to find that every family member's name on my present list had been ticked – and they weren't all vouchers, either.

'Alma,' I told her, 'you're a blooming marvel. The least I can do is to treat you to a late lunch – that's if you don't have to rush back for Les.'

I fully expected her to refuse the offer and was astonished when she said carelessly, 'He can manage on his own for once. He knows where the kettle and the breadbin are.'

Since she would be cooking when she got home and I was eating out we decided on toasted sandwiches and found a table by the window where we could watch the shoppers rushing about, smug in the knowledge that we had finished.

Alma didn't even leap to annoying conclusions when I

inadvertently let slip that Bruce would be there for the meal that night, merely saying, 'That's nice.' In fact, I couldn't believe the change in her and began to wonder what had brought it about.

We ate cheese and ham toasted sandwiches companionably, surrounded by my parcels and carrier bags and I even found myself telling her about the plans for a display stand for my cards in the newly refurbished bookshop when the high street was up and running.

'I envy you,' Alma said suddenly, just as I was taking a sip of tea and I almost choked.

'*You*,' I said, coughed and went on, 'envy *me*?'

'Well, yes,' she said, just as if she hadn't spent the best part of her life telling me I should be envying her.

'But you love your life with your family around you.'

'Yes,' she said slowly, 'I do, but that's because I've never known any different. I've always been a huge advocate of marriage, yet just lately I've been wondering if there isn't more to life.'

Well, to say I was gob-smacked was a huge understatement and, after I'd picked my chin up from the table, I managed feebly, 'Really?'

She nodded. 'And I've come to the conclusion that you're right about being independent.' I stared at Alma, so shocked that I was sure my eyes were as round as saucers. 'Nobody takes you for granted,' she went on, her tone firm. 'I've become a little more than a doormat, but that's all about to change.'

'It is?' I managed.

'Yes,' she said firmly, 'I've got myself a little flat and have told Les I'm leaving straight after Christmas.'

Chapter Seventeen

I DON'T THINK ALMA had even appreciated that I was quite speech-
less, because she was too busy telling me about her plans for her
new and wonderful future as a single woman.

I found myself in a state of total dismay, imagining that my own
negative attitude to marriage was completely to blame for this huge
turnaround. However it soon became apparent that the unexpected
offer of a job might have had something to do with it.

'It's only part-time to start with,' she explained, 'but to hear my
lot you would think I'd be commuting to London every day and
working long hours in the city, instead of just walking the short
distance from home to serve in a little tea shop in the new high
street when it's re-launched.'

A glimmer of light shone into my confusion and I hazarded the
guess, 'The family didn't like it?'

'Didn't like it?' she fumed. 'The kids asked me what they were
going to do about child care in the school holidays – just as if
I hadn't given years – years, Ellen, to caring for their kids in the
holidays without so much as a thank you – never mind a bunch of
flowers – coming my way. Not that I haven't loved having them. Of
course, I have – but they're grandchildren, aren't they? Not actually
my children, or *my* responsibility, at all, are they? Surely I am entitled to a life of my own, aren't I?

'And then there's Les,' she went on, her fury gathering

momentum, fuelled by the belated sense of injustice of the family taking her so completely for granted – just as they had been doing for more years than I cared to remember. 'Les just told me straight I couldn't do it. *He* wouldn't stand for his wife working and how did I think *he* was going to manage.'

I had some sympathy for him – albeit limited sympathy – understanding that the man must have been in a state of pure shock at the sudden realisation that he might actually have to do something for himself for once.

'Well, that's when I told him I was leaving. If he can't support me in this after all the years I've given to supporting him, he can go to hell.'

I wanted to applaud, because she was absolutely right. Only a fool would try to deny her this chance to break out and see a little bit of life outside the family home – and Les, of course, was an absolute idiot. However, I also wanted to preach caution, because Alma was burning her bridges at a frightening speed and I knew – I just knew – that she would quickly become miserable and very lonely without her family around her.

'You never know,' I said, sounding feeble even to myself, 'they all might come round.'

Alma snorted, as if the very idea was out of the question. As I accepted her offer of a lift home and gathered up all my bags and parcels, I had a horrible feeling she might be right.

She chatted happily all the way home and I made an effort to nod or shake my head in all the right places. I was pleased to see her so full of life and full of plans, but not so pleased when she dropped me at my gate and left me with the words, 'You were right all along, Ellen. It's just a pity it's taken me so long to understand it.'

I wondered as I walked up the path and let myself into my silent house what she would say if I told her I had changed my mind and wanted what she had. Oh, not the self-centred husband and selfish kids that Alma herself had encouraged to be that way, but a partnership based on compromise. A bit of give and take never hurt anyone, and so I would tell the dreadful Les if I ever got the chance, which seemed highly unlikely.

I realised I was still a bit distracted later that evening when I looked up from a plate of food that was probably delicious, though I hadn't tasted a thing, and found four pairs of eyes staring at me.

'Don't tell me,' said Jasper, 'you've gone off the whole idea of the card display in the shop, I can see it in your face.'

'There's no pressure of any kind, you know,' Greg hastened to add. 'It can be as big or as small a stand as you want it to be – and the shop won't be up and running again until the grand opening in the spring so there's still plenty of time to think about it.'

'Is it that?' Bruce asked, looking at me closely, 'or is something else bothering you?'

I smiled at him, grateful for his understanding, knowing that if he ever married he would never be anything like Les because he didn't have a selfish bone in his body: single-minded in the pursuit of success didn't necessarily equate to always putting yourself first. You only had to look at the way he cared for his father. Jack was just sitting there with a worried look on his face.

'It's something else – a family thing,' I told them, 'and nothing anyone can help with – there's not even much that I can do – but I am grateful for your concern. Now, I must do justice to this delicious Lasagne and you can tell me about your plans for the shop and its refit.'

'It will be the final store to be refurbished and ready for business when the official launch takes place,' Bruce explained, looking pleased and quite excited. 'It will be out of commission for only as long at the refit and redecorating takes. It's always been very popular, despite its shabby surroundings, so we plan to make it the jewel in the crown of what will be the new-look high street.'

'And allowing us to stock your cards is going to put us head and shoulders above the competition in the precinct, Ellen,' Greg told me.

'Yes, we're so excited,' Jasper beamed at me.

I did my best to match their enthusiasm, and I think I succeeded to a certain extent – even if there was a lot of pretence involved. 'A jewel in the crown' was the phrase Bruce had used to describe the finally refurbished bookshop – and there was no doubt the whole project would be a massive jewel in his crown if the new look high street was the success it was expected to be.

I could see the headlines now. It would be a case of local boy comes back to the area of his childhood and makes good. He would be hailed a hero – and what then? There was no doubt the resulting nationwide publicity would mean Bruce would be in great demand to take on similar challenges in other towns. There were many shabby high streets all over the UK crying out for a similar make-over. What would be left to keep him here?

The change he had wrought wasn't only to the high street, of course, even in this small close people had become closer, more inclined to exchange news and views. Bruce had come back into our lives and changed them, fired us up with an enthusiasm we had somehow lacked before – and turned my world upside down.

I didn't know whom I could talk to. The whole situation was a mess. I'd been avoiding Fiona for some time because she had a crush on the same man, and now Alma and Jonathon had suddenly decided to follow in my footsteps – footsteps that no longer fitted traitorous feet that longed to follow an entirely different pathway.

I slept badly that night, fell asleep at dawn and then woke mid-morning to find a Christmas tree had been dumped in my back garden. I tried telling myself not to be such a misery, but the last thing I wanted to do in my frame of mind was trek into town again so soon looking for decorations to put on it.

Actually – once I'd planted it in an old garden tub I found tucked away under a bush and dragged it inside – I thought it looked rather festive standing under the stairs at the back of the sitting room. Or it would, once it had been trimmed with tinsel and baubles.

My mind made up, there was obviously no time like the present.

I took the car to save time, parked next to the precinct, and headed for a shop that sold everything and, I recalled, was annually packed with all things festive. I was filling a basket with everything a well-dressed tree might need in red and gold, when I felt a tap on my shoulder and found Fiona behind me with a similarly filled basket, though her things were silver and blue.

She looked in my basket and I raised my eyebrows at the contents of hers. Fiona shrugged, 'It matches my decor,' she said without apology.

'Fairy or star on top, though?' I debated, 'that is the question.'

We held up several options in our colours of choice and eventually got it down to two choices for the top of the tree for me and three for Fiona. Then treated ourselves to a turkey and cranberry panini apiece in the nearest coffee shop and chewed for a few moments in companionable silence.

'This is nice,' she said eventually, and when I nodded, she added, 'and I don't mean the food – though it is good.'

'I know what you mean,' I nodded. 'Just lately we seem to have become ships that pass in the night but it's a busy time of year for both of us.'

'Plus the fact,' she said, meeting my gaze, 'I was behaving like an idiot around Bruce. You know me, Ellen, where men are concerned I set my sights and go tramping in where angels fear to tread. Bruce was kind to me when I was upset over James re-marrying, but I misread the signs and realize now that it was only friendship he was offering.'

When I didn't say anything, she continued, 'I never could stand my own company and have always thought the only way to live was as half of a couple. I even seriously considered taking James back, did you know that?'

I was startled by her admissions, though on reflection not particularly so. 'Even after everything he'd done?' I asked softly.

'Ah, well,' she said, 'you know he has a way with words and he almost convinced me he was a changed man.'

'Oh, Fiona,' I gasped.

'I did say "almost", and I soon came to my senses and showed him the door. Just as well he's going to be someone else's problem soon, though, and out of harm's way. On careful reflection I have realised I was probably lonelier when I was actually *with* James, than I have been in all the time since then that I have actually spent living alone. That's why,' she said, beaming at me, 'I've decided to take a leaf out of your book and put all thoughts of marriage and relationships right out of my mind.'

I choked on a mouthful of panini. 'But you've always said—' I began when I had recovered.

'Yes, I know what I've said, but I've decided that you're right and I've been wrong all this time. I want what you have, independence and peace of mind. It makes life simpler all round.'

'You can't give up on love, just like that,' I told her, horrified at the sudden influence I seemed to be having on those around me after years of my opinions and wishes being ignored.

'Why not?' Fiona demanded. 'You did, and as a result you've never found your life in the mess that mine has often been in. I've finally learned to my cost that when you fall in love, you leave yourself wide open to hurt. I won't be making that mistake again.'

We left the coffee shop together and I walked with Fiona to her boutique. I even went inside and had a look along the rails of sparkly clothes geared towards the festive season. Ironically, everything I selected for a closer look was chosen with a particular man in mind and what he would think of me when I had it on. I wondered why – when those around me were busily planning to live a life without love – I could think of nothing but the impossible dream of settling down with a man I could never have and I wondered if Fiona was right and my change of heart was wrong.

The idea of decorating a Christmas tree no longer appealed, because wasn't that something you should share? I doubted Bruce was really interested in joining me, despite what he'd said and doing it alone seemed kind of sad somehow. Even Alma wasn't planning on spending Christmas by herself.

As if the thought of her had conjured him up, I climbed from my car and found myself confronted by no other person than Les – and a very angry Les if I was any judge.

'This,' he said, 'is all *your* fault,' and shoved me so hard with the flat of his hand that I fell back against the car with a thump.

I was shocked that he would touch me, let alone push me, but I recovered quickly. 'Do that again,' I snarled furiously, righting myself and leaning right into his face so that our noses were practically touching, 'and I will slap your face so hard that your ear will ring for a week – and then I will report you to the police for assault.'

Shocked, Les took a step back. Bullies were always intimidated easily, I had often realised.

'Sorry,' he mumbled, admitting, 'I was completely out of order.'

'Yes, you were, and if this is about Alma and her future plans, I think you should accept responsibility for your own part in her decision to leave and stop looking for someone else to blame.' I stood straight and looked him right in the eye.

'What have I done wrong?' he demanded. 'It's you – always babbling about the single life – that's made her discontented. What does she want a job for anyway? She's got enough to do at home with me and the kids.'

'So she's not entitled to want more, after all the years she's given to you?'

'More what?' Les was clearly bewildered. 'I don't keep her short of money.'

'It's not about the money, though, is it?'

'Isn't it?' he looked confused and I almost felt sorry for him.

I shook my head. 'It's about having a life to call her own. It's about having the support of the husband and children she has dedicated her life to all these years. It's not asking for much, is it?'

'We support her,' he argued.

'You take her for granted,' I said flatly, 'every last one of you.'

'No, we . . .'

'You think going to work is enough, but when you come home, Les, you never lift a finger. She's been waiting hand, foot and finger on you for years, can you really blame her for thinking there's more to life?'

He stared at me, and I could almost hear his brain working as he tried to come up with an argument that worked, then he said simply, 'She doesn't have to leave.'

'She does,' I replied, 'if it's the only way to make you listen. She doesn't want *my* life, Les, she wants her own, but with a few more options open to her and a bit of a life outside the same four walls. Can you blame her? She hasn't left yet, but unless you all change your attitude she most definitely will – and it's no more than you deserve. Think about that, Les, and when you get home why don't *you* try putting the kettle on for once?'

It was a different man who walked away from me, his normal cockiness was missing, and I hoped I had given him food for thought. He'd done no more than fall into the trap of the majority of long term or married couples and that was of taking his partner completely for granted. Most never realised anything was wrong until the other upped and left and then they scratched their heads and wondered why.

'Disgruntled customer?' I turned to find Simon hefting a large Christmas tree towards me, and when he stopped and put it down it was even taller than he was. 'He didn't look very happy,' he added.

'Disgruntled brother-in-law,' I said briefly.

'Ah,' Simon nodded, 'I thought his face looked familiar – from the night of the family meal,' he clarified, 'and he didn't look very happy then either.'

'I'm a bad influence on his wife, apparently. Can I ask you – have my reservations regarding being in a couple made you want to stay single?'

'No,' he said emphatically, 'trying marriage for myself the once was quite enough to do that.'

I was curious now. 'Do you think you'll ever change your mind?'

'Possibly,' he nodded, 'if the right person came along. You?'

He asked the question so suddenly that I was surprised into admitting the truth. 'Yes, for the right person.' Then I quickly changed the subject. 'That's a big tree you've got there.'

Simon grinned cheekily. 'Now come on, Ellen, you know size isn't everything.'

I couldn't help laughing at his rude humour. I turned to lift the box of baubles from my car and told him over my shoulder, 'Just as well, given the twig indoors waiting to be decorated.'

'It might be small,' he said trying to keep a straight face, 'but it's perfectly formed. I can give you a hand when I've dropped this at Jasper and Greg's – if you need someone with the festive touch.'

I was very tempted, but sure he must have better things to do, I assured him I could manage to sling a few strands of tinsel on the stunted tree he thought was good enough for me, and smiled my way indoors.

The tree was actually a very nice one, with very full and nicely shaped branches. I stood for a moment admiring it and planning my strategy.

'Lights first,' my dad always dictated and that was when I realised I hadn't bought any.

I went to put the kettle on while I decided whether to make another trip out to buy some or manage without. I sipped the tea and stared at the tree and then around the room as if looking for inspiration. It was when the display board through the arch caught my eye that I recalled the lights I had purchased in the fond belief that draping them around the card samples would enhance the overall impression. In the end I had decided the string of fairy lights had just looked naff, but they were still in the house somewhere.

I wasted far too much time and the light was beginning to fade by the time I'd located them at the back of a filing-cabinet drawer. However, seeing them on the tree was magical and, as I added strands of tinsel and then baubles, the tiny twinkling lights seemed to bring the decorations and the tree to life.

Fairy or star? Star or fairy? I had tried them both and was still undecided and reluctant to spoil the overall effect by going for the wrong choice when I heard the back door open. I felt like cheering, relieved and happy to let someone else make the choice for me uncaring about whether it was Simon coming to offer his expert advice once more or maybe Bruce just popping in to say, 'hi,' or even to join in.

I was smiling as I turned towards the kitchen arch with the fairy in one hand and star in the other – and came face to face with a complete stranger.

Chapter Eighteen

Because the words were already on my tongue, in spite of my alarm, I only just stopped myself from asking, 'Fairy or star?'

I was too shocked to feel real fear and, with the Christmas tree twinkling incongruously in the background, we stared at each other in complete silence in the gathering gloom. He was young, far younger than me, and that gave me courage.

'What do you want?' I said, and then, 'Get out.' Furious at the slight tremor I detected in my voice, I said it again in a louder and firmer tone. 'Get out. Go on, get out.'

Without realising it, I had taken a step forward and for the second time that day I found myself pushed hard. There was no solid vehicle behind me this time to prevent my falling backwards. It was only when I heard the tinkling of glass ornaments and the snap of breaking branches that I knew I had fallen heavily onto the tree. The room went completely dark as the lights went out and seconds later the front door slammed.

It took a minute or two for me to gather myself together and then rage brought me to my feet and racing to the door.

'Help,' I screamed. 'Stop that man.'

The close was, as usual for that time of day, quiet but, in the gloom of early evening, light began to flood out into the street as doors were flung open and people hurried outside. Some of them ran towards me and others took off in the direction of my pointing finger. By then I was shaking from head to foot.

'What's happened?' Jasper reached me first and, after checking that I was in one piece, stood in front of me picking pine needles from my clothes and out of my hair.

'There was a man,' I said, my voice trembling, 'in my house. He pushed me over and ran away.'

'Are you hurt?' Greg asked, looking me up and down. 'Leave it,' he frowned at Jasper to stop fussing.

'No,' I shook my head, 'only my pride and my Christmas tree. He was there one minute and gone the next when I shouted at him. Did you catch him?' I asked anxiously, as Simon, Bruce and even Miles, who had all set off in pursuit, made their way back towards us.

All three shook their heads and Bruce demanded, 'Has anyone phoned the police?' There was a shaking of heads, and he asked furiously, 'Why ever not?'

'What would be the point? It'd be a waste of police time, wouldn't it?' I directed my questions to Greg who always seemed to have the most common sense.

'Well,' he pulled a face, 'if he didn't hurt you, and I assume he didn't take anything since you said he ran off when you confronted him – they won't have much to charge him with if they do catch him.'

'Breaking and entering,' Simon suggested, and I really wished he hadn't because I suddenly knew what was coming next.

When I didn't say anything, Bruce stared very hard at me and then said, 'Please, *don't* tell me that you left that bloody back door unlocked again.'

'Oh, Ellen,' Simon stared at me reprovingly and shook his head.

'Don't you, "Oh, Ellen" me,' I hissed, mindful that this oversight on my part was going to lose me the sympathy vote very quickly, 'because this is completely your fault.'

He took a swift step back. '*My* fault? How do you work that out? I was at the other end of the street putting lights on Jasper and

Greg's outside tree when I heard you shrieking.'

'Yes,' I fumed, gathering self righteous around me like a cloak, 'but if it hadn't been for my going out into my back garden to bring in the tree you left for me – the tree I didn't even *want* – the damn door would never have been unlocked.'

'Come on now, Ellen,' Miles intervened, giving me a reproving look, 'you can hardly blame Simon for the fact you didn't lock your back door as soon as you'd brought the tree in. Home security should always be paramount.'

'Oh shut up, Miles,' I said crossly, recovering quickly now and becoming angrier with myself than I was with him. If they all realised for just how long the back door had been left unlocked, I would never hear the end of it.

'Perhaps we should all calm down,' Shirley said in her quiet way. 'Especially as there seems to be no real harm done – apart from the shock Ellen has sustained.'

'Exactly,' her husband agreed, 'and that being the case, we'll leave you to it.'

I watched them make their way home arm in arm and envied them a solid relationship that suited them so well.

'Sorry,' I said, sheepishly to the rest of my rescuers, 'I didn't mean to bite anyone's head off. Of course it's my own stupid fault, and I've learned my lesson the hard way, so please don't rub it in.'

I turned to go inside, feeling ridiculously nervous at the thought of stepping inside of a house that suddenly didn't feel as safe as it always had – especially as I still hadn't locked the back door.

'I'm coming in with you to check the place out,' Bruce told me in a tone that brooked no argument – and actually, I didn't feel the least bit like arguing as he made to follow me.

'OK,' I said in a small voice.

'You seem to be wearing a set of lights and a few fir tree branches,' he said gently, tugging at something snagging on my clothes that I couldn't see.

I looked over my shoulder to see trailing wires and broken

twigs hanging from my clothes and suddenly found myself sobbing hysterically.

'The guy pushed Ellen onto her Christmas tree,' Greg explained, helping to pick them off, 'it's probably ruined.'

'It must be,' I sobbed, and added, 'and it looked really pretty.'

'I'll go right now and bring you back another one,' Simon promised, already walking away. 'I should have brought the tree right inside for you when I delivered it. I do feel really guilty, and should have known better being perfectly well aware of how scatty you are.'

'Just check that everything is safe and secure,' Jasper was saying to Bruce, 'and then bring Ellen round to ours. The last thing she needs is to be thinking about cooking after such a shock and we have a massive beef casserole almost ready to be dished up.'

'She could just as easily come to mine, 'Miles put in huffily, 'my chick pea chilli is also ready to serve up.'

'I think Jasper gave his invitation first, Miles,' Greg pointed out in his mild tone, 'but perhaps another time. The important thing is to make sure Ellen's house is secure and then to provide her with some company and good food while she gets over the shock.'

I was still hiccupping a bit as I followed Bruce inside and the tears sprang again to my eyes when I surveyed the state of what was left of the sweet little Christmas tree.

'I thought you agreed you would wait for me, and then we were going to decorate it together,' he said, standing next to me. Did he sound disappointed? It was difficult to tell.

'Well, once it was planted in the pot it just seemed to be crying out to be decorated and I'd gone to town for the stuff, and everything. I quite enjoyed doing it, though it's the first time I've bothered with a tree in years, but now I'm not sure I have the heart to begin all over again.' I hated how self-pitying I sounded.

He checked the house room by room, which didn't take very long, and then carried the remains of the wrecked tree outside. It probably ended up in the skip that seemed to be permanently parked in his garden, but I didn't want to think about that too much. I know it was only a little Christmas tree, but I had become ridiculously attached to it in a very short time.

I was still snivelling as he brushed up the mess of pine needles and then went to the door and let in Simon carrying aloft a new tree, followed by Fiona, who rushed to put a comforting arm round me.

'I've never been more horrified,' she said, 'than when I heard what happened to you. Honestly it comes to something when you can't feel safe in your own home.'

'It helps if you keep your doors locked,' Bruce pointed out in a mild tone.

'I know that,' I said, but couldn't help adding indignantly, 'years ago no one locked their doors my mum is always going on about it.'

'That was then, Ellen, and this is now. There are more people out there with fewer scruples and expensive habits,' Bruce said firmly and I nodded, feeling sad that it was so.

Bruce made a big show of locking and then bolting my back door, tutting about the flimsy bolt and making noises about fitting a sturdier one. Fiona buttoned me into my coat as if I was a child, before they all escorted me to Jasper and Greg's house. Although it wasn't many steps to their front door, I can't pretend I wasn't happy about the thought that there was safety in numbers – despite the certainty in my heart that the guy had just been an opportunist thief in the area looking for easy pickings close to Christmas. The main lights had been off and he'd probably thought his luck was in, finding the door unlocked and no one apparently at home.

Of course, everyone ended up staying for dinner. Jasper and Greg were well known for their generosity and their love of company.

'We're lucky,' they told us as they served up generous helpings, 'having each other and though, sadly, we haven't got children, we've come to look on the people living around us as our family.'

'In fact,' Greg confided with a glance at Jasper, who nodded encouragingly, 'we thought we'd open our home up to any residents of the close who would like to come and share our Christmas – and that includes Jack, of course, Bruce, and you, too, Simon. We've always found it a bit sad when just the two of us sit down to share a roast turkey dinner – not to mention wasteful.'

The four of us looked at each other, but none of us said what we were all obviously thinking – that it could be a whole lot sadder to find yourself sitting down to a microwaved turkey dinner alone.

Then we were laughing, and saying all at once how much we would love that and a time was arranged that suited us all. I'd have plenty of time to visit my parents before they set off to Alma's for lunch, and then enjoy spending the rest of the day with my friends without anyone taking every opportunity to remind me that Christmas was a time for families – especially when you had your own. Christmas suddenly seemed a lot more appealing.

Bruce left first, explaining that he'd taken to popping into see his dad of an evening. 'He'd go mad if he thought I was checking up, but I feel better for knowing he's all right – especially after the ankle business. I know I could phone, but I've spent too many years keeping in touch with him that way.'

Shortly after that Fiona took herself off, and I knew I should do the same, but the thought of returning to my empty house suddenly seemed vastly unappealing. Ridiculous, I knew, since I had heard and seen Bruce check both the back and front doors, all the downstairs lights had been left on, and the chance of the same guy chancing his luck twice in the same neighbourhood, let alone the same house, was extremely unlikely.

In the end I felt I had little choice, because the suggestion was made that we go outside to see the lights on the tree that Simon had been working on when I'd rushed into the street yelling blue murder. It was late, I already had my coat on, and had no excuse to return to the safety and comfort of Greg and Jasper's home.

I left them with Simon, discussing the merits of putting a Santa, complete with sleigh and reindeer, up on the roof. Their laughter followed me along the street and I was taking comfort from the fact they were close at hand when it suddenly went quiet and I knew they had gone back into the house.

I reached my own gate and peered up and down the familiar close with a fear that was strange to me. A fear I had never known in all the time I'd lived there. I would have taken comfort from the feel of the mobile phone in my pocket, if I hadn't left it indoors when I left earlier. A dog barked somewhere, and then a cat wailed closer making me jump.

The sooner I got myself inside the better, I told myself, and feeling for my key I held it ready to slide into the lock, but when I tried I realised that my hand was shaking so much I was going to have trouble inserting it. Hot on the heels of that realisation came the one that told me I really didn't want to go through that door.

Something rustled in the shrubbery close by, an owl hooted, and I almost died on the spot when someone behind me spoke.

'What are you doing still outside?'

I almost sank to my knees with relief when I recognized Simon's voice and, without thinking twice, I raced back down the garden path and threw myself in his arms.

'Whoa,' he laughed, 'what have I done to deserve that kind of welcome?' Then he quickly became serious. 'Hey, you're shaking.' He looked down at me and then, maybe seeing the fear on my face, he pulled me close and held me tight.

My teeth were chattering so much that I could barely get the words out, but I managed, 'I can't go in there. I just can't.'

'I could try telling you that there's no one there, but you already know that, don't you?' I nodded, the top of my head brushing his chin. 'What if I come in with you?'

'Would you?' I pleaded. 'I'm sorry to be such a wuss, but. . .'

'I know. You've had a terrible fright. It would be remarkable if you weren't a bit nervous.'

'A *bit*,' I managed a tremulous giggle.

Simon went in first, leaving me to follow. Lights blazed in every room downstairs and a glance in each was enough to show they were unoccupied. Feeling more than a little foolish I went to put the kettle on while he checked upstairs.

'Are you OK?' he asked, coming to stand in the archway between the rooms.

I nodded but pulled a face. 'I keep re-living the moment I realised what I thought was a friendly visitor was actually a complete stranger. I've never known fear like it.'

I carried the mugs of tea through to the sitting room and we sat side by side on the couch, Simon talked easily of this and that, encouraging responses that would take my mind off something that refused to be forgotten – which to my mind was hardly surprising. My gaze kept straying to the stairs and the thought that soon I would be climbing them to struggle for sleep above the room where I had come face to face with the reality of one of my deepest childhood fears.

'Are you going to be OK if I get off now?' Simon asked.

'Of course,' I said at once, my tone as sharp as a shard of glass. 'I'll be fine.'

'Sure?'

'Honestly. Don't you be worrying about me.'

We both stood up, and I fought a real battle with the urge to beg him to stay as we moved towards the front door.

Simon already had his hand on the door handle, when he asked for what was obviously one last time, 'You're sure you're all right about me going?'

'No,' I whispered, 'not really.' I sounded so pathetic I was actually embarrassed, but not embarrassed enough to keep my fears to myself.

'I'll stay if you want me to.'

'Really?'

He nodded and gently taking hold of my upper arms and looking down at me he said, 'You must know that I'd do anything for you, Ellen.'

His words were so unexpected that I was almost ready to let him go and leave me on my own – almost, but not quite – and I couldn't let him stay without first making it clear that this was not an invitation to share my bed.

Ignoring his statement, I said, 'I'll go and get you a quilt and pillow. Will you be OK here on the couch?'

'I'll be fine,' he said, and if he was disappointed, he hid it well.

There was no repeat of the night that Bruce had stayed. I slept like a baby knowing Simon was downstairs to protect me against anything my imagination came up with, and I woke up alone with a December sun shining through the gap in the curtains. Of Simon there was no sign when I got downstairs and when I checked the bedding had been tidied away. He could have had toast or cereal, but if he'd eaten breakfast, he had also cleared up behind himself and left no sign. It was as if he had never been there, but I didn't think he'd been a figment of my imagination.

I had a few last minute things I was keen to put together for Christmas and I worked steadily throughout the day. The only difference I noticed in my behaviour, after the fright of the day before, was that I jumped at the slightest noise and continually checked that the doors and windows were securely locked. I was quite sure that I would relax again with time.

Fiona turned up on my step late afternoon after she closed the shop, bringing with her pizza and tree decorations. 'I thought you'd like some company and a few new baubles,' she said, beaming. 'Luckily I was with you when you bought the others so I was aware of your taste in tree bling. I thought we could eat the pizza and then decorate the tree together.'

'Thank you.' I hugged her. 'That's so sweet of you and I am actually starving.' I hesitated, 'Thing is though, I'd invited Bruce to help me decorate the tree the first time around and then went ahead and did it without him. I wouldn't want to offend him for a second time.'

Fiona was already crashing plates about in the kitchen 'Oh, don't worry about that,' she said, coming to poke her head round the arch. 'I bumped into him outside and invited him to join us, but he mumbled something about having a lot on and then drove off.'

'Well, he is a busy man,' I pointed out, trying not to imagine that he could still be miffed from before. My sensible side reminded me that he was a man and therefore incapable of being that shallow.

The pizza was delicious and the tree looked a picture when it was fully adorned and settled in its place in front of the window, and not under the stairs as before. Fiona had even remembered to buy a new set of lights.

It felt just like old times and when she suggested purchasing something new to wear for lunch on Christmas day, I knew she wasn't just keen to make a sale, especially when she added, 'Mate's rates, Ellen.'

'Least we can do is turn up looking stunning when Greg and Jasper are going to all that trouble,' I agreed. 'We're so lucky to have them as our neighbours.'

'Talking of neighbours,' she said with a nod in the general area of Bruce's property, 'how's the extension going? Have you been round there to have a nose yet?'

'No,' I replied abruptly, and then I softened it by adding, 'but the wall out the front looks great, doesn't it? Almost makes me think of having mine rebuilt.'

'You don't think seeing Bruce's other improvements will make you think of making some of your own in here?'

I shook my head. 'I did all I intend to do when I moved in. I never wanted a mansion and this suits me very well. What about you?'

'Oh, I've had the mansion,' Fiona reminded me. 'Having it all is not everything it's cracked up to be, I can assure you, especially when there are those eager not only to share it, but to relieve you of it as well. I'm probably much happier these days being accepted for who I am and not what I have. In my experience, the more you have, the more you have to worry about anyway.'

I'd never had that much, so I refrained from comment, and

changed the subject instead. 'Have you thought about relocating to the refurbished high street when it's ready?' I queried. 'I hear there are still premises available.'

'Mmmm,' Fiona looked dubious. 'Not sure it would be worth the upheaval because I'm doing all right where I am, though I must admit the competition from the big name stores is pretty fierce. Have you had any thoughts about opening the card shop everyone was trying to convince you to open? I think you'd do really well.'

'Like you, I feel I'm doing all right where I am and I never was that ambitious. However,' I continued, 'I have agreed to have a display stand in the book shop and Greg and Jasper will get a cut of whatever they sell.'

Fiona looked thrilled for me. 'But that's brilliant and a clever compromise. It will be great for all of you. Another feather in the bookshop bow, *and* it will make your cards more accessible to your local customers. The high street is going to make such a difference to the local economy and for the local people.'

'Not all of them,' I said, pulling a face. 'It's going to sound the death knell for my sister's marriage.'

'I don't think the high street can be blamed for your sister cheating on her husband,' she said.

I stared at her and then I laughed bitterly. 'Not that sister,' I said, 'Alma is starting work in the new teashop and her husband stupidly tried to put his foot down. He's a male chauvinist of the first order,' I explained, adding briefly, 'even expecting him to put the kettle on all by himself is asking too much, apparently. According to him Alma's place is at home waiting on him.'

'He's stopped her from getting a job in a teashop?' Fiona sounded scandalized.

'Not exactly,' I corrected. 'He tried to forbid it, so she said she was leaving and *that* apparently, is *my* fault. He came round here and had a right go at me.'

'Ah, yes, I remember him from the family meal, so now it doesn't surprise me. He had your sister doing everything for him all evening and was too lazy even to help himself to the salt and pepper right in front of him, as I recall.' She pulled a face, 'As opposed to my James, who was far too keen to help himself – especially to all my worldly goods.'

'Suddenly, instead of everyone trying to change my mind about relationships – which is what I'm used to – you all seem to think I have the right idea. Even my brother Jonathon, who's spent his whole life in and out of relationships, seems to have come to that conclusion,' I protested, 'and I don't actually want to be carrying the responsibility for you all being alone.'

'I think it's our own experiences making us want to follow your lead,' Fiona paused, and then added, 'but your example is encouraging. You always seem so contented with your life.'

When I said nothing, she stared at me and then the penny dropped. I could almost hear the clang when it did.

'Oh. My. God,' she said, an expression of awe on her face. 'Don't tell me – you've changed your mind and would actually consider being part of a relationship – after all these years. Am I allowed to ask who the lucky man responsible is?'

Chapter Nineteen

'I DON'T KNOW WHAT you mean,' I retorted, immediately regretting my hasty words. I might have known that Fiona would put my change of heart down to a man – and, of course, she was absolutely right to do so.

She burst out laughing. 'Yes, you do, Ellen. If you're suddenly hankering after a relationship after all these years of swearing that it's the last thing you want, you definitely have a man in mind, and there's no way you can just leave me here guessing.'

'How do you know it isn't just my age?'

'What,' she scoffed, ' "Life begins at forty," or the fact you might be over the hill, and all the baloney the media dish out is driving you to change the vow of a lifetime?'

'It might be.' I shrugged in what I thought was a nonchalant way.

Fiona shook her head. 'I'm not buying that for a minute. Come on – who is it? I wonder.'

'Stop it,' I said, beginning to panic.

'Not Miles,' she decided, ignoring me. 'I couldn't even believe *that* particular choice when you went out with him the *first* time around. No,' she shook her head again, more emphatically this time, 'he wasn't your type then, and he isn't your type now. So-o that leaves just Simon or Bruce.'

'They aren't the only single men in Brankstone,' I pointed out, getting desperate and trying to make it sound as if I might have another option hidden up my sleeve.

'No, but I don't see that many of them beating a path to your door.' She put her head on one side as if she were giving the fact there might be others vying for my attention her full consideration. 'Jasper or Greg maybe? Highly unlikely, and I don't see you as a home-wrecker.'

'Now you're just being silly.'

Fiona relented, and I gave a huge sigh of relief as she said, 'It's OK, I won't tease you anymore. I just want you to know that nothing would please me more than to see you settling down with the right person. I do still believe in love and marriage – despite my only foray into the world of matrimony going so wrong.

'I'm not stupid enough to believe that all men are like James, but what I've finally learned from you is that there's also nothing wrong with being alone either. You can be a lot more alone if you're in the wrong relationship – and, believe me, I should know. It's just taken me a long time to realise that. Now that I've stopped being so desperate to snaffle another man, I'm actually quite enjoying my single life. Now – that's not something you thought you'd hear me say in a hurry, is it?'

We'd been friends for a long time and, for the first time that I could remember, we found ourselves in total agreement. I didn't say a word, just gave her a big hug.

However, Fiona still couldn't resist putting her head on one side, just as she was about to leave, and giving me a long look, she said, 'Mmmm, Simon or Bruce? Nice guys both of them, but one of them obviously has the edge and I wonder who it can be?'

'Shoo, go on with you.'

I'd pushed her towards the door and had merrily waved her goodbye before I remembered that I was about to face a night in the house alone. I slammed the door shut and leaning back against it, realised my heart was thumping alarmingly. Reminding myself that I'd been alone all day didn't really help, because though I did appreciate that break-ins were just as likely in daylight hours, my unwelcome visitor had arrived with the on-set of darkness so that was what I feared, however irrational that might be. I quickly locked and bolted the front door and then rushed to check that the back door was still secure.

Bruce had been right, I thought, when he said the bolt was flimsy. I gazed at it fearfully, wondering if it would withstand a determined kick, and remembered he'd mentioned replacing it with a sturdier one.

'Well,' I told myself, straightening my shoulders resolutely, 'you're supposed to be an independent lady. You are quite capable of dealing with such jobs yourself or, if push comes to shove, you have two grown up brothers to give you a hand.' I suddenly realised I was talking out loud and managed a nervous grin.

Keen to help myself and not allow my fear to paralyse me, I did the best I could with the resources I had and placed a chair beneath the door handle of both the front and back doors and went to check the windows. Then, satisfied that everything was as secure as it could be, I took myself off up to bed, where I put another chair under the handle of the bedroom door, and placed the mobile phone I rarely used on my bedside cupboard and left the light on.

I didn't drop off immediately, as I listened to every tiny sound and fought with an overactive imagination, but once I was asleep, I slept until morning.

'But I thought you'd at least pop round to Alma's with us,' Mum reproved me on Christmas morning. 'It wouldn't seem right without you. All the family will be there.'

That was exactly what I was afraid of. It was odd that they were strangely silent on the subject of Alma's imminent marriage break-down. My family weren't known for holding back when it came to voicing an opinion. They held strong opinions on most things, particularly what went on in each other's lives – and mine, of course. I wondered if Alma had saved her big announcement for when everyone was gathered together. I could just imagine the furore that would follow, especially if she started holding me up as the example she intended to follow. It was all I could do not to shudder.

'You know how I hate get-togethers,' I protested, reminding her, 'You had to trick me into going to my own birthday party.'

'But you're going to a get-together at the home of your neighbours.'

'It's not the same. There will be just six of us there, Mum, because even Jack has decided to join his widowed neighbour for Christmas lunch.' I pointed out gently, 'There'll be a cast of thousands at Alma's, what with your other children, their children, not to mention the step-children, and grandchildren.'

'Just pop in with the presents,' Dad suggested, giving me a look and adding, 'you don't have to stay, but it will make your mother happy.'

I knew when I was beaten – and reminding myself that it *was* Christmas I gave in with a fairly good heart – just making sure my parents remembered that I must get away promptly so as not to be rudely late for my own lunch.

The house was heaving with people, as I had known it would be, and my eagerness to begin distributing presents was helped along by the younger children swarming around me, equally eager to relieve me of them. It was a while before I realised that Les wasn't ensconced in his usual armchair. My heart sank as I realised this could mean only one thing – that he had been the one to leave. I cringed when Dad asked where he was.

'In the kitchen,' Alma said cheerfully. 'You'd better go on through, Ellen. I think he wants a word with you.'

I couldn't gauge from her expression what the word might consist of – but somehow I could guess and I forced my reluctant feet to go in that direction, admitting this was becoming even more of an ordeal than I had expected.

Finding him standing at the sink was a shock, discovering that he was peeling potatoes brought me up short and I stood there on the threshold staring at a sight I never thought I would live to see.

I must have made some slight sound because he turned slowly, a knife in his hand, and I waited for the mouthful of abuse that was surely coming.

His smile came slowly, but it was genuine. 'Surprised, eh, Ellen?' he said nodding. 'I've surprised myself these past few days. You might think I didn't listen to you that day – and I'm so sorry for the way I treated you – but I thought about what you said all the way home. In fact, I've thought about little else since then.'

'Oh, dear,' I muttered.

'It would have been "oh, dear" if I *hadn't* listened,' he said, a rueful expression on his face, 'because I would have lost the only thing in life that really matters to me – my family. Even the kids would have taken Alma's side – never mind that they were as guilty as me of taking her for granted. But that's all going to change because I've had a word with myself, and I've had a word with them.'

'New Year, new start then,' I managed, through the teeth I was gritting to stop my mouth from hanging open.

'Oh, I couldn't chance waiting until the New Year.' I'd been half joking, but Les looked deadly serious. 'My marriage might have been all over by then. I'm not saying it's been easy, because old habits – especially bad ones – die hard, but I'm trying.' With a flash of humour I had never seen in him before, he added, 'But I had to draw the line at wearing an apron – even if it is Christmas.'

I was relieved when he put the knife down before he came towards me and then, to my complete astonishment and before I could guess his intention, he had wrapped me in a bear hug.

'I'm glad to have the chance to thank you,' he said simply.

'We both are.' Alma spoke from behind me.

'But I didn't do anything,' I protested, taking a step back the minute Les had released me.

'According to Les, you wiped the floor with him,' Alma said gleefully, 'and he's admitted it wasn't before time because, as unpalatable as home truths often are, they usually need to be told. Pity you didn't tell me one or two, Ellen,' she grimaced, 'because I can see now that I wasn't helping myself.'

'How's that?' I was mystified.

'By seeing myself as indispensable and, in the days when Les and the kids did try to help, taking over because I felt only I could do things right. See the way he's peeling those potatoes.' We both looked at Les, knife back in one hand and part-peeled potato in the other. 'The peel is far too thick, but,' she put up her hand as Les and I both went to speak at once, 'I realise that, in the scheme of things it really doesn't matter and it's lovely not to have to do everything myself.'

'If she'd criticised in the past,' Les said, pulling a rueful face, 'I'd have got into a mood, thrown down the potato and the knife and told her to do it herself but, as you can see,' he carried on preparing the vegetables with a little grin, 'I'm learning to turn a deaf ear.'

Alma laughed and came to give me a hug as well. 'Oh, I wish you would stay, Ellen. I can promise you we've all learned our lesson and won't try to interfere in how you live your life. You obviously have more sense in your little finger than the rest of us have in our whole bodies.'

I hugged her back and wished I could be honest about how wrong I'd been. It had taken a long time, but I finally learned that my family had been right when they'd said repeatedly that everything would change when I met the right man. My problem now was that even my choice of Mr Right wasn't going to believe that I was finally ready to settle down even if he was ready himself, so I was probably going to get my long stated wish to live the single life and be left all alone to enjoy it.

Releasing her reluctantly, I urged Alma and Les to enjoy their Christmas together, and reminded myself that now wasn't the time or the place to unburden my soul. Issuing similar wishes all round before I left, I found myself crying before I even reached my car. I drove away wondering if I would ever know the joy of a family

Christmas of my own and, for the first time in my life, I actually did feel lonely.

By the time I got home, I had shaken myself briskly, given myself a good talking to, and worked out that I was only feeling this way as a result of the attempted burglary. It had obviously left me feeling vulnerable.

I had nipped inside to collect the presents and cards that I was taking along to Greg and Jasper's when I heard Bruce's voice and stepped into the sitting room to find him standing there.

'You'll never learn, will you, Ellen.' He sounded absolutely furious. 'You left your front door wide open.'

'But I only popped in to pick up these,' I nodded at my armful of parcels. 'I haven't taken more than a minute.'

'It was long enough for me to make my way inside,' he pointed out. 'Wasn't it?'

'OK,' I accepted the rebuke as justified. 'I know you're right, and I promise it won't happen again.'

'Family OK?' he asked in a gentler tone of voice.

'Fine,' I said quite abruptly, making my way outside and leaving Bruce to secure the door behind us.

My head was full of the happy Christmas atmosphere in the house I had left behind with children racing round the house playing happily together, and my siblings – for once – showing every appearance of appreciating their married status. I pictured each couple as they had been when I left them. Alma with the recently domesticated Les working together side by side in the kitchen, my other sister Molly cuddled up on the sofa with her husband Gordon, and my brother Richard apparently enjoying a truce with his wife Sheila as they joined in the children's games and – as always – my lovely Mum and Dad at the centre of it all. That left just me and my other brother Jonathon happily – and I used the word loosely – single. What a pity we couldn't all have learned from our own parents' example of a genuinely happy marriage.

However, I had shrugged off my melancholy by the time I

walked past the tree in Greg and Jasper's front garden twinkling with the lights Simon had strung through the branches – and I would absolutely defy anyone not to raise a smile on entering a house that hadn't missed a trick where Christmas decorations was concerned.

Forget the old-fashioned garlands I had grown up with – pinned by my father diagonally across the room, and drooping lower as the holiday progressed until the grown-ups were forced to duck to avoid them. This large house was a veritable grotto of singing Santas, lit-up snowmen and instrument playing animals – though there was also a bow to the traditional with the holly wreath on the front door and the banister inside similarly entwined from hallway to landing with garlands of greenery. To finish it all off a massive spruce tree bedecked to within an inch of its life dominated the hall.

'Ellen,' Greg enveloped me in a huge hug, 'what do you think? Not too much is it?'

I grinned and felt myself relaxing. 'Not too much at all,' I said firmly, 'and, anyway, if you—'

'. . .can't overdo it at Christmas, when can you?' He finished and we roared at the bemused look on Bruce's face.

'He and Jasper use the same excuse for every occasion,' I explained. 'They even manage to overdo the hearts and flowers on Valentine's day – you should just see it.'

'I hope I do,' Bruce said, and I could tell he wasn't sure if I was joking or not.

I handed over my parcels and we were ushered through to the dining room at speed, following Jasper's urgent tones beseeching us to, 'Hurry up, do. This turkey is crying out to be carved before Boxing Day.'

'Sorry, sorry, I know it's all my fault but Mum and Dad insisted I drop the presents off to the rest of the family personally and it took me longer than I thought.'

'Oh, no, not squabbling among the siblings again, I hope.' Fiona came to give me a sympathetic hug.

'On the contrary, obviously the season of goodwill has had an effect and all was calm – well, as calm as it could be with the children running around in a state of high excitement.'

'Sounds great to me,' Simon kissed my cheek, and pleased that someone understood I found myself saying, 'Do you know, it was actually.'

The dining room was a picture. The long table, sporting a red and gold runner along its centre, gleamed with silver cutlery and the light from the candles sparkled on the glassware. I wasn't surprised to see yet another Christmas tree flashing its lights in the corner.

'Sit down, sit down,' Jasper urged hidden behind the enormous turkey he was carrying into the room on a huge silver platter.

There was enough food to feed an army, but I felt that even the six of us managed to do it justice before moving to the sitting room. Everything was going beautifully until the subject of future plans came up and it was my own gifts of personalized calendars that had brought the subject up.

'These are just gorgeous, Ellen.' Jasper was running his fingers reverently over the raised stacks of books that adorned the front of his and Greg's. 'Are you thinking of branching out? We could definitely find a spot for some these in the new shop.'

I said I might think about it for next year because they were all so insistent. In fact, I'd only made them because I was running out of ideas, it was getting very close to Christmas, and I'd felt the need to treat each of my neighbours – and Simon – in a similar fashion. I used the same 3D method as I did for my cards so, even if I said it myself, the books looked exactly like the real thing in miniature. There was just the one main page for the artwork and small rip-off sheets attached gave the dates and months. I was quite pleased with them and the pleasure they seemed to give the recipients was gratifying.

Fiona's sported the same sort of glamorous clothes that hung from the rails in her boutique and I'd even managed to make use of real silk and lace to make them appear more realistic. Simon's calendar held a reminder of what each month could bring for the gardener in the form of shrubs and flowers around the parameter. Finally, after a good deal of thought and a fruitless idea or two, for Bruce's calendar I had managed to come up with rows of miniature shops from the artist's impression I had seen of how the refurbished high street would look, with tiny shoppers created to bring it to life.

After all the oohing and aahing over my gifts had subsided, the thought of the New Year ahead started a discussion on what the future might hold for each of us.

'Well, as you know we're taking ourselves off for a break in the sun as soon as the Christmas festivities are over,' Greg stated.

'We'll be back –rejuvenated – in time to get the newly fitted out shop ready for the spring opening,' Jasper added, topping up glasses with alcohol for those who were drinking and soft drinks for those who weren't.

'Well, thanks initially to you, Ellen,' Simon turned to me, 'and then the rest of you. It hasn't been the lean winter I've been expecting and, with spring on the way, I'm expecting to be rushed off my feet. The move back to Brankstone has proved to be the right one for me.'

'And I also have a move in mind,' Fiona said. 'I've been giving serious thought to whether or not I relocate to the high street. It seems sensible to move away from the sort of competition I will always come up against with the chain stores so close by. That's if there's anything left in my price bracket.'

'The rents have been kept at a reasonable level to attract the right kind of retailer,' Bruce assured her. 'We can find something for you, I'm sure – in fact I have just the thing in mind.'

'And you, Bruce?' The question came from Greg. 'The house is almost finished, and you must be pleased with what you've achieved in Brankstone. Will you settle here? Now that the job you set out to do is nearly done – is there anything left to keep you here?'

We all turned to look at Bruce and I found that I was holding my breath. Here it was, the question I had been desperate to ask him for so long but been far too afraid of the answer.

He seemed to give the matter far more consideration than it needed and I was almost at screaming point by the time he began to speak, slowly and deliberately. 'I can't deny that I am pleased with what I've achieved here. It's been quite an experience coming back to the town and meeting again the people I grew up with,' his glance rested on my face for less than a second, 'and I've long wanted to do something for the town.

'I'll definitely stay around for the grand opening but, once the high street is up and running for business, my job here is done and I will be moving on to the next project. Apart from Jack – whom as you know has recently developed an interest in one of his neighbours and has his own hopes for the future – there is nothing to keep me here.'

There, it was said, and I suddenly realised it was the exact answer I had been expecting – and also the one I had been dreading. I had no choice but to accept – not that it was over, but that it had never been.

Chapter Twenty

I SETTLED BACK INTO my single life – the one with no thoughts of marriage or a relationship – with surprising ease and forced myself to ignore all the dreams of what might have been with Bruce. After all, what had really changed? One night of unbridled passion wasn't going to make a love affair any more than one swallow was going to make a summer. I couldn't make the man love me – though there had been times when I had really thought. . .

Right after Christmas Greg and Jasper took themselves off for a well-earned break in a sunny climate. It was the first holiday they had been able to take together in years because they would never close the bookshop or leave it in anyone else's charge. For the moment everything in the store had been put into storage while the refurbishment took place.

The work on the high street itself continued apace. I heard from Fiona that completion was expected well ahead of the original timetable and the grand opening had been re-scheduled for early February. That gave me the month of January to come up with enough stock to fill the sizeable display earmarked for my cards in the book store. I must admit to finding it bitter-sweet that a good portion of the cards were aimed at the Valentine's Day market.

With two of my neighbours away and Fiona working flat out in preparation for the move from one boutique location to another, when I did pop up for air the only person I ever set eyes on was

Simon, who was hard at work putting the finishing touches to the outside space next door. Every day I was expecting the For Sale sign to go up.

Arriving back from town and a quick visit to my parents I saw him bent over in the front garden and called a greeting.

Simon straightened up from rolling out turf and watched me unloading groceries from my car. 'It's not really the best time of year to be laying a lawn,' he explained, viewing his work with a frown. 'Not when there's still the chance of a frost, but Bruce wants it all done and dusted, so who am I to argue?'

'You've done a great job.' Already inside my own front gate, I paused to admire his handiwork across the top of the shrubs dividing the two properties. 'Shame it's too early for bedding plants, to give it all a bit of colour. You look cold. I'm just about to put the kettle on if you fancy popping in for a cup of tea – might even run to a slice of cheese on toast, if you're lucky.'

I didn't need to make the offer twice and Simon followed me through the front door carrying the rest of the shopping bags. 'I was saying to Bruce that I haven't seen much of you, for all that I'm working right next door most days,' he was saying. 'He seemed surprised until I pointed out that you'd be working flat out, like everyone else, getting ready for the grand opening.'

He put the bags down and wandered off, probably to see how I'd been spending my time. 'Wow,' I didn't hear him come back so I jumped a bit when his voice suddenly came from just behind me, 'you *have* been busy and, in your case, quantity definitely hasn't been at the expense of quality. The selection of cards is fantastic and the ones I can see are all beautiful.'

'Thank you,' I said, and wished his praise gave me more pleasure. I had always taken a pride in my work but, somehow, my satisfaction in the cards I created wasn't what it had been just a very short time ago. I hoped I hadn't made the wrong decision in agreeing to join a venture that was going to mean more pressure and maybe less enjoyment.

'Laps, is it?' Simon put out trays and cutlery with easy familiarity. 'Not a lot of space left on your dining table.'

'That's what happens when you work from home and agree to expand,' I smiled, but Simon must have noticed a disgruntled edge to my voice.

'Not having regrets, are you?' he asked as we sat side by side and tucked in to the food on the trays in front of us.

I shrugged, 'It's a bit soon for actual regrets. We'll see how it goes.'

We ate in companionable silence for a while and both jumped when the front door suddenly flew open and Bruce burst into the room. I hadn't seen him for ages and discovered in a swift rush of emotion that absence actually *does* make the heart grow fonder.

'Will you never learn, Ellen? Your bloody front door was on the latch again. Oh,' he came up short when he took in the sight of us sitting side by side, our mouths full of food, and then glaring at Simon, he growled, 'I wondered where you'd sloped off to.'

'Lunch break – I got an offer I couldn't refuse from the lady of the house,' Simon said easily, adding, 'and the front door is my fault. I was helping to carry the shopping in and couldn't have pushed the door hard enough to shut it properly.'

'It might help to be a bit more careful,' Bruce said shortly, 'and have you done anything about that flimsy bolt on the back door yet?'

'Erm, no.' Simon looked confused, as well he might, since we were both well aware that Bruce had said he would take care of it. 'But I'll get on to it right away.'

'Do that,' Bruce said, and with that he was gone.

'Well,' I said, as the door slammed behind him.

'No idea what's eating him,' Simon shook his head. 'Probably the pressure of a deadline looming, but then he didn't *have* to bring it forward.'

'I guess he can't wait to shake the dust of Brankstone from his shoes and move on to pastures new.' I could hear the bitterness in my tone and despised myself for caring so much.

'Well, I can't understand it,' Simon replied. 'Fancy spending all that time and money on a house he's never going to live in. He seemed dead set on making a life for himself here. It's where his dad is, and Jack isn't getting any younger, after all.'

'I wouldn't say that,' I found myself smiling at last, and was glad to have something to smile about. 'There's a definite spring in Jack's step since he started seeing that neighbour of his, and she was right there under his nose the whole time, apparently.'

'Just goes to show,' Simon stood up and took both of our trays through to the kitchen, 'you're never too old, and there's hope for us all.'

'I thought you were a confirmed bachelor these days, but you sound as if you're changing your mind,' I stood up, too, and stared at him as he came back into the room.

'It wouldn't take much,' he admitted. 'Business is booming and I'm feeling good about myself. For the first time in a long time I feel as if I have something to offer. There is,' he said wisely, 'more to life than work and I've had the feeling lately that you've come to believe that, too.'

It would have been such a relief to agree that I had come to believe that, to confess that I, too, wanted someone to share my life with, but before I could find the right words, Simon carried on talking.

'I know you said, right at the beginning that you weren't the marrying kind – and I was right with you. Having just gone through a bad experience I was quite definite about once being more than enough, but things, change – feelings change – and I'm wondering if you still feel the same way.'

He was going to tell me that he was getting married, and I couldn't have been happier for him. I reached out to take his hands, smiled up at him, but the smile froze on my lips as he said, completely out of the blue, 'Marry me, Ellen. I can make you happy, I know I can. We'd be perfect together.'

I couldn't actually believe it, but for the longest moment, I was very, very tempted. Simon was easy to get along with, a funny and a genuine all round lovely guy and, like Jack's lady he was here right under my nose. I could almost see us making a home together. Almost, but not quite and it was his final sentence that brought me back to reality with a bang.

'We'd be perfect together,' he'd said, but he was wrong – quite wrong.

I didn't love him. It was as simple as that, and I had always known that for any relationship to work, love was the glue that held everything together. My family were cases in point. For all their ups, downs, break-ups and reconciliations Alma, Molly and Richard and their partners kept on working at their relationships and you had to believe that was because of the love they obviously still shared, in spite of everything. My brother Jonathon and I hadn't found that yet and we never would if we settled for less that we *really* wanted – which was probably a relationship just like our own parents had.

Simon was looking at me so eagerly that I felt what I was about to say was tantamount to kicking a defenceless puppy. I had to take a very deep breath and try to soften the blow with a careful choice of words.

'Don't think I'm not tempted,' I said and then put my hand up to stop him when he started to speak. 'But,' I continued, 'though I love you dearly as a friend, I'm not *in* love with you and you deserve better than that.'

Simon looked at me closely, and I thought I saw understanding dawn as his next words confirmed. 'You're not in love with *me*, but you are in love, aren't you, Ellen?'

My instinct was to deny any such thing emphatically, but the solitary tear that slipped down my cheek rather gave the game away and so I just nodded.

'I think he feels the same about you,' he said, taking me by surprise.

'And I think you're quite wrong.'

It was obvious we were both talking about the same person, though Bruce's name was never mentioned.

'Because he's leaving?' Simon asked.

I nodded again.

'Does he know how you feel about him?' was the next question.

I don't know. I think so.'

'You *think* so?'

I stared at Simon and gave the matter a bit more thought. Surely the fact that when I discovered Bruce in my bed I had kept him there was a good indication that I must feel something for him?

'Do you know how he feels about you?'

I didn't hesitate. 'No, I don't. You heard how he spoke to me just now. Does that sound like a man in love to you?'

'Actually,' Simon said, nodding his head, 'now I think about it, yes, it does. I put his abruptness down to the stress of the deadline looming, but now I think about it he sounded, well, just plain jealous.'

I stared at him, and then burst out laughing. '*Jealous*? That's the most ridiculous thing I ever heard.'

'Is it, though?' Simon stood up, said, 'Now, I'm going to fetch my tool box and fix that bolt Bruce is so worried about – and why is he so concerned for your safety, I wonder? I suggest you give the whole matter some thought and ask yourself what you're going to do about it. Else before you know it, the high street will be up and running and then Bruce will be gone.'

True to his word, Simon did just that and I did as he suggested. In fact, I thought about nothing else as the days slipped by and the deadline crept ever closer.

I went over conversations we'd had, wondered if we'd been trying too hard to convince each other that neither of us wanted anything serious in spite of all the indications that told us otherwise. In the process I realised what might have been a fledgling romance hadn't been given half a chance to flourish.

Where to go from here, though, that was the question? If I opened my heart to Bruce and was completely wrong I was going to make a complete fool of myself. I cringed at the thought, but if I said nothing he was going to disappear from my life and then I would never know and I would always wonder what might have been.

I put down the card I was working on. It was, predictably, a Valentine's card and that was certainly one way of letting someone know you cared – but if I waited until the day itself to make my feelings clear it might already be too late. Then my gaze was drawn to the card on the display board and I knew what I was going to do.

I hadn't wasted a glance in the direction of the house next door or stepped inside the gate since the renovations had been completed. I didn't want to be impressed as I glanced around but I couldn't help being pleasantly surprised.

Simon had done an amazing job re-laying the pathways and lawns, and the green shoots looked ready to burst into bloom among the old and new shrubs planted in the flowerbeds against the hedges and walls.

The house itself had been very sympathetically renovated so that it lost none of its old-style charm and cottage style. The bulk of the extension to the property had taken place at the back and wasn't visible from the road. In other words it had been planned by a man who knew what he was doing. Thinking of the accusations I had levelled at Bruce that first day, my face burned with embarrassment.

Best get this over, I told myself and, dreading the thought of being caught skulking around, I hurried to the front door and put my hand out to lift the letterbox flap. The door swinging open took me completely by surprise and I fully expected to find Bruce standing in front of me, but no, obviously the door had just been left unlocked. When I thought of all the fuss he had made about me doing the same, I couldn't quite believe it.

I stood there on the threshold listening to the sound of complete silence from within for several long moments until I was sure there was nobody at home – and then I stepped inside. My heart thudded against my ribs as I moved forward through the porch and into a sitting room that – apart from redecoration – looked just like my own, though this one was unfurnished. The kitchen, though, had been extended and completely refitted, it even had an island in the middle and it opened into the dining room. I could also see a conservatory beyond that seemed to go right across the back of the house.

I should leave, and I knew that, but my feet seemed to find their own way towards a door where the archway in my house led into my office cum dining room. I was curious to know what lay behind the door in this house and my hand stretched out and closed around the door handle.

'What are you doing in here?' I jumped at the harsh sound of Bruce's voice behind me.

I held out the card, pristine in its white envelope. 'I came round to deliver this and found the front door open. Ironic, isn't it, after all the lectures you've given me about leaving my doors unlocked?'

'I'll be having a word with that estate agent,' he said, without a trace of rancour in his tone. Then indicating the card, he asked, 'What's that?'

'It's for you,' I said, holding it out. Watching him take it I wondered if I was making the biggest mistake of my life because there was nothing in Bruce's demeanour to indicate he had a shred of feeling for me.

'You didn't have to go to the bother of bringing it round,' he said, but he was looking at me and not at the envelope in his hand.

'Actually, I did,' I murmured, but it was so quiet that he must not have heard me.

'Go on.' He indicated the door in front of us. 'I can see you're dying to take a look.'

I could have flounced out, told him that I wasn't interested, but curiosity got the better of me. Again I reached out and grasped the handle. The door opened silently. I peered inside and I gasped out loud. Despite the fact that the dining room was blocked off, the room remaining was large and fully fitted with office furniture, work tables and even display boards on the walls. It was a room absolutely perfect for card making. It was a room absolutely perfect – for me.

'Laughable, isn't it?' Bruce said, and looking into his eyes, I replied, 'You don't see me laughing, do you?'

Tearing his gaze from mine he looked again at the envelope he still held in his hands and then began, very slowly, to tear it open.

For long, silent moments he stood looking down at the card, and then finally, his voice so hoarse that I could hardly understand him, he asked, 'This is really for me?'

I nodded. 'It always was,' and then I turned and stepped into the room, 'And this is for me.'

It wasn't a question, but Bruce still replied, 'It always was.'